...by

...ary Tower
... N.W.
...da T2N 1N4
...m

...by Dennis Johnson
...n by Erin Woodward
...y Super Stock
...in Canada by Friesens for Red Deer Press

...ledgments
...provided by the Canada Council, the Government of Canada through the
...dustry Development Program (BPIDP), the Alberta Foundation for the Arts,
...Lottery Fund of the Government of Alberta, and the University of Calgary.

Canada

THE CANADA COUNCIL | LE CONSEIL DES ARTS
FOR THE ARTS | DU CANADA
SINCE 1957 | DEPUIS 1957

...nal Library of Canada Cataloguing in Publication

...a, 1948–

.../ Kristjana Gunnars.

...2004   C813'.54   C2004-905057-5

Publishe

Red Deer Press
813 MacKimmie Libr
2500 University Driv
Calgary Alberta Can
www.reddeerpress.c

Credits

Edited for the Press
Cover and text desig
Cover image courte
Printed and bound

Ackno

Financial support
Book Publishing In
a beneficiary of the

ALBERTA
Lotteries
COMMITTED TO THE DEVELOPM

ANY D

Nati

Gunnars, Kristja
Any day but this
ISBN 0-88995-311-
I. Title.
PS8563.U574A6

This is a work

Red Deer PRESS

Acknowledgements

Thanks to the following people for information and permissions and other gracious help during the writing of these narratives: staff of the Vancouver Public Library, staff of the B.C. Ferries Corporation, staff of the Office of the City Clerk for Burnaby, the online publication *Saskabush* and friends who told me stories. Thanks to Per Winther for reading the manuscript in early stages and to Dennis Johnson for encouraging me along and editing for publication. I have consulted far and wide for these tales, including the libraries of the University of Alberta, of Sechelt, B.C., of the University of British Columbia and Simon Fraser. Also *The New York Times*, *Berlingske Tidene*, *Morgunbladid* and source books on everything from tonsillectomies to Alzheimer's, and personal interviews with people whom I have pestered with questions. The driving force during the whole project was my fascination for the Sunshine Coast and its people, whom I ultimately have to thank.

contents

Directions in Which We Move

Arne Ibsen had a dream during the night from which he woke certain it had been real. It took him longer than usual to figure out it was actually a dream. He was on board a passenger flight—a big airplane, maybe a Boeing 737. The plane was being piloted by one of his colleagues at the University of Alberta Sociology Department: Art Van Hoors. Art (who specialized in criminology while Arne did social policy) had an office down the hall from Arne in real life. In the dream, Arne was noticing that the plane slowed its motors and prepared for a descent, which was then abandoned, and the plane revved its engines and ascended again into a lull while it circled at a higher altitude. It happened three times that the plane tried to descend but didn't. On the fourth try, Art Van Hoors got on the speaker system and told his passengers they were trying to maneuver through turbulence at the beginning of their descent, and they would try one more time. This time the plane charged onward, right into the weather. The pilot—Art Van Hoors, that is—lost command of the aircraft and it pirouetted around in the air like a car spinning in circles on a slippery highway. It was a surreal experience to sit on the plane that had gone out of control and was spinning like a Frisbee—made more eerie because it seemed to be happening in slow motion.

Arne's first thought after realizing he had been dreaming was that it doesn't matter if this is a dream or not. The conclusion is still the same. The fact was, or the fact certainly appeared to be, that Arne Ibsen did not think he was safe. In the hands of his colleagues, in the workplace he had become part of, even at home with his family, he knew for certain: *he was not safe.*

Arne did not have to teach today, so he could take his time coming in—if he chose to do so at all. Today was his research day, and he was fiddling with his latest article. All the research was done, and it was simply a matter of putting it together on his computer in the study. It was a tiny study, and the old Mac was perched on a computer stand on casters that he had bought in a Mac store in downtown Regina long ago. He wheeled the computer around, depending on where he wanted it.

His little house was all one floor, a tiny bungalow of seven hundred and forty square feet with no thresholds between rooms. So he freely drove the computer station around between the miniature study, the bedroom and the living room—which in bigger houses would have been called the great room because that's what it was. The house was over forty years old, and he could see a line in the hardwood floor that indicated a wall had once divided the living room in two. This was the kind of tiny hovel a family of ten would have lived in forty years ago, cramming themselves into a minute space on the enormous prairie. As it was, the house was just barely big enough for one, and whenever anyone else was there, the setup was simply too small. When his wife, Gro, left him, Arne had sold their big old albatross in Mill Creek and bought this bungalow for much less money.

The old house was located on a hillside in Edmonton with a view north of the river valley—just where the North Saskatchewan cradled the downtown high-rises. Full of trees green in summer, the view provided a soothing spectacle. But there was so much wrong with the place. The plumbing didn't work, the windows were draughty and the old forced-air gas furnace gave out a month after they moved in. Plus, Gro didn't like the layout. She started renovating the house with her bare hands, attacking the walls and floors and plumbing with what he could only describe as Viking fury. She tore out the whole bathroom upstairs—the linoleum, the plaster, the bathtub and tiles. Trouble was, it took her ages to finish the job, and it was very inconvenient to have to find your way to the basement toilet all the time. Gro was unhappy in this town, that was the problem. She could never forgive him for taking her to Edmonton, Alberta. She wanted to go home. Not just home to Norway, but to the village where they both grew up: Svelvik, a town of six thousand in southern Norway. She wanted the pastures, the woods, the apple orchards, the flower gardens, the fog sidling along the water in the morning, the hiking paths up the mountains, the fishery platforms, the boats in the harbor, the world's smallest ferry. . . . And she wanted to head for the mountains, to some *hytte* or other. It wasn't something he could reason with her about: that you go where the jobs are in this life, and there were absolutely no jobs in the village of Svelvik.

(The glory days of Svelvik are over! He had yelled at her even, absurd as it was. It hasn't been livable there since the eighteen seventies when there was real ships' traffic, when it was a genuine harbor town, and when sand mining and ship building and pulp and paper making were going on! It's over! And he smashed the glass against the wooden floor.) Fact is, these things are not matters of the intellect, but of the heart.

Gro was a large woman; a *bountiful* woman, Gro was, striking in her largeness. Her hair was fiery copper-red, shoulder length and curly, and she towered above most people—but only a little above Arne himself, because he was also a tall man. When she wore her black full-length dress with the ivory collar and satin trim, with her silver Saga pin in front, she looked dazzling in her Brynhilde aspect. But she gave up here and went home, leaving Arne to fend for himself in a little house on the prairie, where he was free to develop whatever addictions he wanted, and there was no one to take him to task for it.

Because it was true he was getting by with one addiction or another going at all times. He varied them a bit, but he was well aware that without the assistance of alcohol, pain killers or just plain shopping he would go insane too—the way Gro continually claimed to be going crackers in this place. He bought tools, he loved tools, but they were expensive. He would eventually use them to fix this little place, but mainly he just wanted the tools: a circular saw, a variable speed reversible drill, chisels, a level, whatever. So long as he could start the day—and then keep it going—with his tall crystal tumbler of club soda or Canada Dry tonic, ice cubes, and Bombay Sapphire Gin, he was all right. After all, he had been abandoned by his whole family—or so it seemed. Their son, Magne, finished high school in Edmonton Old Strathcona and then took off to study marine biology at the University of Bergen. Their daughter, Hedvig, (beauty queen material, that's what they all said) went to Tampa, Florida, to the Academy of Design and Technology to study fashion design and clothing construction. And finally, to top it off, Gro just went home. She didn't even have a place to live when she left. She just wanted to get in her old Mazda, which was still parked at her parents' house in Drammen, and drive into the country. She had no plan! Well, he couldn't stop her. And he himself, what was there to keep things up for now? He gained a little weight, let his beard grow rough and scraggly, and combed his hair, which had gone from a pale blond to somehow colorless, straight back from his forehead. This morning, after reading his email, he filled his glass with a good helping of gin and tonic and took it outside to the back steps. The back porch of his small wooden house on 88 Avenue was pretty worn down and leaning a bit with all the paint weathered away and the wood rotting, but it was a nice place to sit when the first days of spring appeared, washing away another harsh winter and making the soul more free; happier, lighter. Arne was looking at the dry, brown patch that was supposed to become a lawn when the summer started, thinking about his life and the email he got this morning. He still had the lyrics of the Bay Ridge Band in his head, which he was listening to before he went to sleep and had his airplane dream (*How many members gone? Gone, gone. How many members gone? / Won't be back until Judgment Day. / Done took that train and gone, gone, gone. / Took that train and gone. . . .*)

The e-post was from Dusty Cameron, his co-author in Vancouver. They were working together on an article called "The Politics of Marginal Space" and were coordinating their research this week (finally, after Arne had waited over two months for the man to get his material together). Dusty sent him a newspaper story from the *San Francisco Chronicle* about a dog. There was a picture of a sorry-looking mutt, a ten-month-old mixed-breed named Dosha, and with it a sorrier tale of how the dog got run over by a car. A policeman named Bob found him by the road, thought he was a stray and shot him in the head to relieve him of the pain of dying like that. Then the dog was taken to the dog pound and put in the freezer. But an employee named Denise decided later to check, and when she opened the freezer the mongrel was still alive—suffering from hypothermia, but alive. It was a funny story, but also pretty brutal. They were nursing the dog back to health, and they said it would survive this onslaught. Arne found elsewhere that, at the moment, this was the most e-mailed story in the world. The sheer sense of the triumph of life must be what attracted people to the tale. *If it's not your time, then no matter what happens, it's not your time.* For some reason (maybe he was just feeling weak these days?) Arne suffered a slight sense of alarm. He wrote Dusty back and said, "I hope they don't do that to me!" The story had triggered a memory, a Proustian-like moment when he vividly recalled a trip to the doctor in his childhood. He was ten years old, back in Svelvik, and his dad, Olaf Ibsen, took him to the nearby town of Drammen to have his adenoids removed. Or that's how it ended up, although Arne had no idea what was coming. He just trusted his dad. His dad took his hand, and Arne let himself rely on him blindly.

It started when Arne lost his hearing in one ear—an infection—but he had no idea what that was about at the time. His dad, though, was pretty upset about it, and Arne picked up on that. He could feel in his own nerves the fright of his father. Olaf was a tall man who became the village schoolmaster and who told tales of living in Haukeligrend with reindeer meat and mountain trout and freshly picked berries to eat. His folks' cabin had grass planted on the tin roof and a sauna, after which he said they jumped into the ten degree lake—all of which put little varicose veins into his cheeks. Arne knew his father was never completely happy away from his mountains; he didn't understand why, but he picked up on it in a form of emotional transference.

His dad took him to see Dr. Eide. Dr. Eide was the family's "court physician," about whom his mother, Asta, only spoke in reverential, hushed tones. Whenever the subject of Dr. Eide came up, his mother lowered her voice and talked like the announcers on NRK radio when they described classical composers in their moments of inspiration.

They went to Dr. Eide's messy office—a corner of his living room actually, in an otherwise picturesque white house facing the sun in Svelvik, next to the church on Storgata. There was a Persian rug on the floor, an oak cabinet with a bowl and jug on top, a big umbrella plant on the floor and a picture of trees on the wall. They were taken into the inner room, which had wooden closet doors like Venetian blinds painted white, and there was a round fan for air and a white chair his dad could sit in. Dr. Eide—a rotund man with a sonorous bass voice and a Bergen dialect—came into the room wearing a long white doctor's coat. Dr. Eide stationed Arne against the entrance door to his office, which was padded with green felt to muffle the sound (so people wouldn't hear the patients crying out their pain?) and turned the boy around at a ninety-degree angle. The doctor then stepped back to the end of the room (Arne could see the consternation in his father's face) and said something he asked Arne to repeat. It turned out that the bad ear was practically deaf. So Dr. Eide decided he should puncture the infected eardrum then and there, perhaps to drain off the puss that had collected in the ear canal. He inserted a needle into Arne's ear. Suddenly, there was a loud clash, an attack of blaring sound. A pop in his ear, like when someone turns on the music full blast all of a sudden (a whole new level of sound; *condition red*). Dr. Eide chuckled, peered at Arne over his round reading glasses with his smiling eyes, and said in his bass Bergenese voice, "Now little Arne can hear whatever he likes again!"

The two grown men must have decided that Arne should have his adenoids removed, so his dad made an appointment with Dr. Haugen in the town of Drammen. Drammen was a long way off—at least for a ten-year-old boy. It was 1957, the year Kong Haakon died. Arne and his dad went on the Svein Helling A/S bus, number nineteen it was, painted white with red and blue trim, from Svelvik to Drammen, on the narrow and winding road, partly along the coast with the boulders and birch trees jutting out sideways, and the hills and valleys, the sharp turns. The occasional gray heron or swan could be glimpsed on the sea or an eagle dipping down for a fish where the waters were shallow. Stops along the way (Hella, Tangen Gard, Oscar Kjaers vei, Rundtom) were still sharp in Arne's memory. Part of the dread of the episode, he realized now, was that his dad was himself terrified of medical procedures. They got off the bus in Drammen at Stromso—just a back street bus depot in a poor part of town—and they had to walk across the bridge to get to Dr. Haugen's office at Bragernes Torg. Arne remembered his dad stopping strangers on the way to ask for directions because he couldn't find it. They got to the doctor's office: it was at Tollbugata three, on the third floor of an old Victorian building with wide, stone stairs and a tall, brown door with Dr. Haugen's name on it. Arne noticed the white, shiny, convex, porcelain sign, with tall letters, reading DR. C. HAUGEN, ORE, NESE OG HALS-SPESIALIST, KUN TIMEBESTILLING.

Arne and his father Olaf walked inside and sat down in the waiting room. There was a white desk with a typewriter and an electric calculator, a desk lamp swinging under some black and orange notebooks on a shelf, and messy papers and yellow boxes on other shelves. Coats were hanging on hooks in the corner, and a rusty rug lay on the floor. And, memorably, a white couch along the wall, clad in some cold, fake leather. After what seemed a long while, they were led into Dr. Haugen's office by a Draconian nurse. Today, in Arne's mind, the most fitting resemblance to this nurse was the figure of Big Nurse Ratched in *One Flew Over the Cuckoo's Nest: capable of swelling up bigger and bigger. . . .*

The doctor's office was huge and contained assorted examination and surgery equipment—blood pressure monitors, scales, thermometers, lotions in jars, tapes and bandages, a stethoscope, a neck collar—and a model ear of papier mâché, with veins and canals distinctly showing. Dr. Haugen wore a strap wrapped around the top of his head with a shiny disk in front, which he tilted before his eye as he inspected Arne's throat. The blinds were drawn, and the room was very dark. Arne figured it was so the lighted pharynx would show up better under the spotlight for Dr. Haugen with the disk over his forehead. After the diagnosis, the nurse accompanied him back to the couch in the waiting room, where he was told to lie down with two steel pins, tipped with cotton swabs dabbed in an anesthetic solution, placed firmly up his nostrils. There he lay, two steel pins sticking out of his nose. Then he was taken back to the inner office and put in a black leather chair, the kind found in barbershops and dentists' offices. The nurse stood behind him, holding his head firmly in a vise of her two hands. The doctor directed a beam of light down Arne's throat and put that Cyclops disk in front of his face. (All Arne could see at that moment was the disk, larger than life.) Dr. Haugen held a curved medical basin under Arne's chin and then inserted a T-shaped instrument into his throat and began to scrape the adenoids out of there. At least half a cup of blood trickled from Arne's mouth and nose during the procedure with that steel torture device.

Here is where Arne's imagination failed him. He was never able to adequately describe the incident to anyone. He tried with Gro once, but it didn't come out right. The pain he felt at the moment his adenoids were scraped off was intense. It was as though his whole head exploded in an instant: he imagined glass shattering into a thousand pieces, burglar alarms shrieking, Molotov cocktails smashing through the office window, bursting into flames. And in the very next instant, Arne felt completely betrayed by his father, who was in the room watching this. *How could his dad let that Gestapo-doctor do this to him?* His sense of betrayal was almost sharper than the physical pain.

The telephone in the doctor's office rang at that moment, and the nurse let go of his head and went to answer it. Arne was left sitting opposite the doctor, who was now poking with his instrument in the medical tray full of Arne's blood, in which floated a piece of flesh the size and shape of a squashed cherry. Dr. Haugen poked in the tray the way someone would push his fork around in his stew, to see if there were any good bits of meat left. Then the doctor said what were unforgettable words to Arne for the rest of his life: "I think we will have to take a bit more out."

After a few moments, the nurse returned, grabbed his head again and the procedure was repeated for the second time. In a daze of pain and emotional paralysis, Arne was taken out afterward into the waiting room and back to the couch, where he was told to lie down with medicinal cotton up both his nostrils, so the bleeding would stop. There was blood all over his face and some even in his yellow curls, but no one wiped it off. The cotton in his nose was soon completely drenched with blood. In the waiting room a girl of about five, with a ponytail and bangs and big brown eyes, wearing a white frock with pictures of strawberries on it, was waiting to see the doctor with her mother. The girl sat in the chair staring at Arne in disbelief. After a few minutes she turned to her mother and said, "They're not going to do that to me!" Her mother kept glaring at a women's magazine—*Alt for damene* it was—studiously avoiding looking at the boy on the couch.

Getting back home again remained hazy in Arne's memory. He walked back over the bridge to the bus depot holding his father's hand, still mortified by the recent assault. Someone must have wiped his face clean by then. They rode back in the bus that wound its way on the bumpy road, twisting and turning with the irregular coastline, and then the number nineteen reached the stop in Svelvik, where they got off. They must have made their way up the hill to the house in the afternoon sun—not too fast, but walking in silence. What Arne did remember well was the lush sympathy he got from everyone afterward. His mother Asta and his brother Leif were fawning over him. He got nothing but soup and ice cream for the next three or four days. Arne could still smell the steep yeast and cinnamon, maple and strawberry odor in Baker Nielsen's bakery and konditori, where he went to get the homemade vanilla ice cream (made with lots of whipping cream and sugar and egg yolks) he was allowed so liberally. In the bakery with its deep red sign out front, all the employees wore white from top to toe, and the air was fluffed with flour dust. That was where they got the cut-off ends of the *wienerbrod* they baked daily—a paper-cone full of yeast cakes with almond paste for five Ore. After having his little world destroyed (to Arne all of civilization was obliterated in a moment in Dr. Haugen's office at Tollbugata three in Drammen, Norway), the universe had to be reassembled. It was put back in place, bit by small bit, at Baker Nielsen's Konditori, and with the taste of creamy vanilla ice cream, made in the backroom of a flour-dusted bakery. Arne had been supremely fond of vanilla ice cream ever since. Feeling the cold, creamy, pungently soft vanilla-milk in his mouth always gave him a sensation of happiness that flushed through his whole body like soothing, mollifying cool water. Later he learned Dr. Haugen's wife had left him and gone to Canada. No wonder! he thought already then.

But had he not also gone through life with a huge sense of betrayal? Suddenly, today, on an average day in April in Edmonton, Alberta, a gin and tonic in his hand, the ice cubes rustling when he shook the specially purchased tumbler to and fro (a glass he bought at a store so far east on Whyte Avenue that no one knew about it: The Glass House, where you bought diamond-cut crystal wine glasses, goblets, decanters and vases, in clear crystal, made by a Russian named Tutchev)—an early spring day with the occasional wasp wending its way across the scraggly, ugly yard, and the old white Buick (twenty-five years old now) in the too-small garage—suddenly today he felt he understood why the betrayal. His wife, Gro, his children, Magne and Hedvig, even his colleague Dusty Cameron, who was slow to respond and kept this project going for too long, thinking more about his tulips than his work—somehow, none of them could be trusted. He had in fact depended on each and every one of them and been led blindly by them all into—into what? This backyard? This endless succession of glasses of Bombay Gin and Tylenols at night and Aspirins every morning? Did it really all start with his father, Olaf, the tall man with the early lines of age on his forehead, in his tweed schoolteacher jacket with the reinforced elbows (which he thought very swanky, no doubt, that touch of suede on the elbows and the collar) and their trip into Drammen the year Kong Haakon died? Now he knew that adenoidectomies were no longer considered useful. Adenoids protect your body from toxins that invade at every turn. Tonsillectomies, appendectomies, adenoidectomies—all these were no longer practiced. He even apprehended the betrayal of science itself. The flesh at the back of little Arne's throat, which in medical pictures looked like a cluster of grapes, was of course enlarged because he had an ear infection. The adenoids were working overtime. But he could have kept them; they would have shrunk on their own. Like so much else. If you leave things alone, they'll right themselves.

He tried to tell that to Gro, but she wouldn't listen. Even as late as when he drove her to the airport, he said, "Stay and you'll be all right. We'll find a way." But she wasn't hearing. She was completely deaf to him then. Perhaps she always had been? They got in the Buick that morning, she with her purple headband to hold back her violent hair and a brown all-weather jacket, her American Tourist suitcases packed, headed for home, and he keeping up a good front. He was so depressed that morning that he didn't even bother to shave or tie his shoelaces, but just threw on a pair of old off-color corduroys and a vomit-green sweatshirt. They drove out on Calgary Trail, south past Devon and Beaumont, out to Leduc and the airport. Into the parkade and the walk to the terminal building. They were early, so they stopped at The Bush Pilot for a drink while they waited. Gro didn't want that; she wanted to go to the Second Cup and have coffee, but he had already then decided a drink would be the only adequate response to what was happening. She had no reason to be dictating his lifestyle to him now. Not at this moment. It was live and let live. They picked something up at Smith Books for her to read: the *New Yorker* and the *Globe and Mail.* Then it was her through the gate, and she flew away on WestJet to Calgary, where she was taking a KLM flight to Amsterdam.

He went outside as the plane taxied on the runway to see it take off. The day had become hot. A wind was blowing. He went to the side ramp of the terminal building where no one was, only an aircraft hangar and a Quonset hut and then bald prairie with the open wind on it. He watched as the plane taxied to the end of the runway, turned and headed up into the sky. The engine roared, the plane made a slight turn to the right and then got smaller and smaller as it faded into the cloudless sky. It seemed surreal to him then; he couldn't really believe this was happening. Could she actually be leaving now? On that Boeing 737 from Gate 14, this Friday morning? Gro

Ibsen, coasting above the boreal forests and the ranchlands—over Camrose and Red Deer and all the wheatgrass and timothy and foxtail and orchard grass everywhere, as far as you look, grasses and horses and cows grazing and a hundred blue lakes dotting the flatland like sapphire jewels in a gigantic gold crown.

She did not feel safe either, did she? This was dawning on Arne Ibsen as he stood outside in the hot breeze watching the plane fly away. You were safe nowhere as long as you were alive. He was dreaming while awake: he was thinking of going home to his backyard stoop, to his tall crystal glass of ice and Bombay Gin, to the bottle of Tylenol, to the freezer of his seven hundred square foot home in the middle of the world's emptiness, nursing his wound, with the still-seeping sore, the blood that runs and runs.

Dreaming of the Coliseum

Karl Heffner had a little time on his hands. The reading was at 7:30 and it was only 6:20. When he arrived at the Vancouver Public Library, he was a little disoriented. It was such a huge library—not like the one he worked in, West Vancouver Memorial Library. In Ambleside the library was homey and cozy. Actually, it *was* home for some people. There were people in the neighborhood who came there every day and stayed for several hours, mostly in the newspaper room. Kind of a social center. But people hanging out there bothered no one, and it made the place warm with human bodies. An empty library is pretty dreary. A library is like a *giant brain*. A 3-D brain experience. Karl loved the whole construct: the encyclopedias, the search catalogues, the indexes, the super searchers and bibliographies—the whole paper trail mechanism of people trying to find out things. Trying to *know* something. The downtown library, however, was something of a colossus. Library Square, where he now found himself, was basically two separate buildings enclosed by glass. A curved atrium, actually. No artificial lights: all seven stories of the space, with its twenty-four kilometers of shelving and its one point two million books, were dressed in filtered and patterned daylight coming through square panes. There were big events here: weddings and ceremonies and trade fairs.

He walked along the promenade—a kind of courtyard or circumscribed town square. A concrete quad, he thought—no, a *book garrison*, that was better—looking for the room he was supposed to go to. The Alma Van Dusen Room. He noticed a stairway to the left of the front entryway. When he peered down from the bridge to the floor below, where the Moat Gallery was, he saw the doors on the left. It occurred to him that the architect (well, it was Moshe Safdie, and it dated back to 1995, although what he obviously did have in mind was a classical Roman Coliseum) had the deck of an ocean liner in mind when he designed this space. (Karl would be a passenger staring into the gloom below the ship's deck, wondering whether to throw himself overboard.) The Van Dusen Room was at the bottom of the stairs, the sign large and visible above the double doors. He walked down. The gallery (now he noticed this space too was naturally lit) was showing a photographic exhibit: Vancouver historical photos; he made a mental note to look at it more closely later. The room was large, like a big classroom but without the desks: a lecture theatre with bare ivory walls and stark theater lighting in the ceiling. A pale parquet floor, red plastic chairs and a lectern at the end. No one was in there. His "minder" was nowhere to be seen—a Julie Barthe, who worked here and who was supposed to look after him—meet him and introduce him and all that. He stood for a while in the stark room and thought how grim it felt. Nothing decorative or brightening. No windows. He began to feel oppressed and went upstairs again. He was thinking about the words of Christian Bök he had read earlier that week—how fitting! Talking about the plasticized epoxy resin polypropylene blob world of our language NOW. The man was a maniac, Heffner thought, but a great maniac! He was out there on the Web calling for a poetics of explosion, like language terrorism: *incendiary literature* written by "misfits" *still dizzy from the fumes, after having melted a platoon of plastic army men with a match*. . . .

Just as Karl rounded the corner at the top of the stairs, a woman in her early forties, probably, with short, black hair (darkened with tea, perhaps; he had read about how Gypsy women made their hair black with nettle tea), and very bourgeois clothing—black and white hound's-tooth wool slacks and a marled ruby cardigan—stopped him with her hand (dressed like a schoolteacher, Karl thought. He read a briefing once on the dress code for schoolteachers: "They shall be neatly attired and groomed." Jeans and T-shirts not allowed).

"You must be Karl!" she said effusively, her big smile genuine, although well rehearsed.

"Yep, that's me," he replied.

"I spotted you from your picture. That curly brown hair is recognizable anywhere!"

"I was just downstairs looking at the room," he informed her.

"Okay, so you've seen it. It's a bit early now. We need to get you to sign some forms beforehand, so we can pay you!" She leaned over as she said this, the way people do when they tell secrets to each other.

"Good. Let's sign away."

"I'll have to go up to my office to get them—my office is upstairs—and I'll bring them down for your sig. You can hang around here if you want. Would that be okay?" Karl looked at the concourse activity as he thought what he might do there. He saw two coffee shops, a L'Express and a Café Arabica, with sidewalk tables outside of both of them, and an SAK Newsstand.

"That's fine. I had dinner a little while ago, but I didn't have coffee. So I think I'll get a coffee here." He was thinking of the surprisingly excellent Greek *spanakopita,* with fresh parsley and dill, and lots of feta and egg, he had eaten at the diner called The Gardens on Capilano Road—a quaint, tiny place, but all the food was homemade and fresh: *tsatziki* with fresh cucumber and pressed garlic, *gigantes* with new tomatoes and pepper ground at the table, and *skorthalia* made with today's boiled potatoes. The proprietor, who was also the chef, kept running out from the kitchen in his checkered shirt and dishcloth apron, asking him, the only customer, "How's the food? How's the food?"

"Which of these is the better café?" he asked.

"I'll tell you," Julie half-whispered conspiratorially. "The coffee is the same in both places, but the one on the left is cheaper. We always go there."

"Okay, I'll go to the one on the left. You can find me there."

"Great!" Julie enthused.

She ran off to the inner sanctum of the library, and Karl wandered over to the café. A man with a heavy Middle Eastern accent (Karl could never figure out which accent for which country: Syria? Iran? Egypt? Or *Iraq?*) stood behind the counter in fervent, loud conversation with a countryman in a language Karl did not know. The men were gesticulating, animated about something. Karl walked up to them and ordered a dark Arabica coffee, which he got in a Styrofoam cup with a sleeve on it. The man serving him half-shouted over the counter as he took Karl's money: "No burnt sticks or stones in this one! Just the good *Maragogipe!*" Karl nodded cheerfully and raised the Styrofoam cup for a mock-toast. He took it to one of the sidewalk tables and sat down. Only one other customer was there—a young Chinese looking woman, reading a paper with Chinese script on it. She was raptly focusing on the curious symbols, and Karl wondered what might be so interesting. Something mighty engrossing, that's for sure. He remembered an absorbing article he once read about an evangelical Christian sect in China called the Little Flock. It came with a story: *On a chilly night three autumns ago,* a woman walked past Granny He's courtyard, past *the chickens scratching,* and proceeded to *knock on her red wooden door.* Then Granny He was taken to an evangelical meeting at a house where *the pulpit is a red flounce curtain draped over a desk* and where the *broken windows let the swirling central China dust coat the white-washed wall.* It was a great story. Karl loved it. They said Jesus was back, *and she is Chinese and she will destroy the earth.*

Karl put his nylon tote bag on the floor at his feet and leaned back in the café chair (one of those wood-and-steel constructions you get at Ikea, he thought). His mind began to wander as he watched people go up and down the walkway. They entered the main portal from Georgia Street and walked down to the front door of the library, located exactly halfway down the promenade. An old man (black baseball cap, shoulder-length charcoal-and-ashes hair, black corduroys and purple velveteen shirt, with a shepherd's hook walking stick and a dry bowl-pipe in his mouth, carrying two books under his arm) made his way to the door with difficulty. A young Chinese couple, the boy pushing a mountain bike, wandered in blithely, smiling and conversing. A middle-aged woman in a navy raincoat, looking businesslike and professional, walked briskly out of the library door, holding a leather briefcase. (*Famous blue raincoat.* Karl remembered talking to his mother about the lyrics to Cohen's song, one of the many discussions they had about poetry and the main thing they actually had in common. His mom said, "You know, the lyrics do have some ambiguous lines! I mean, it's just not obvious what he's talking about." And Karl: "Don't get bogged down with it that way," and his mom: "Isn't it important to be talking about something, though?" and he: "Well, everyone knows what a love triangle is, to start with," and she nodding and he again: "If a woman has an affair, say . . ." and she: "Yes?" and he: *And thanks for the trouble you took from her eyes / I thought it was there for good, so I never tried*—the husband to the lover, for example. It makes sense emotionally when you look at the whole thing." And she, nodding again, the tea getting cold in their ceramic cups.) Inside the library, Karl could see dozens of people, mostly young student types, perched on chairs at desks or standing by computers or milling about among the book stacks. What a busy place! It was almost like an airport, he thought. But out here on the covered sidewalk, it was actually quite peaceful. As the minutes passed, Karl began to feel quite calm and contented. He wondered why he wasn't stressed at all: you'd think he was just flaneuring downtown and not here to do a reading from a book he once wrote and which a publisher in Victoria had taken a (big!) chance on publishing.

Annoyance. That was the title of Karl's book of poems, published by Shachter-Holmes. Not quite his first, but almost. He'd done a chapbook at the Horsemen's in Toronto—had even been there to read from it at a bar called Ravenna's. It was a curious night. He came to read with about seven other poets. Jazz was being played beforehand. The poets and the minders were having beer (Enderby had a Martini—Karl thought that was a bit passé)—and Fiona was wearing something he could only describe as *underwear.* A dress that looked like a smudgy nylon slip with lace on all the edges and that barely stayed up, the straps over the shoulders falling down as she read. And the stuff she read was stranger. Quoting from some early dissertation by a reverend of an English country church: *Thus does the case stand with the doctrine of the second advent. It will be progressively better comprehended as the various second comings are brought forward in history. Only when the last of those events, the final coming, has been reached, will a completed true doctrine be made possible. . . .*

That night, before he read, he struck up a friendship with a cellist, a very serene woman named Elly Winthrop, who taught cello in the music department in Alberta somewhere. They decided to go on the stage together, with Elly improvising to what she heard. They went up cold. Karl read his word-constructions (his mother said they weren't poems, but "word constructions") and Elly ad-libbed on the cello. It was cool. Very.

Actually, Karl had done more readings already than he had published poems. In this world, you did lots of readings, beginning way before you ever got anything published. Well, he published in the UBC student newspaper when he was undergraduating there, and in *Geist* magazine and in *Open Letter*. But this book, this was the real thing. He was a poet, always wanted to be a poet and never wanted to be anything else.

Still, he had to support himself and pay the rent. He had been at the West Vancouver library for seven years now and had liked every one of them. It didn't bother him that his mother worked there too. Everyone thought it would, but it was all right. He was assigned to the computer division down in the basement, where he kept track of the computer users and helped them out. Sometimes he was at the lending desk upstairs. He kept to himself, didn't socialize much. It didn't bother him that his mother was keeping an eye on him. "Why don't you go out more? Why don't you mingle during lunch more?"—criticisms that had mostly died down now. If you kept your style long enough, your parents had to accept you as you are.

The good thing about working in a library is that you have your research at your fingertips all day long. Literally. He could snag a moment in a workday to look up something for his own writing, and it appeared as though he were working. It really did. It was impossible for anyone to tell that he was doing his own research and not working for the library at that moment. He might branch out from poetry and do something else soon—interactive essays, for example. Or Wendy Kramer-style word collages. He might write texts that were "about" things (which had actual subject matter) and interrupt them with photos and things that were nontextual. He might publish on the Web someday. Start his own blog. But mostly he was a poet, and he lived the life of a poet.

Karl's mother, Betty Heffner, was what he could only describe (in the language of lovely ladies) as a lovely lady. He liked her. He even liked working with her. She was cheerful, helpful, sociable, well-adjusted. They bantered occasionally. She was fond of roses, and he discovered the "Lovely Lady" rose in a book, which was a huge pink hybrid tea rose, originally from Ireland. He later found for her that it was used for a rose essence called "New Energy" that cleaned out the *chakras*, all that "karmic drama" of your misdeeds. It was a joke—or was it? Sometimes he helped her out (her computer skills were almost nil, although she did do email), and sometimes he covered for her (days when she wasn't "feeling good," as she said, which meant she was feeling rotten). There was a tendency to get sick there, whatever that was about. She was pretty good at avoiding things she didn't like talking about. Pretending: the way women do when they come from "polite society" and have learned to behave themselves. But it was better than being whiny. He would get tired of a whiny parent real quick.

He was good at avoiding things too—like not talking about his parents' relationship, for example. Their relationship was "cool"—

meaning not cool but cold. His parents liked each other and relied on each other and all that, but where was the love? Oh well. He happened to know (just deduction, putting two and four together) that his mother (yes, his Mom) had been having affairs with not one but at least three different men in the time he had known her, which was thirty-two years now. But it made no difference to their daily lives. Everything continued as usual, and he never mentioned that he knew, and his dad never mentioned that he knew something too (because he did; Karl would swear that he suspected his wife's infidelity—faithlessness? duplicity? inconstancy?—to the point of almost knowing; suspected it with certitude). Fortunately, Karl didn't know who the last man was, and he didn't try to find out (although he accidentally discovered the first one—some writer she met when his parents were vacationing in Santorini in Greece and who got her started liking poetry so much, a Sanderson Waits. Karl made a point of not reading his stuff). Some things you just don't want to know. But he did cover for her when she had to disappear due to "not feeling fair and square," as she put it. (Karl's dad, Arnold Heffner, a tall, handsome man with a wind-battered face from going fishing on weekends in his own boat, was going to retire from B.C. Hydro soon and wanted to move to Galiano Island. Maybe to get his mom away from West Vancouver? Did his dad know how many people had affairs on Galiano Island? It's a hotbed!)

Karl didn't "mingle" at lunch like he was supposed to in order to seem well adjusted. (Who's to mingle with? There were no men working there whom he would like to have as his buddy. All the women at the library were "taken" and he didn't fancy them anyway, except maybe one girl, someone who used the library every week, name of Millie something; she sat at the circular desk reading books on Nordic mythology. Karl could take an interest in her; she was so quiet and, well, studious). Instead he took his homemade cucumber sandwich to the seating area in the back garden and read a book. It was like an outdoor atrium, with a brick patio, teak garden furniture, ash-gray clay flower pots with small trees in them, peace and quiet away from talking noise. Karl loved to read books there—the more the merrier. At the moment, he was fascinated by W.G. Sebald. That was more intriguing than almost anything he could think of right now. Sebald wrote novels that were not really novels, but compendiums of all sorts of data, details of architecture and history and complete facts about mechanical stuff and maps of places and so on. Narrators told stories in layers, so you have a story inside a story inside a story, because the narrators are telling other people's narratives and so on. There were photographs and documents everywhere. Karl hadn't been able to decide whether the photographs helped or not, or what they did, but they made the reading experience really *strange.* Curious, odd, ominous. Ominous, yes. The photographs haunted Sebald's text like ghosts—dead people who hovered in stories about the living. W.G. Sebald's almost-casual observations (which he attributed to someone else's "casual remarks") were sometimes breathtaking. For example, the way he described the light in a McDonald's restaurant. The light in those places is so intense and bright and unreal: Sebald says it's a *glaring light which . . . allowed not even the hint of a shadow and perpetuated the momentary terror of a lightning flash.* No wonder, Karl thought, he was so uncomfortable in those "food courts" in shopping malls and in places like Wendy's and McDonald's. They were terrifying. The lighting alone (not to mention the acoustics!) did actually prolong the "momentary terror of a lightning flash."

Karl had in fact started on his "subject-matter" work (because it was a principle of his never to discuss poetry in terms of "what it's about." You don't ask what a poem is *about.* You ask what it's *doing*). He was just in the beginning stages, but was following up a story he was interested in. It was something he first read in the *New York Times*, which he liked to read on Sundays in his flat on Lonsdale in North Vancouver. He looked forward to Sunday mornings when he didn't have to go to work and he went down to the newsstand and bought the $10.95 issue of the *Sunday Times* and took it upstairs and read it for about four hours. The story was about some bloke in Beijing who had put his dad's essays online for him and was then arrested for it. His dad, it turns out, was retired and liked to write essays and wanted to publish them. But he didn't know how to put them on the Web, so his son helped him out. The essays were critical of the government's handling of the American spy plane issue. But the son was arrested instead of the father. The controversy was that the guy who put the essays on the Web was punished for their content, while the writer was not. In larger terms, this meant that a publisher could be arrested for what a writer writes, while the writer is free to keep writing.

Karl found himself researching this matter further. An organization called China Labor Watch was taking this as an indication of the "vulnerability" of the government—that they think "any voice detrimental to the government is considered a threat." (It would be just interesting if it weren't so *sad*, Karl was thinking, that statements like that make sense when they're about a place like China, but people don't see it when it happens in North America. Sometimes what's right in front of your nose is the thing you don't see). In some reports the father was a "retired army officer" and in other reports he was a "scholar." In some articles his essays were reported to be reasonable but critical, while in other news blurbs they were just plain "cranky." It was hard to tell whether the father was writing really silly stuff or reasonable critiques. If they were that silly, why would the son help him out? (Karl enjoyed the story in a perverse sort of way: It's the middle of the night, state security agents enter the house of Hu Dalin with a search warrant, remove his computer and bill the family forty-six dollars to keep the son in jail for fifteen days. "You have to pay them to be kept in jail," Lu Jiaping is reported to have said). Why wouldn't Hu Dalin (just a guy in Shaoying with an art supply store who likes computers and the stock market) say to his dad that it wasn't worth publishing? What was the relationship there anyway? Do you do everything your parent asks you to do? Filial devotion? Do you always cover for your parent, even when you know it's wrong-headed and dangerous?

Karl saw the figure of his minder, Julie Barthe, come out of the library entranceway. She was holding a small folder and tramping briskly around the corner toward the stairway. He roused himself and took his half-finished cup of Arabica with him to the staircase. It would be good to have a coffee on hand while he read. Downstairs in the Van Dusen Room, Julie was fixing the podium and the stray chairs, putting things in order. There were already two people sitting in the front row—two women of middle age, come to the weekly poetry reading. Both were very handsome women, Karl noticed. Fashionable, suave, cool. One was wearing a light wool skirt suit, pale lime-colored, her hair tied up loosely; the other wore a kind of matador jacket, chocolate-toned, and black trousers. She had sleek, dark, drawn-back hair. This was good. Hopefully, there would be more people. He had ambiguous feelings about readings because there was always a small moment of dread beforehand. The dread was about the audience. It was too embarrassing to read when no one came. Karl would much rather be at the local pub getting completely pissed on cheap beer than reading to empty seats. On the other hand, reading to an actual audience (even a half-full room would be satisfying) was a gas. It felt good. Every reading was taking a new risk, hoping for something of an audience but conceding that it might not be there. Things can go wrong, he reminded himself, and not just at readings. That's true for everything. It doesn't mean you don't do it at all. (Karl loved the comment E.M. Forster apparently made about the poet Cavafy, that *he stood at an odd angle to the universe.* It was true for all poets.)

Julie noticed he had come in and moved to a back row with her papers and gestured for Karl to join her there.

"I just need your social insurance number here, and your signature there," she half-whispered. He dutifully filled out the blank spaces and handed her the form back.

"I once worked in this library, you know," he told her. For curiosity's sake.

"Oh! It's a nice place to work!"

"Well, it was a long time ago. I actually ironed call numbers onto book spines in the backroom." She laughed at that.

"That must have been long ago!" Then she looked at him curiously and asked, "Do you get nervous before readings?"

"Sometimes. The fewer in the audience, the more the nervousness," he said. "Oddly enough. I once tried to figure out what people do for it—like what's the medicine for audience dread or something."

"Oh, do tell me what it is. I find it really hard to give speeches myself."

"There are some tips, I guess. I like the one that tells you to 'Use Simple Anglo-Saxon Language.' That's good!" They chuckled, although Karl was not sure they were laughing at the same idea. "I also really like the advice they give you to 'Choose Visuals.' And this one: you should 'End with an Appeal for Action!'"

"That's more for speech writers than poets, though, isn't it?" Julie asked. Karl was smiling broadly.

He picked up his bag and went to the front row, where he sat down to wait. Another ten or fifteen minutes passed. He marveled at the strange emptiness of the room. No windows, nothing on the walls. It was hard to think of putting on cultural events in a completely "dis-cultured" room like this. In such a denuded atmosphere. What were they thinking? he wondered. You'd have to work three times harder to overcome the unfavorable energy of the room itself. There were other readings he had done in other environments, and it made a difference. One reading he did in an art gallery in Regina. There were paintings by a Saskatoon painter; Honor was her name. Her canvases were all around: huge panels with frightening images of dead roses upside down on a wall, taped with masking tape; things like a dress without a person in it, hanging on a bare wall; or a leather chair without anyone on it, in a barren room, but a full cup of tea with milk in it on a table, too far from the chair for easy reach. The whole scene looked like the person drinking tea had been unnaturally removed. Karl was so distracted by the paintings that he could hardly concentrate on his poems. Another reading he did in a restaurant. It was an eatery attached to a bookstore, on Circle Drive in Saskatoon, in a strip mall way out in the suburbs, which was more like a business district where no one ever went. There was a microphone in the corner and huge windows on both sides, where people could look at the intermittent traffic going by. Absolutely no one was there— except for the bookstore owner who was hosting them and the other reader, Maggie from Edmonton. He had a brief spell of complete empty-headedness. He wanted to cancel the reading, but then again, he was getting a small honorarium, which he needed. If he didn't read, he wouldn't get his two hundred bucks. And he had come all the way there. So he would have to do the reading, but it would be a farce. He decided to read to the chairs. What's to lose, anyway? (Except your dignity or something, which didn't count for much). He and Maggie read away, and then they went to a bar called Amigos on 10 Street and drank "Banker's Dooms" with melon liqueur and whiskey and vodka. Maggie smoked about twelve Parliaments. They had to "get over" the fiasco of the evening—which strangely enough, wasn't that much of a disaster either, because they didn't actually mind. It's something you have to take for granted.

As Karl was remembering these moments, a few more people were coming into the Van Dusen Room. A short, plump woman with a bun right on the top of her head and the rest of her long hair hanging down her back, short bangs, cherry-colored lipstick and wearing a bust-revealing velveteen top with white lace along the edges, stood in the aisle for a while and then picked a seat close to the lectern. A middle-aged man, his face heavily lined, his straw-colored hair cut very short, with sad-looking eyes and wearing a white T-shirt under a red checkered shirt, seated himself square in the middle of the room. Another woman, who struck him as a typical suburban housewife (someone with a cookie-cutter home and a square lawn, who was white and owned lots of Tupperware?) with shoulder-length straight brown hair and big round glasses, sat in the back. A nice couple from one of the better neighborhoods came and sat toward the front. Elderly with gray hair, they looked happy together, going to cultural events in the city. They sat there smiling. There were some student-types as well: an Asian girl in a bright red T-shirt with a cartoon on the front and short, slightly unkempt hair sat reading her book, and behind her, two Chinese men (one of whom looked very intense, with a crew-cut and a rain jacket, the other with his hair almost completely cut off and wearing all white). They were sitting and chatting. Interesting motley crew, Karl thought. What would be the glue that binds these disparate people together?

Julie stepped up to the lectern and started her introduction of Karl Heffner, the young poet of North Vancouver, who "made waves" with his first book *Annoyance*. Reviews called the book "dazzling" and "perplexing," but she figured Karl himself would be able to explain some of it to us. While she was talking, Karl realized she knew nothing about him. Not that she should. Where would she get information from anyway? But he thought she could have asked him some questions. There had been time. But maybe that didn't matter. He got up when the smallish audience applauded and took his stance at the rostrum. He decided he should try to "explain" the stuff he was going to read—not an easy decision. A poet doesn't want to have to explain anything. But these people didn't seem to be literary types, so what did it matter anyway? He was here to give them as good a time as he could. He started to explain. He had concocted this series of poems from a mathematical principle, he told them. He treated the letters of the alphabet as if they were numbers, and formulated specific patterns with the letters that became verbal patterns as well. The geometry of the poems was such that the patterns expanded in concentric rings, ever larger: from the individual letters to single poems (which took a square shape in the middle of the page—he held up the page so they could see the shape of the poems) to the whole series of poems together. The same patterns persisted. The idea behind the whole thing was to explore the geometries of language and the mathematical impulse of the Roman alphabet. So here goes—and he read away. There was not much to say about each individual poem, so he just kept on reading one after another for about thirty-five minutes. Then he stopped and told his audience they could ask him questions if they wanted, but he would understand if they didn't have any. While he was reading, he noticed the two fashionable women in front were very attentive and engaged. The plump woman looked quite clued-out. The happy elderly couple were enjoying themselves, but he had no idea why. The Chinese students were quiet, and he couldn't tell what they were thinking at all. The newly retired gentleman in the middle of the room had a stern expression on his face, and he had gone from looking sad to positively grim. Julie in the back was blithe as a bunny, smiling cheerfully but probably without an inkling of what he had just read to them.

To Karl's surprise, there were questions. People *had* been listening, and even thinking—in a disoriented, unfocused sort of way, but they were following. The woman in the front row in her matador jacket with her tied-back hair asked where he got the idea for such a book. He told her it came from reading books on architecture (a hobby, he said, that came from working in a library). The elderly couple asked (seemingly with one voice) whether his parents understood his poems (No, not at all, he assured them, but they liked the fact that he wrote them—especially his mother, who wrote poems herself. But her poems were more the garden-variety poetry, which they might have liked a little better). The plump, dark-haired woman in the amazing velvet-and-lace outfit, her heavy makeup and nearly bared breasts, finally spoke up and asked how you get poems published. Karl considered for a moment whether he should answer this at all, and while he was pondering, she kept talking; said she had heard publishers take all your money and don't ever send you royalties so she said she didn't want to give a publisher her poems. Karl assured her this was not true, but tried to say as little as possible to her. Afterward, people were dispersing, but the bespectacled woman, who looked like a very nice housewife out by herself for the evening, came up to him.

"Do you know the work of Dr. Anthony Felix?" she asked. "He's a professor at Alberta, and he wrote a book called *The Physics of Poetry*."

"Yes, as a matter of fact. Someone sent me that book," Karl remembered.

"I have it; my friend sent it to me," she said, looking intently into his eyes. Karl was momentarily uncomfortable. There was an essay in that book entitled "Amazing Geometries" about Karl's poems, which was why he had been sent a copy. It was Dr. Felix himself who sent it to him. Karl came home from work one Tuesday and found the book in his mailbox with a note from the author (*Hope you like what I have said about your work, Regards, A.F.*). "You're all over that book!" the friendly woman was saying.

"I know," Karl replied. "I read the essay in there."

"But it's not just the essay itself—he's referring to you all over the place, in all the other essays as well. He keeps mentioning you!"

"I didn't know that. I haven't read the whole book yet." Karl was packing up his bag.

"I read the book. That's why I came tonight," she confided. He smiled, looking as grateful and appreciative as he could. He was actually pleased with the essay (he had seen it in a journal too, the *Journal of Canadian Poetry*, on one of his excursions into the new crop of journal issues. He went through the table of contents as he filed them onto the stacks, and he enjoyed seeing what people were writing about in the literary world). He nodded to the woman. On second thought, he liked her. She was completely natural, with her unassuming straight hair and awkward glasses. She was wearing brown well-pressed slacks and a yellow windbreaker. They exchanged a few more pleasantries, but Karl couldn't keep track because the two dashing, swanky women from the front came up and thanked him for the reading. They were all smiles.

Just as suddenly as everyone had appeared, they were all gone. Karl found himself sauntering out of the room with Julie. They walked slowly up the steps, and he heard her talking about practical things—but he was only half-listening. He often got unfocused like this after a reading. What he most wanted now was a beer. He had three Labatts in the fridge, so he was just going home to drink them. All three. Julie was saying something about how he should send the receipts if he had any expenses in coming down and they would reimburse him.

"Something happened there," he broke in, his mind wandering about.

"Oh?"

"Yes, something quite genuine actually." He said this as if he were surprised—and in fact he was. His astonishment betrayed the fact that he hadn't expected anything at all out of this reading. Usually, readings in public libraries were dead events. There was no "cult" thing happening, no real dynamic. Julie was looking at him quizzically. "It was that woman with the mousy hair, I never got her name," he explained. Julie was nodding questioningly. "She looked like a housewife or something," Karl explained further. "You know which one I mean?"

"Yes, the woman in the back with short hair and yellow jacket," Julie recalled.

"Yeah. Well, she came because she read an essay. That's really remarkable." He looked at Julie to see if she understood what he meant. "I find that remarkable—the kind of domino effect that happens when people are really interested in something."

"Oh yes, well we get such a variety of people here!" Julie had picked up on an idea and was launching into a kind of spiel she must get into frequently. "You never know from one reading to the next who's going to be there and from where. We've had all kinds of people show up."

"I bet you have," Karl agreed. "What I'm trying to say is just that people often come to readings for the wrong reasons. They're either just getting 'culture' or getting away or finding a place to read a book or whatever. I even heard students like poetry readings because they resemble computers! Quick succession of information, etcetera. But I very seldom run into people who come for the right reasons. Like that woman."

Julie was still smiling, and they were parting company at the entrance to the library. They shook hands, and Karl thanked her for being the host. He had to remember to thank people. His mother had scolded him several times after they ended up working in the same library and she discovered how awkward he was socially. He forgot to be polite half the time, and it was a sore spot with her (her voice on the phone: "Try the *honorific approach* Karl, just show respect for the other person sometimes! And be more fuzzy—hedge your bets more, Karl.") Then Julie was gone, and he was wandering out of the Coliseum again.

When he got outside the air was fresh and cool. There was a lingering dampness from an earlier rain. The cars and streets were glistening with a rime of wetness that covered them, and the air smelled of fresh cedar and damp steel. It was a good smell. Bark mulch in the flower patches exuded a stark, tannin odor that penetrated. Karl crossed Georgia Street to catch the bus for North Vancouver. He stood at the bus shelter holding his black nylon bag. Another reading finished. There were no more readings lined up just now, but no doubt the next one would show up in a couple or three months. A slow trickle of readings, a review he would find once in a blue moon. Being a poet was such a quiet occupation. Hardly discernible. Almost unnoticeable. That's the way he liked it; that's what he liked about it. The least conspicuous occupation in the world. Karl Heffner was a quiet person and lived a quiet life. He was discreet, like his mother, and a little awkward like his father. But he relied on them. When they left, whenever that would be, for Galiano or wherever, he would be alone in town. He wasn't looking forward to that. Somehow, his parents were enough of a social life for him. He didn't need any more. But when they were gone, he would have to replace them with someone. Something. The thought gave him a headache.

The bus came and he got on, taking a seat in the nearly empty coach. They drove down the avenue, and Karl was observing the fashionable people downtown: people dressed up in party clothes, and some very elegant couples, and groups of businessmen in suits. Then there was Stanley Park and the marina before it, and the view of North Vancouver on the other side. He liked looking at that. The construction equipment was parked for the night on the sidewalks. They were widening Georgia Street to the south, adding another couple of meters for cyclists. They were replacing the streetlights. All that for six hundred thousand dollars, he had heard, and the whole street was supposed to accommodate an average of sixty-five thousand vehicles every twenty-four hours. Right now the traffic was very sparse. He liked that. There was the all-glass exterior of the Vancouver Centre. Nicola, Cardero, Bidwell, Denman, Gilford, Chilco—he read the street signs as if they were important. The flags were outside of Hotel Vancouver at Hornby, a limousine parked out front. From his reading of architecture, Karl had learned they were going to build a fifty-one floor skyscraper on the Hotel Georgia parking lot, something that was going to tower over everything and look like an icicle. As he pondered the view, trying to imagine the appearance of that behemoth, his mind wandered to the woman in the yellow jacket with the straight brown hair and the book by Dr. Felix. He couldn't quite get her out of his mind. Why should he, anyway? Why should he? During his lunch-hour breaks at the library, he had been reading *The Thousand and One Nights*—for no reason. But he was at "The Porter and the Three Ladies of Baghdad." Right at the very beginning, he was intrigued. Couldn't put it down:

> Once upon a time there was a Porter in Baghdad,
> who was a bachelor and who would remain unmarried.
> It came to pass on a certain day, as he stood about the

street leaning idly upon his crate, behold, there stood before him an honorable woman in a mantilla of Mosul silk, broidered with gold and bordered with brocade; her walking shoes were also purfled with gold and her hair floated in long plaits. She raised her face veil. . . .

Code Pink and Denim

The Faculty Club was large and wintry, as usual. Not cold in temperature, but in atmosphere. The carpet was a seaweed-green, and the walls were pale brick. There were huge windows in the formal dining room and the Saskatchewan Room (aptly named, Elly thought); all around the space was nothing but glass. The coldness was amplified by starched white tablecloths and linen napkins, sticking up like icebergs by bone-white plates. Elly assumed that was why the place appeared so cool and unwelcoming. The view from the windows was usually a view of frost: ice-caked sidewalks, snow-covered fir trees, a frozen North

Saskatchewan River where nothing moved and high-rises on the other side, standing still as sentinels.

Twenty minutes earlier, Elly had showed up at the office of the Chair's secretary, as prescribed, to meet Anthony Felix and a candidate for a job who was being interviewed. Anthony Felix, a man with two first names (Elly found that so interesting that she assumed there was no last name at all), was a newly retired colleague brought in for the occasion. They were taking the job applicant to lunch; he happened to be from Nigeria and had just flown in for his lecture and job interrogation. When the three of them got to the front door and stepped outside, the visitor put on a cap he had bought the night before at Army & Navy, which happened to be across from the Varscona Hotel where he was staying. He hadn't prepared for this extreme chill, he told them. Elly could not help laughing quietly at the hat: it was a joker's cap, with five appendages sticking out in all directions from the top of his head, and a tiny bell at the end of each. "It was all I could find!" he explained laughing.

The usual lunch buffet was spread out on the long table: hot dishes that changed every day of the week (today was pork kebab, beef stroganoff, *samosas*, Kiwi mussels, filet of salmon, quiche Lorraine), steamed cauliflower and broccoli, cold macaroni salads with and seafoods (imitation crab with mayonnaise), lettuce leaves with sliced radishes, desserts (chocolate cheesecake, raspberry pie, Nanaimo bars), juices, coffee, bottles of white wine (Okanagan Grey Monk). Elly looked at Anthony Felix, who was signing their names in the guest book.

"I don't belong to the Faculty Club any more," she warned him. "I can't actually pay for this."

"That's all right!" he said loudly. He always talked as if he were about to break into laughter. "I'll sign for us. The department pays anyway!" Then he actually chuckled. Elly decided she liked him then.

She didn't see him much. Hardly ever, in fact. He was of medium height, with bronze-colored hair not entirely gray yet, a broad smile, gleaming sky-tinted eyes. Slender but not thin, always well dressed in professorial tweed jackets and white shirts. A man of considerable charm, Elly had always thought.

"I think it's all the house rules that got to me, finally," she joked to Felix. "Seems more like a military than a club. You may have nine guests and no more," she recited. "You may not come more than three times without being a member; jacket and tie only; you may not be disruptive; whatever—kind of scary rules." He laughed and shook his head as if to say *so it goes.* What she didn't know, but learned during this lunch, was that Anthony Felix had spent a good portion of his life in Africa. He spoke with a British accent and was enthusiastic about all things African. Elly got the sense that he was an old-fashioned colonialist with very liberal views, in love with the "native" cultures. But that was not it either, she reasoned. He was in love with everything. A life-enthusiast. A dramatist. The Nigerian visitor, who turned out to be a poet as well as a scholar, sat facing the view of the frozen river, picking at the green beans, which would have seemed pale fare to anyone. Anthony Felix was chatting away good-humoredly. Elly wanted to look the visitor from Nigeria square in the eye and get to the point, but of course couldn't say the inappropriate things she wanted to. Such as, *Do you really want to come to this climate? Are you sure about this?* His wife would surely leave him. Isn't that what happened to her colleague over in sociology? His wife took off for Norway because she couldn't stand it here?

After lunch they came out again into the subzero weather and headed for Anthony Felix's old Toyota, so he could drive them back to the Arts Department building. The Faculty Club was a rather nice building, when looked at like this outside in the snow. Dark brown wood and glass. Elly looked at Felix's tanned face and broad, energetic smile.

"You seem to be faring well in your retirement," she said. He laughed a little bit at that.

"No," he said in a half-confidential tone. "I'm terrible, really. I have prostate cancer and I'm going in for surgery next week."

"No!"

"Yes. I only just discovered it; it was such a surprise." He opened the door for the two of them.

"I didn't know," Elly said. "I'm sorry to hear it." They were caught up in packing themselves into the car and driving off, making small observances along the way. The inside of Felix's car was messy: plastic bottles with blue liquid in them, a flashlight, a suede cloth. She remembered a poem she read somewhere about "boys who keep secrets under the front seat. . . ." She took another look at her colleague. He seemed so healthy, but was clearly masking his distress. They started to talk about the build-up of war with Iraq.

"We don't need a war," Elly exclaimed as they pulled into the staff parking lot. "Life itself is a war."

"Yes, you're oh so right," Anthony Felix concurred, with his near-laughing smile. "Right you are." He was silent for a moment, as if thinking something over. "We really mustn't be silent about things that matter, don't you think?" he then said. "That's what Martin Luther King Jr. once said, I believe." A broad smile. "There is a whole domino effect, I think, with Iraq, then Iran, then Syria—or so it seems, you know!"

"Dangerous stuff," Elly conceded.

"Oh yes, right you are. I was in the military once, and I'm sure glad it was then and not now."

"British military?"

"To be sure. There's even the chance of invading North Korea after Syria, as far as I can see. Or am I too pessimistic?" He was chuckling at himself.

Later, Elly kept thinking about how mystified Anthony Felix seemed to be about his health. Perhaps his interest in politics was taking up all his attention? These things had a way of colonizing your mind, it seemed. As time went on, she followed the news of his sojourn into hospital and back out. The surgery went well, and nothing happened. Surprisingly, though, the next news was that Anthony Felix's wife, Sarah, had died. A notice went around with a card to be signed. Elly was not surprised. How often had she not seen that happen: the husband is sick, and all the attention is on him. Meanwhile, the wife is the caregiver whom no one notices until she suddenly, always unexpectedly, just dies.

Elly went home early on Wednesdays. Her workday was short that day because the day before and the day after were prolonged. Tuesdays and Thursdays she worked until ten at night. She had a string of workshops with individual students for seven hours straight and did not get home till half past. She did not like walking home so late, when the temperature had dipped into the minuses and the air was icy and a frigid wind blew down her neck. (She liked walking in the summer when it was hot, though: the Devonian Botanic Gardens, with its vaulted bridge over calm, mirrorlike water, trees of all shades of green and orange lining the view, sculptures on the grass, park benches where you could sit and think . . .) On this wintry day, the sun was shining. It was three in the afternoon, and she did not have to button her fake-sheepskin coat. She let herself into the apartment. It was right next to the music department building, where she kept her cello in the piano and woodwinds room. Cymbals and harps were in there too along with anything too big and cumbersome to take home every night. The air in the apartment was dry but warm with the sun beaming in from the southwest. It was an industrial building, the ceilings raw concrete with the pipes exposed. Something typically urban—meant for a lifestyle of restaurant eating and cinema going, café haunting and art gallery cocktailing but not for domestic living. Still she liked being home. It was the privacy. To be able to close the door on the world and choose whether to answer the phone, decide yourself what you will hear and when, what news to listen to, what not to. She could play Bach's cello suites or Vivaldi's cello sonatas as much and often as she liked here. Privacy was, for Elly Winthrop, a near-synonym of *peace*.

Tranquility was hard to come by. She figured stillness and harmony were not actually sought after. Not really wanted, for some reason. She hung up her winter coat, shed her boots and went into the small bedroom with the April Corneille quilt on the bed, displaying its lilac and russet print pattern, and threw off her brown office suit. She stripped naked, put on a light day-pajama set she picked up at Save-On Foods once, and went to the kitchen in her bare feet to make afternoon tea. The space was silver-quiet, but there was a muffled sound of traffic outside. Cold tires on iced streets. It was a sound she had become used to. As she put on the water in the Ikea kettle, she found herself thinking there was only one really good reason for all the conflict and strife surrounding us all: discord and friction were wanted. They were what makes people feel alive, she thought. She remembered an interview with journalists who cover war, who go to the frontlines and end up being excited by the whole experience and can't settle down to regular life after such an assignment. Up in her summer cottage in the Shuswaps a few months earlier, Elly remembered showing her friend Cath pictures of a seaside village in southwestern Sweden. A quiet place with red houses, cinder-colored cliffs, hazy blue sea, forests of beech and Norway spruce stands and serenity all around.

It was Elly's plan to move there. What she remembered now was Cath's response: "But it'll be boring."

"What do you mean 'boring'?" Elly asked surprised.

"Nothing going on!"

"What's supposed to be going on?"

"Something. I don't know."

"But quietude. It's what you want," Elly suggested then. "The calm life."

Then she and Cath were staring at each other for a while in silence. Elly surprised. Cath at a loss for words, having blurted out something quite real to her. From the guts: Cath did not want the quiet life, but she did not know what she wanted in its place.

The water boiled and Elly put two bags of Moroccan green tea into a bone-white teapot. She poured the water in and waited for it to steep. The steam rose from the pot and made her feel momentarily contented. Steam from a teapot was a safe feeling. The strong sun radiating and filling the room with warmth was a safe feeling. The colorful quilt on the bed, the comfortable pillows underneath. Books in the bookshelf waiting to be read. Quietly secure.

"All you need is enough money to live on," she said to Cath then, finally. "That's all you really need."

What she meant but could not find the words for just then was that life itself—just the way you got it, the way you had to live it in any case—was dangerous enough. You do not actually have to do anything to have too much going on already. Every minute is full of potential. Even if you never lift a finger, there it is: danger, harm, terror, morbid awful anxiety and fear, and then, dreadful death. Of course she would not say that. Could not say that. It would make her sound melodramatic. She had an old copy of George Herbert's poems on her coffee table by the television. Sometimes she read the poems—just for fun. They harbored the intense Biblicalism, she called it, of her upbringing in Washington: she knew some of the poems by heart:

> *Lie not; but let thy heart be true to God,*
> *thy mouth to it, thy actions to them both:*
> *Cowards tell lies, and those that fear the rod;*
> *The stormie working soul spits lies and froth.*
> *Dare to be true. Nothing can need a ly:*
> *A fault, which needs it most, grows two thereby. . . .*

"Dare to be true." She liked that—a thought that lay behind her movements. *All* her movements.

The quiet life. *Blest who can unconcern'dly find / Hours, days, and years slide soft away / In health of body, peace of mind, / Quiet by day. . .* She remembered this verse from Alexander Pope from her schooldays. *Thus let me live, unseen, unknown; / Thus unlamented let me die. . . .* The quiet life had a bad name now. History sped on irrevocably, and the public mood was for action—any action. Movement for movement's sake. Every year, Elly felt more like an anomaly than before. Because everything unassuming appealed to her. Everything graceful and considered. Sharp movements and harsh noise repelled her. Bright lights and chaotic relationships made her dizzy. She had begun to think that silence—a hushed space—frightened people.

She first got this idea when she lived in a townhouse on 109 Street. It was a two-story row house with gables and a picket fence, a fireplace and an attached garage. One of the new residences that had been built recently, loosely constructed with cheap materials. Elly moved there after she sold her house and wanted to rethink her future. She bought two large leather chairs at Eaton's, burgundy-colored lounge chairs with brass buttons down the sides. She put one on each side of the fireplace. She placed her mother's antique furnishings about the rest of the house. Things she inherited from her mother's house: a dining table and eight chairs, upholstered with handmade weaving from her mother's loom. A china cabinet with stained glass doors, created in her mother's art studio. Everywhere, all her mother's things. The dwelling was soundless, except for the hum of the refrigerator. Even the busy noise from 109 Street around the corner did not reach into those walls.

One of Elly's students came to visit on a Sunday afternoon. They sat down in the leather chairs and had their conference ("I've got an offer to Victoria and another to Berkley, and my mom wants me to go to Victoria, and I want to go to Europe, but I haven't been accepted yet, and what should I do next?" the student went on, because she had a host of conundrums she wanted Elly to decide for her, and Elly couldn't help remembering the sign in the doctor's office that read: OUT OF CONSIDERATION FOR YOUR PHYSICIAN'S TIME PLEASE BRING ONLY ONE MEDICAL CONCERN AT A TIME, an order she found almost amusingly absurd) and suddenly the girl sighed, looked around, and exclaimed: "I've never seen such a quiet place!" It was not so much what the girl said that caught Elly's attention but how she said it. With apprehension, as if she were afraid. It made Elly think of young people and how they surround themselves with noise. It must be for comfort, she thought then.

She took her cup of green tea to the sofa and leaned against the russet pillow she once hauled back from the Hudson's Bay on Bus 06. The hiss of passing cars could be heard outside. The low rumble of busses stopping at the shelter across the street. Occasional shouts between people walking by. Students and staff went to and fro along the street. The University Hospital, the largest in the city, was also across the street. From her front window, she looked right at the EMERGENCY sign, lit up in scarlet neon all night long. Often at night the burp of a siren could be heard from an ambulance that started off on a journey to fetch the sick. Elly watched the beams of sun filtering in through the window as they lit up the partition opposite. On the wall were two photographs she had framed, pictures of boats in a marina that she had taken in Malmö, Sweden, the place she wanted to live in someday. When the sunlight landed directly on the photos, the azure of the sea became shadowy, and the white boats austere. The sofa was by the outsized window in the living room. Where she was sitting, Elly could watch the activity on the street below. People were bundled up in overcoats, fur caps, clumsy looking mittens, carrying bags under their arms or weighted down with heavy-looking backpacks. It was minus thirty-two out there. The cold breath of winter hung suspended in the air.

Now she thought back to the lunch with Anthony Felix at the Faculty Club. As it turned out, the man they were wining and dining that day did not get hired. But another academic from Nigeria did, and he had accepted. Elly had seen him around in the halls. There was a funeral for Anthony Felix's wife, and then things went on as usual. (She was known for doing things like weaving and pottery and painting—all sorts of creative things. She had a kiln outdoors, and did her weaving on a balcony above the living room. Elly used to think she must have the better life of the two, but she realized now she may have been wrong. There's more to a life than what you hear in the halls.) Carolina Bilmington, their renowned colleague, was giving the Atquest Lecture one week, and Elly went to hear her along with everyone else. The topic was the indigenous music of Tazmania. On the way back to her office, she ran into Anthony Felix on the stairwell. Elly was thinking of the stone steps at the University of Washington, where she spent all those years; the nice way they blended natural stone and huge oak trees and autumn grass full of leaves, with benches inside alcoves where you could sit and meditate between classes. . . . And she was thinking of the survey course of western music she was about to go teach. (She taught applied music, she participated in the Campus Choraleers, she did Instrumental Ensemble—it was all wound tightly in to a short term. Too much to know and too little time to learn it in.) Felix had come for the address as well and was looking as perky as usual. But he was emotional. He gave Elly a tight hug in the middle of the stairs.

"I know you have a broken heart," she said. It was all she could think of.

"But I do!" he said. "These things seem so pointless sometimes, don't they?"

"They seem so."

"I didn't know it then, but I know now that caregivers often die first. We should plan for that, shouldn't we? We shouldn't put all the stress on one person. I wish I had know those things. Isn't that part of making your own plans and will and all that? That's what I have to think."

"You're probably right about that. There just doesn't seem time to think about everything when you're sick."

"No, you're so right," he said.

They chatted for a while in the stairwell. Elly recollected the conversation in fragments. She mainly recalled the affection, the neediness, that had surfaced in her otherwise flamboyant and worldly colleague.

Elly wavered between ennui, comfort and anxiety this Wednesday, like all other days. It was never one or the other; sometimes the three shifted in balance, one becoming more prominent, then another, like a symphonic arabesque, almost *Mahlerian*. But on a day like this, they were all there at once. She had office hours in the mornings. Students came to see her, and she subjected them to her counsel. Then she invariably wondered whether she had said the right thing. Was her advice good guidance, after all? She could never be certain. It required a much higher level of self-confidence, even arrogance. An ability to be patronizing, even. That was not her. Not her any more, anyway. Oddly enough, when she was younger she was more self-assured. Now it was only the daily renewal of a wish for a good day, not a bad day. Her morning mantra, silent, sometimes unnoticed even to herself, but always there: *hoping today will not be a disaster.* Hoping she would come home of an evening after a day's work, like today, and there would be some daylight left in the sky, perhaps even some sunshine, and she could drink in the last dregs of daily relief. Because there had been days when she came home just plain anxious, harboring those recognizable psychic tsunamis. The best she could hope for, she had learned, was that the Machiavellian impulses that surround her would not be directed at her this time. "Pass over me," she could wordlessly pray. Her own little Passover.

On the table in the corner of the apartment kitchen (a table Elly had bought from a discount furniture store on 82 Avenue and lugged home in big packages in a Yellow Cab) was her apple bowl with two apples left in it. It was a $10 glass bowl she got at Southgate Mall. She had furnished her new home in the least expensive way possible because she knew she would leave it. She was going to stop working at the university and start doing something else. Well, she was going to play her own music in a white wooden house outside of Malmö, watch the midnight sun dance on the sea between Sweden and Denmark, and take long walks among the birches. . . . Some of her friends thought she was crazy to give up her security, but she had known for a decade that she would do this. It was inevitable. When she met Anthony Felix in the stairwell on the day of the Atquest Lecture, he had heard the news.

"I hear you're leaving us!" he said plaintively.

"Yes. . . ."

"You're leaving too soon! Is there no way we can entice you back?"

"No." He hugged her then, a sad and intense embrace. His body expressed itself better than language could. And besides, there was not enough time to say much.

For Elly, everything had to link up. She had come to a point in life where things were not connecting. She had to work at it. The apple bowl, for instance. She had to have such a thing because there was always an apple bowl on the dining table when she was growing up in Bellingham, Washington. She grew up in an old plywood house with plank flooring and braided rugs. Her mother sought out folk furniture in the antique shops all over Washington, with considerable success. Her mother was fanciful about it. The dining table was actually an old Mennonite table dating back to the eighteen hundreds. It had originally been bright blue—the blue of pansies—but the paint was worn off and only showed in patches here and there. The table legs were rusty red. But her mother left the table as it was, rough looking and rustic. Along the sides were four wooden chairs with high backs and seats she upholstered herself. On the floor she kept carved decoy ducks and swans, painted white with red bills. And the windows were covered in plain white silk tied in loose knots. The model for them had been the peasant windows of Czechoslovakia. Elly loved her mother's house. She was sorry to leave it because time did not pass so quickly there. Time was unhurried and went by effortlessly, without friction. One of the memories she had managed to keep alive from those years was the smell of apples. There were apple groves everywhere, and apple tress with ripening fruit. The smell of apples in all stages of maturation—that was the scent of her childhood. There were always fresh apples in the brightly painted Mexican apple bowls. Rotting apples on the grass. Apple cider in the press, the fragrance of cinnamon and nutmeg in them.

She took the book from the coffee table—a light birch box-table from Ikea. The book was a newly purchased copy of Frantz Fanon's *Wretched of the Earth.* She had an old, smudged paperback from Albert's Books in Sycamous, B.C., where her summer cottage was, because she could not find a new copy in any regular bookstore. But the day before she tried one last time, at the University Bookstore, reasoning it might be there for some course or other. She found a new edition and cheerfully took it home. Back in the Sixties, when this book was so popular and everyone in Seattle was reading it and talking about it, Elly was a Taoist and a pacifist and didn't want to be influenced toward violence. Her understanding was that Fanon spoke of violence in a positive manner. Now, almost forty years later, she returned to it and finally read it. No, he was not prescribing violence as a solution to colonialism the way she had thought. He was simply describing why natives of a colonized country take to violence. The explanation was quite straightforward, understandable and sympathetic.

She found herself thinking about a comment Fanon makes in his chapter "National Culture," about how culture doesn't matter. This she found hard to take, but decided to ponder the question from Fanon's point of view. What did he mean, exactly? Making cultural objects and texts in a colonized condition doesn't matter, he claims, because they are gestures towards exoticization and are not liberative. They are more likely to be "dead" than to be helpful or vigorous. For something to be alive, he writes, it has to be changing and developing. Anything that does not change and grow and evolve is dead. The only thing that matters, he says everywhere in that book, is the struggle for the liberation of one's people. It is the struggle for the nation you call your own that matters, and struggle is action. A true citizen and patriot is engaged on the physical plane, not just in the realm of ideas and imaginings. Then Elly leapt automatically to a comment she remembered Virginia Woolf making about patriotism and struggle, in 1938 in *Three Guineas*, a treatise she was reading again. Woolf said: *If you insist upon fighting to protect me, or "our" country, let it be understood, soberly and rationally between us, that you are fighting . . . to procure benefits which I have not shared . . . in fact, as a woman, I have no country. As a woman, I want no country. As a woman my country is the whole world.*

In the gathering dusk of late afternoon, the sunshine disappeared as abruptly as it had come. The gray of nightfall took over. A kind of gloom descended. Elly heard a helicopter in the distance. The piercing machine echo, low and angry sounding, approached and grew in volume. It was one of the hospital helicopters, coming for a landing on the hospital roof opposite. It was an emergency. Everything was an urgent situation, she thought. Life itself was a disaster. She could not help recollecting the day she took a cab to the food store in south Strathcona. It was minus thirty-four and windy that day, and driving and walking were out of the question. She had decided to stock up for two or three weeks, so she wouldn't have to go anywhere in this weather. When the taxi turned the corner of Whyte Avenue, she looked over to the Cross Cancer Institute and saw people were amassing. A hundred, two hundred, three hundred. They had signs and placards. "Don't Beat Around the Bush." "Drop Bush, Not Bombs." An anti-war march—the first of many, she knew. It was the start of something. A grassroots movement. Why was she not there too? She berated herself. Next time she would go. She wanted to think about this: were there not many ways of protesting? Could we all not do what we are best at so long as everyone does something?

She went off and bought food and necessities for two hundred and fifty dollars. When she carried the grocery bags into the apartment that day, she couldn't help feeling some sort of indefinable kinship. With all women everywhere. How many women around the world were not hauling food from one place to another—or water? Sometimes it was just a daily task, other times it was an emergency. She had seen news programs on television about how people in Iraq were hiring well-drillers to drill for water in their backyards, just in case. People there were stocking up on food for their own reasons. They got two months' worth of food coupons every month. That meant in six months there would be no more coupons, no more food. How close to catastrophe life was for some, Elly thought. And then the next thought: why were we doing this? Why were people creating artificial crises when they didn't have to?

The cup of tea in Elly's hands was warm; it warmed the palms as she cradled the white porcelain in both hands. She watched the steam slowly rise from the hot tea into the air. She put her bare feet into the muffle of soft, fuzzy slippers. The slippers were fur-lined moccasins with beadwork on them in Indian style; something she picked up at Safeway. Odd little purchases, spontaneous at the time, which grew to become important small components of daily life. The slippers felt velvety and gave a comfortable sensation when the temperature outside dipped to the minus thirties and the wind began to howl among the concrete buildings, moaning like bereft mothers. Slowly, it began to snow.

A peaceful moment in the afternoon. An ordinary day in the middle of the week. Nothing special. Elly had learned over time to take these moments that were given to her—that are given to any-one, really—and take pleasure in them. They are moments people often try to avoid, as if there were something dangerous in them. She thought again about the strange conversation she had with Cath about boredom. Cath was afraid of being bored. To Elly, there was no such thing. She had never experienced it. Ennui, yes. But bore-dom? What she really wanted, she knew already, was to slow down time. Everything was moving too fast. Life catches you unaware, and before you know it, you look in the mirror and don't recognize the face looking back. It's you all right, but you look much older than you should be. In fact, you still feel fifteen. The person in the mirror is at least three times that. This gap between perception and reality was what was upsetting. These moments, when you stop what you are doing, put on your slippers, have a cup of hot tea and watch the snow coming down outside—they were moments she stole from the storehouse of time, so she could really feel time passing. So it would not just go by without her. She remembered once reading a novel by A.S. Byatt, *The Biographer's Tale.* She sometimes thought about the core in that book, which is not so much affirmed as it is implied: it is the fantasy of quitting writing. And she remembered Vikram Seth's novel all of a sudden, *An Equal Music.* That was about the fantasy of quitting music. Of quitting teaching, playing, performing—even hearing. The fantasy of deafness. Perhaps many people have fantasies of giving up the work they are doing. The reverie of quitting work. Of being set free from the self you are in. Even from the body you are in. For what? So you can feel time passing, so you can follow along as it inches forward.

"Where are you going?" Anthony Felix had asked her at their chance meeting in the stairwell after that spontaneous hug on the day of the Atquest Lecture. "Where will you be?" She hesitated to say. She had so much more to tell him than there was time for. How to condense everything into one answer?

"I'm going to where there is magic," she said. "Where life is magical."

In moments like this the mind could wander. The snowflakes were very tiny, coming down like dust over the city. Dry, miniature snow pellets collected like dandruff on the shoulders and hats of people walking. How was the ending of Fanon's *Wretched of the Earth* anyway? He ends on a diatribe against all of Europe. Europe is at an

end, he says; the European game is over. And America, which set out
to catch up and be better than Europe, has become a monster. Real
liberation is not found in that direction. How then? *Comrades*, Fanon
closes as he himself sets out to join revolutionary fighters instead of
practicing psychiatry in a hospital, *we must turn over a new leaf, we must
work out new concepts, and try to set afoot a new man.* And a new woman,
Elly thought. Fanon had been criticized for the way he viewed
women, but it didn't matter now. That was also the writer's job, he
had said: to find a new way of being human. It was a good thought.
It was the real answer she wanted to give to Anthony Felix when he
asked her what she was going to do next. Learn how to be a new
human being.

She picked up the small, hardbound volume of George
Herbert's verse she had carried with her from Washington to B.C. to
Alberta—the little blue book was always there. It was given to her
by her grandfather, who was an English teacher in the high school
system of Washington State. First she left it on the shelf and never
opened it. Then one day she happened to be leafing through it, and
she found her grandfather had underlined certain poems, had made
comments in the margins, signs and symbols that meant something
to him. She got interested in deciphering his private code. He
marked one poem with a red pen, and she knew it was special for
him. She began to read it. Now she knew it by heart:

> *I got me flowers to straw they way;*
> *I got me boughs off many a tree:*
> *But thou wast up by break of day,*
> *And brought's thy sweets along with thee.*

> *The Sunne arising in the East,*
> *Though he give light, & th'East perfume;*

If they should offer to contest
With thy arising, they presume.

Can there be any day but this,
Though many sunnes to shine endeavour?
We count three hundred, but we inisse:
There is but one, and that one ever.

The cup of Moroccan green tea was soothing. On the table she glanced at an advertisement for a concert at Convocation Hall nearby. The Edmonton Chamber Music Society was hosting the concert Sunday night of Alessandro Marcello's concerti. *La Cetra,* all the oboe concertos, performed by the Edmonton Camerata. Suddenly, Elly took her own thoughts to heart. She could invite Anthony Felix to come out for the concert with her. He would be surprised; after all, they hardly knew each other. But it was a nice thought. As the steam from the cup in her hands diminished and the snow outside fell more thickly, Elly let the afternoon slip into evening. Her bare feet were warm in the fluffy slippers. The sound of a distant fan in the ceiling hummed almost imperceptibly. She was thinking, there is nothing but this moment. This minute going by—it is the only minute we have, the only hour, the only day. The black telephone she bought at Army & Navy sat on the raw pine tea table next to her. She reached for the receiver.

Dancing in the Marketplace

"*B*ut I enjoy wearing them," Randolph Outlaw said with his carved smile on, the smile that made Nancy think he had the face of one of those tree sculptures that were carved with chainsaws into trees uprooted in storms. They were everywhere: howling wolves, sitting owls, honey bears on hind legs, and old men's faces with long stringy beards and sad hair and ancient mouths. (At the Shell Station they had a fox sculpted into a tree trunk, which they wound the hose around.) Chiseled lines and deep expressions. "I enjoy it. Don't you? Come on, admit it now. They feel good!"

"Yes, but you know," Nancy hedged. "You're a man!"

"So?" He looked at her aggressively, as if she were demented or something. She didn't like that look. She definitely didn't like it.

"It's just . . . Randy, it's just that these things were meant for women. Don't men have comfortable undergarments? I always thought comfort was the main thing for men's underwear. Lots of women envy men for getting that, when they have to make do with things that snag and cut and creep and stab." It was true: those wire-boned bras and demi bras that cut into the middle of your breasts; those tanga panties and lace garter belts that scratched along your stomach; those so-called hip-slimmers and body enhancers that cut off your blood supply.

"Oh but nothing like this! Nothing compares with this tight, silky, sexy feeling!"

"Okay, okay," she gave up on him. Every time they mentioned this topic, she had to give in. He just wouldn't budge. But he could do something about that name, though. She wanted him to go change his last name. It was three years now since she first started bugging him about it. He would have to get a new social security identity, but—Outlaw! She would not marry him until that last name of his was changed to something more proper. She was never going to bear the name Nancy Outlaw. Never!

"But you will go to the government offices in town, though?" she asked demurely. Once again. "See about that name, won't you?"

To this she got the usual silence. He just munched away at his scrambled eggs and didn't answer. (At least it wasn't the brains and eggs he always made a joke of getting as a kid up in Pender; he said they were made with bacon grease and pork brains and gravy—well if that wasn't Canadian?) Someday he would. He would have to do something someday.

Nancy Hedgecroft was of British origin, and she took pride in that. (Liverpool, where she used to take the bus from Queens Square to Merseyside regular as clockwork every day at 10:20 to meet her grandma, something she thought of now with a foggy dissatisfaction. She also—more often recently—thought of an encounter with a young soldier. Tony—Anthony Felix was his name and she didn't forget it either—a boy she knew for exactly one day at the Liverpool Moat House on Paradise Street. He was sweet, he was, in his khaki uniform, up for the weekend; they were smoking together, walking by the Mersey, visiting the Albert Dock museums, wandering around, and at the Lime Street train station they exchanged numbers—then she left for Canada! Why did she do such a thing?) When people watched film versions of Jane Austen and George Elliot, things like *Mansfield Park* or *Silas Marner,* on television, she could say to them "I know what that's about." She meant she had the inside track; she had the tone and the atmosphere. She knew. (She could for example tell them the scene where a gentleman is smoking in the same room as the ladies—well, that was inaccurate! And people just didn't address each other by their first names, the way it was in the movies!) She hadn't lived in England for twenty-two years, but that didn't discount anything, did it? Now Nancy was getting a little older and she felt it more necessary to keep up appearances. Not that she didn't before, when she was younger. It was just easier then. It came naturally to look good. Now the business of being pretty actually took time and was a lot of work. She was careful, though. After all, she was out here *in the colonies,* so to speak. Even though Canada was an independent country and all that, it was still an old colony of Britain, and she had what she felt was *special dispensation.* So she groomed herself carefully. Every morning, she bathed and then began the lavish arrangements of looking the part.

First she applied undertone to her face, then her neck and arms, and sometimes all the way down her chest. Then she applied powder on all the same areas. There was her Revlon Shopper's Drug Mart kit:

eye shadow, blush, mascara, eyeliner, lip gloss and lipstick, and finally a dimple to paint with her eye pencil. She had her bottle of *Graffiti Vanilla de Naf Naf,* a perfume she splurged on. Her hair needed elaborate care. She had it colored a deep mahogany, with a slight tinge of red. Underneath the color, her hair was really mousy and gray, but no one needed to know that. She painted her fingernails and toenails raspberry red, and once a week she removed cuticles and filed them down and applied Alba Botanica hand lotion liberally every day. She also put Elizabeth Arden lotion all over her body to make her skin "silky smooth" as they said. She had a wardrobe of outfits—a different dress for each day of the week. She started over again every Sunday with the week, so it seemed like she had a lot of outfits. Today, Monday, she was wearing her black Rayon dress and jacket. The skirt was long, almost down to her ankles, and it was black and straight, but roomy and comfortable. The jacket was short, almost bolero, but colorful, with tan and ivory patterns in bold display. She put on a fake pearl necklace over that. No one needed to know it was not real—who was going to peer up close with a magnifying glass anyway? Besides, she was only going shopping.

Nancy was going to the IGA Marketplace first off. She was going to wheel one of those new, upright and handy carts around and buy some groceries for herself and Randolph. They would have something proper for dinner, she would see to that. Some *Coquilles St. Jacques,* perhaps—scallops in mushrooms and shallots and cream—something they wouldn't be making in every house around here (and she had some cherry red clay ramekins she found at a thrift shop once to serve it in). Well, of course, in her special neighborhood, what people lived in couldn't properly be called "houses" even though they were perfectly good things. The mobile home she shared with Randolph was actually very prim. They got it at a good price, and it only cost three hundred dollars a month to be there. Randy had added to the back portion, and there was more room now. (He renovated the thing; removed the outside metal, repaired two leaky windows, changed some patches of damp insulation and covered the outside walls with sheathing.) After the IGA, she was going to the new Canadian Tire store on the highway. She was going to get a couple of begonias or maybe one of those cute elves they were selling for $12.95 or maybe a gnome wheelbarrow planter. Just something to put by the front step; a little booster. People need that, Nancy knew for sure; they needed little boosters along the way.

Nancy always went to the IGA, rather than the Safeway or the Supervalu or the Extra Foods store. It was obvious why a woman would go to IGA—any dolt would know. It was the lighting. Some very clever manager of all the IGA stores had discovered the advantage of lowering the lighting. Who wants to buy groceries in what was like the inside of a refrigerator? Where the lighting was so fluorescent and crass, punching through everything, rotating, highlighting, coming from inside meat cases and on tracks over vegetable bins, so powerful that every dimple on your face and arms was instantly visible? No, the dim lights in the IGA were soothing, and better yet, people just plain looked better. She looked better there than in any other of the stores, so there she went. Obviously, there were no women managing grocery stores nowadays. It also alarmed her when she watched television—which she did a lot, that had to be admitted—how they were always photographing people up close. Why did they do that? It used to be you got a picture of a person from a proper distance. Now, they swing the camera right up to the face and you practically see up a person's nose! She used to want to be photographed for television, but not any more! Oh no. She wouldn't want those cameras prying into her nose and ears and making obvious every single hair and freckle and blemish. Obviously, no women in charge of cinematography nowadays either. She mentioned this to Randolph.

"Why do they do that?" One of those evenings with beer and chips—a concession to Randy's Canadian manhood. He was not of British origin, so she had to concede. But the beer was good. She enjoyed the beer when it was cold, so what of it? "Why do they plaster the camera lens right up against a person's awful looking pasty skin and show the grossness of it all?"

"Because they can." That was his easy reply.

"What do you mean, Randy? People don't just do things because they 'can.' There has to be a better reason."

"No. Sometimes people do things just because they can. It doesn't mean they should, but the temptation is too great. The thing about this is, there are cameras now that take close-ups so clearly, that it's much easier to do. They've got micro-lenses and zooms they put on tripods that can focus down to the fingertip. They think they're being intimate that way."

"Well, you know what they are being," Nancy retorted with a bit of scorn in her voice.

"What are they being?" Randy wasn't focusing on their conversation. He had his eyes plastered on the hockey. But he could carry on a multitasking situation pretty well. He could watch and converse rather well, she had to admit.

"Pornographic!"

"Pornographic?" He was amused and surprised, and he looked at her while he stuffed a potato chip into his mouth. He was laughing in a way.

"That's what I said." End of story. That was the point. Finito.

Nancy Hedgecroft went in her pointy-heeled shoes to the grocery store. She got into the now twenty-year-old Ford station wagon with the hole in the gas tank. For the most part it was still a good car, and the hole in the tank was something no one could see. Nancy kept the vehicle clean, for the most part, and it had a lot of room if you needed it. The color was not so great maybe—Randy used the words "piss and shit" to describe it. But he was just being awful. He liked being awful, to give her a turn. Playing with her, that's what. She preferred to think of it as a "vintage car," the way people had vintage cars all over this place. There was a real mania going on in this part of the world for collectible vehicles. People had cars from the twenties and thirties and forties and fifties, and they repainted them and spruced them up and then they drove around like crazy— never too fast, because pedestrians and onlookers had to get a chance to really look. It was like a perpetual parade. You'd see, on any day, a 1927 Chrysler Model 60 Roadster with a soft top, painted baby blue, or you'd see an orange 1954 Mercury Sun Valley with a black roof. Randy liked looking at them when they parked at the mall. Daimler Drop Dead Coupe or Studebaker Champion—he knew them all. Sometimes car collectors parked their vehicles by the highway, and you could see them shining in the sun, the chrome glistening, the new paint gleaming. Same with clothes: Nancy used to feel awkward and humiliated getting her outfits at the Salvation Army, used by others before. But then she discovered that "vintage clothing" was chic, and it was just fun—little jet-black crepe dresses sprinkled with rhinestones, or pink and green floral summer outfits with flowers and ruffles and elastic sleeves.…. She enjoyed *vintage*. If anyone asked where she got something, she lowered her voice and moved up close and half-whispered, "It's vintage, you know." As if that meant something incredibly rare and special—which it was, let's face it.

Nancy Hedgecroft had several things to purchase today: Kleenex boxes, chicken livers, potatoes, cabbage for coleslaw, barbecue sauce (Randy insisted—it must be his cowboy background!), real cream for the Coquilles, light bulbs, Tide detergent and, well, pantyhose, size large and tall. She wished she didn't have to.

Sometimes she wondered if she should talk to someone about it. But who? She couldn't go to a counselor, really; they charged over a hundred dollars for just talking for fifty minutes. Besides, it did no harm, did it? She had asked him to explain his behavior to her again, several times, because she didn't get it. She had never run into this before—well, there's a time for everything!

"It was just an accident at first," Randy explained one night. The lights were off (fortunately, because it felt as though the words alone would be visibly embarrassing to her). "I put Cindy's pantyhose on just for fun. They felt really strange. But I had them on under my jeans and was at the bar in them. I just noticed the women started looking at me, like they thought I was really sexy—like they were saying to themselves, 'Hey, who's that good looking guy with those sexy legs,' and I noticed that. They do something to you: keep you really trim and hard where you want to be."

"Do other men do that?" Nancy persisted, hoping he would see things in perspective. "Do other men secretly wear pantyhose under their jeans?" And Randy laughed aloud, like he thought this was fun.

"I don't know. I haven't asked anyone. . . . Only your hairdresser knows for sure!"

The other reason why she went to the IGA Marketplace rather than the village shopping center, where the liquor store was, had to do with Randolph. She didn't want to run into him where he worked. "Worked" was perhaps an over-use of the term, but looked at another way, it was of course work. He did make more money than you'd expect, playing his guitar outside the liquor store entrance (he said it was because he "knew how to do it," meaning he made himself visible; he wore something not too dark, he found a good quiet location, and he said you get good hats!—that Randolph!). He might come home with as much as forty dollars in his bag after a summer afternoon. Crass people might call it busking, but it was more than that. Nancy Hedgecroft had been around during his playing, and it was not just busking, with people rushing by, annoyed at the performer, never dropping in a penny. Randolph Outlaw played classical guitar—he played Beethoven and Schubert and Rodrigo—and people appreciated the soothing music when they were shopping. They stopped to have a listen and take a moment to enjoy the sound. She said to Randy: "They're stopping to smell the roses," and he thought so too. He knew his playing was appreciated and that kept him at it.

On darker days Nancy wished he would have a proper job, but you couldn't tell a man like Randolph what to do. He was his own man. He had his own opinion about things; he liked his guitar and the easy way of keeping his own hours. And of course not having to claim all his earnings to the ever-growing tax department. Oh well, she would say no more about that. She let him do it, but that didn't mean she had to go watch him. She preferred not to think about it. If she didn't think about it, she could almost convince herself Randy was just working "at the office" when he was down there. His charcoal-colored hair was too long, almost to the shoulders, but other than that, he was perfectly presentable. Actually, his face had taken on a weathered look, like someone who's been outside too much, but that wasn't anything he could help. No more than she could help having gotten a little bit older. Sometimes Randy stopped her after she had got herself ready to go out and said in his inimitable Canadian way, "Nancy you look like a doll! You don't have to put on that much makeup—it makes you look like you're made of wax! Honey, you're pretty enough without it!" *Pretty enough without it.* She didn't think so. Not at all. She needed a little help from Max Factor, and she was the first to admit it.

The road from Evergreen Trailer Park to the IGA took Nancy past the new Cedar Pub. She liked the new building, set off as it was up high, with a nice driveway up to the parking lot in the back. It was a classy building that looked more like a resort than a restaurant-pub. It had bay windows on both sides and in between a nice entrance. The front was landscaped, and people could sit outside too on benches. The pub used to be in an old building down in the village by the highway, and it was dark and noisy. The new pub was bright, cheery, served food (specialty: fish and chips, halibut and fries with vinegar and ketchup) and attracted different types of customers—whole families in fact, not just single men out to watch a hockey game and guzzle Labatts. She had worked in the Cedar Pub for five years. It was only temporary, while she was making ends meet, but it lasted five years. When they were in the village, she was running around in the dark, the air full of smoke and the smell of piss everywhere. But when they moved to the new building, it was very different. There was a much more classy feel to the job, and she didn't have to worry about being a bar waitress like before. She could say she was a "hostess" because sometimes they let her run the hostess podium in the front. Then she didn't wait tables but greeted customers instead and showed them to their tables. That was a good time. She lived for the days they let her be a hostess.

But then they asked her to leave. It was pitiful; she had to admit their behavior was a disgrace. The boss, Alan Kusinsky, said to her, "I think you need a little break, Nancy." But what he meant was *you're fired,* and what that meant was *you're too old. We want a fresh young thing who looks like she got lost from her cheerleading troupe.* That's what that was. So she quit and said she had a better job waiting for her (she lied). By that time she had already met Randy, and he had this trailer and somehow they managed. (She met Randy in a bar—yes she did! He sat down beside her, put his arm around the back of her chair and placed a post-it note right on her back. He was going on with one of his anecdotes (he had a collection of them from somewhere), one about *Doctor, doctor, I have a ringing in my ears that sounds like "Why, Why, Why, Delila . . ."*)

Nancy had to tell herself that being fired was actually a good thing. Sometimes things are not so obvious, she said to herself more than once, but when you look at the big picture, it's clearly a good thing to have been fired. She shouldn't be working in a bar anyway. When you got right down to it. That was for students during summer break, not for an English woman (a true Liverpoolite) who was getting a little older. She was feeling something, though, and she couldn't put her finger on it. A strange and stinging feeling in her chest that went right up into her throat. A kind of sadness she didn't know the meaning of. Maybe it was restlessness? She felt like she had to make a decision, but let's face it, she didn't know what the decision was she was supposed to make. Or even what it was all about. She had just come to a place in life where some sort of decision was necessary. What would be her next step? How should she view her life to this point? Where should she go from here? Should she stay with Randy? Was her life what she thought it was? Because, when you got right down to it, Nancy suspected something was wrong here. She didn't know what it was, exactly, but something was terribly wrong with this picture. She had thought of going back to England, but at her age, she realized the only job she could get would be as a charlady. Well, then she might as well work in a bar if she could get even that. She was not going to get down on her hands and knees and start scrubbing floors where snotty grade school students in uniforms tramped thoughtlessly around all day long. Not her. Not Nancy Hedgecroft.

She was pondering the issue of her decision as she held onto the wheel of the old Ford station wagon. Where do you go when you have serious life-thinking to do? Then she saw on the left-hand side of the road: St. Aubert United Church. Of course, she thought with a little self-mockery in her tone. You go to your church and speak with your Pastor.

Nancy swung into the St. Aubert United Church driveway and parked out front. It was a bungalow-style building made of plain cedar, with a wheelchair ramp and a single, simple cross over some wide steps that led nowhere. There were California lilacs in front and some junipers. The sign facing the highway always had something worth seeing written on it; today it was SPEAK LORD, FOR YOUR SERVANT IS LISTENING. It was nothing to be ashamed of, visiting your church, so she didn't mind her station wagon standing visibly in front of the church. There were things said in there that you could remember and think about. The last time she went to service (admittedly, she rarely ever went), the pastor said something that stayed with her: *You can't command love, but you can act lovingly and if you do, love happens. . . . Unless you love each other, you cannot have complete joy.* Why not? The door was open and she walked right in, even though it was Monday and it might easily have been closed. The main hall was terribly empty-looking on a bright day like this when no one was there. The pews were stark and cold, the Psalters in their pockets so forlorn, the choir benches so open. She walked to the side and back where the sacristy and the pastor's office were. The door was ajar and he was in there. What good luck, she thought, as she tapped on the door gently with her knuckle.

"Come in," she heard in a slightly raspy voice. Pastor Smith had that croaky voice, but not because he smoked or anything. It was just the way he was. He was of medium height, with a long face, rather big mouth, curly hair and very very big smile. She stepped into the office. It was a big room with a Persian-style rug on the floor, umbrella lamps and ivies going up in the corners, an old oak side table in the middle of the room, two low pale rose sofas, lots of prints on the wall and of course the Pastor's desk by the window. "Hello Nancy!" Pastor Smith effused.

"May I talk with you a moment?" she asked timidly. Might as well get to the point and not beat around the bush. Pastor Smith was a busy man, she knew that. He had a congregation of several hundred people to attend to. All those baptisms and weddings and, yes, funerals too. He came from Abbotsford, where they were even busier.

"Of course, of course," he said, standing up and extending his arm to show she was welcome. Nancy thought he was a nice man to welcome her in the middle of the day without an appointment. "Sit down," he suggested and pointed to the sofas. She did. She sat down on the end of the lily-of-the-valley patterned sofa, and he turned his desk chair around to face her and sat down. "What brings you here?" That big smile reminded her of Anthony Robbins on television.

"I hope I'm not interrupting," she began, to which he gestured a complete no with his hands, like it was very right that she was there. The sudden thought came to Nancy that he might even be lonely here, all alone in the building, large as it was. You never knew these things. There was a brief silence. "I just came here on the spur of the moment," she began. "I was driving by and saw the church—you know—and felt like I wanted to talk with you for a minute."

"Of course, of course." He was placidly smiling.

"I don't know . . . it's not necessarily easy to . . ." Now she was getting caught in her own words. What a nuisance! Why couldn't she simply say whatever it was outright? But then, she wasn't sure what to say. She waited a minute. He waited too.

"No rush, Nancy," Pastor Smith comfortingly suggested. She cleared her throat and pulled herself together.

"I just have a feeling I need to make some changes, and I don't know what they should be," she finally blurted out. There, she thought. That was good. Well done, Nancy Hedgecroft. Pastor

Smith sat in his desk chair nodding understandingly. She looked into his kind hazel eyes. That gave her more confidence. "I think I took a wrong turn somewhere in life, and I want to set it right." She was pleased with her ability to suddenly be so articulate; however, she was starting to cry. Darn it! The lump rose from her throat into her face and spilled out of her eyes in tears and she got a grimace on her face—the very grimace she would like to avoid after all that careful makeup treatment. But there it was: she was crying and then wholeheartedly sobbing. Her shoulders started to shake up and down and her chest to heave. She put her well-manicured hand on her sobbing chest, right over where her heart should be. "Sorry," she whispered in a voice so hoarse from the phlegm of her crying that it was embarrassing.

"No worry, no worry," Pastor Smith said softly. He got out of his chair and sat down right beside her, like a brother would, and put his hand on her back. "You just have a cry. That's all right." She did. She just went ahead and cried her heart out. He had his hand on her back. Then he put his hand on her shoulder and pulled her toward him to give her even more comfort. He squeezed her shoulder tight. "There now. It can't be all that bad," he consoled her. She took a Kleenex from a box on the corner of his desk, within easy reach, and wiped the mucus that was beginning to fall from her nose.

"It's a hard time of life for me I think," she tried to explain. He was nodding. "I don't exactly know what to do next, you know."

"You don't have to know that," Pastor Smith was saying. "You just have to take care of every day as it comes."

"Shouldn't one make long-range plans and try to do something with one's life?" she worried out loud.

"If you can, yes. But you don't have to berate yourself if you're a little confused right now. Just come here and we'll talk about it. Hmm?"

She looked at him gratefully. His face was very close. He gave her another squeeze. Then he kissed her on the cheek. That was nice. She smiled gratefully at him. He smiled back. This seemed to encourage him because then he kissed her on the lips. Just like that. A smack on the lips. She smiled a little at that too, more demurely. He kissed her again. This time he let his mouth stay on her lips a little longer and—well, something quite unexpected!—she could feel his tongue. His tongue stole out of his mouth and into hers. Pretty soon his tongue was all inside her mouth and running along her teeth, and he was opening his mouth more so he could get better access to hers. Then, without warning and before Nancy Hedgecroft could figure out what was happening, she and Pastor Smith were French-kissing energetically. But it was not with her consent—she knew that even as she was opening her mouth for him.

It didn't last long, and pretty soon Pastor Smith had put more distance between his face and hers. He sat back comfortably, patting her back with his hand. She looked at him again as if she hadn't quite seen him before this. He was a youngish man, early forties probably; he still had minute freckles all over his face (at his age!), and he was really quite athletic and bouncy all the time. He had unheard of energy. People always commented on how Corrie Smith, Pastor of St. Aubert, was hyper-energetic. Sometimes they even just said hyper. He was bouncing from one person to another during Sunday services, both before and after. She had never seen such a sociable pastor before, actually. And he wasn't even married. There was talk of him having had a girlfriend while he was at seminary in Saskatoon, but that obviously came to nothing. A bachelor pastor with empty hands. Oh my. Maybe not such a good combination.

"I am very fond of women of a certain age," he said in his jubilant manner, smiling from ear to ear. She straightened the collar of her colorful jacket. She didn't really have to, but she needed to find something to do with her hands. This was all unsettling. She cleared her throat and smiled forcedly.

"I was actually on the way to the grocery store," she said, not able to think of anything else to say just then. It was awkward. "I should probably stop bothering you and get on with my shopping." He was still patting her back and grinning at her.

"You do that. Perhaps you'd like me to look in on you some-time? I can do that. That's what I do during the week—I visit peo-ple and talk with them!" She was nodding as if that would be a pos-sibility, quite likely, and she would like to do that, yes. Then she got up and he did too. He gave her a slight squeeze as she was about to step out the door. The exchanged goodbyes, and she walked stolidly back to her Ford station wagon. She got inside, sat behind the wheel, straightened her skirt and started the car. *All right, all right,* she said to herself, nearly out loud. *All right, all right.*

Nancy got the Ford onto the highway again, a little roundly, but when she was supposed to turn right she inadvertently turned left—toward the village and not to the IGA. She didn't think, just drove. The Ford was veering into the midsection a bit too easily, and she swerved away from that and onto the shoulder a bit too quickly again. But then she got the car back on track, going down the mid-dle like she should, although she seemed to hit the dividing line fre-quently. She looked in the rearview mirror: someone in the car behind was giving her the finger. Oh my, they probably thought she was drunk or something—but why do they have to be so vulgar about it? Leave off that finger! She wanted to shout, but they would-n't hear. And anyway, what did it matter? She swerved a little but managed to make it all the way to the shopping center where the liquor store was. She parked the station wagon in the large parking lot there and got out. It was good to stand up again, although her knees seemed a little weak. That was inexplicable.

She walked to the liquor store with sea legs, in fact, but when she got there she saw that Randy had set up his post and was playing away. A woman in white from head to toe—white sneakers, white jeans, white jean jacket, white headband—was standing there holding the hand of a cute two-year-old boy in too-big shorts and a green *Sesame Street* T-shirt. "Put this in the basket there," the woman was telling the boy, "and say thank you for the concert. Go ahead, you can do that." The boy dropped a coin into Randy's basket and said in inimitable two-year-old language, "Thank you for the concert." Randy smiled sweetly. He enjoyed this. The woman and the boy left, and Nancy made her hesitant way toward the guitarist on his stool outside the liquor store, with the basket of coins beside him and the guitar case open at his feet. He was concentrating on something by Barrios; she recognized it. She walked up to him and he noticed her. But she was starting to cry again—she couldn't help it. Her shoulders were shaking. She had a coin of her own and quietly placed it in Randy's basket. He looked up. The corners of her mouth were twitching. Her eyes were watering. She stood there, shaking a bit.

"What's the matter, honey?" Randy was saying quietly. He stopped playing and put his elbow on the curve of his guitar. He looked at her sweetly with a little smile. She could tell he had *those things on* under his jeans. An old conversation between them was replaying in her mind, and in her chest had the same sweet, anguished, sad sensation.

"It's not a disability or anything," Randy was saying in their mobile home with the flowery living room seating. "I've been doing something like this since I was ten, at least. I never said anything to anyone at first. Even tried to give it up. But then I figured, you want to do something, who's going to say you can't?"

"But it makes a person think you might be gay or something, like a cross-dresser or whatever it's called. . . ." Nancy protested, but not exactly arguing, just trying to bring in another point of view. He seemed to have thought it all out and then closed the subject.

"Fact is," he announced like he knew this, "most cross-dressers are actually heterosexual. Did you know that?" She had to shake her head, because she did *not* know that. "I just don't worry about it. Some cross-dressers started out with stockings under their jeans, but I, that's as far as I go."

"Have you ever?" Nancy had to get the confession because if he had, then she was going to be . . . "Have you ever actually dressed yourself in women's clothes? Just tell me and have done with it."

"No, honey. Once I bought a dress, but I didn't ever put it on." Silence. What did he do with the dress? And the high-heeled shoes she once found in the linen closet of the mobile home? Where did they go? What were those tights for? "Once I mentioned it to my friends," he said, "and they were real good about it. Real cool. No problem. Just relax."

"It's hard to get this into my head," she started to confess.

"Yea, hon," he broke in, giving her a hug the way he always did when she was confused. "But I'm still me, aren't I? I'm still your same-old same-old, aren't I?" She nodded gently with her face squished up against his manly, guitar-playing chest. A few tears, a couple of wet spots on his denim shirt.

"What's the matter, honey?" Randy repeated as he got up from his stool by the liquor store and packed up his guitar and bag of coins. All while she was standing there a bit transfixed, her mind nowhere and everywhere. He put his arm around her, turned her the other way and walked her toward the car across the parking lot with the people swarming back and forth, cars bouncing in and out, seagulls flying over the lampposts, skateboarders careening down the sidewalk, Nancy Hedgecroft's little miniature suitcase-shaped change purse hanging from her shoulder and banging against her thighs inside the loose, rayon dress and Randolph Outlaw's slim, hard hips swinging into his guitar case as he strode beside her.

The Swans of Chesapeake Bay

That morning, while having her second bowl of continental roast in the leather chair she used every morning while getting awake—a slow process these days—Élise opened the letter she pulled from the post office box in the village the day before. She had taken to going for her mail at two that afternoon. Just in time to deal with problems if there was a notice from the bank or to deposit cheques if they came in. But also late enough for all the day's mail to be in the box, so she only had to go once. This was a personal letter (they were less and less frequent these days, with email and faxes and telephones having taken the job over) with a postmark from Virginia. Élise knew only two people in Virginia well enough for personal correspondence. One was her cousin Francine, who married an American working on semiconductors and who moved to Richmond in her twenties. The other was Holby. He had moved to Chesapeake Bay from Toronto almost a decade ago and had settled in Virginia Beach. She thought the letter was from him and decided to wait until morning to read it. It was one of the luxuries of life these days: she did things in her own chosen time.

Dear Élise: are you surprised to hear from me? I decided not to send you an email because they're so easy to disregard. I didn't want you to disregard my attempt to get in touch with you. I was in Richmond yesterday and saw a book of yours in the Book People bookstore on Granite Ave. Brought back thoughts and memories. I actually drove all the way from Virginia Beach—stopped in Chesapeake and Newport News, and am staying in Richmond for a week. Did I tell you I've been doing some work at the Currituck Beach Lighthouse? You said you always loved lighthouses! They're becoming "surplus federal property" and are being optioned to nonprofit organizations. I was on the Chesapeake Bay Bridge-Tunnel last month, bird watching. I've taken up a bit of bird watching lately. The Bridge Tunnel, all steel and concrete, asphalt and rock, right there on the open water, makes a place to stop for the migrators in the spring. There are four islands there, and wax myrtle trees for the birds. You can see white pelicans, northern gannets, Harlequin ducks, black-tailed gulls, peregrine falcons—all kinds . . .

Élise stopped reading. It was a long letter; the kind Holby used to write when they were younger. He wrote her last about six years ago, when he was involved with the mute swans. So it was with the swans of Chesapeake Bay: they didn't know whether to kill them (and cull them) or protect them. Some said the swans were a menace because they over-breed and eat other wildlife, endangering more species in the Bay. Others said they should be protected because they have such beauty and romance, and culling them would be dangerous. The mutes might themselves die out. It was the seal debate all over again, Élise thought. Except swans have a much higher standing in the repertoire of beauty. Seals are more metaphors for people themselves: they are often people in bondage to some sort of force. But swans are arbiters of love and longing. What people love is not just that they are graceful, but they are always together, two by two, for life. They don't appear in gaggles or noisy groups, but glide by in twos, serene, mysterious. . . .

I know from Suzette that you quit your job. Did you know Suzette is work-ing as a legal assistant now? Go figure. But you—congratulations on taking the big plunge. . . .

It was true. Élise had broken away (*from the flock*, perhaps), although it was not her intention to get away as much as it was to just change course in life. But deep down, she knew it was also about cutting loose. Sometimes you have to move on, that was clear. Everyone should: there is a time for everything in life. You don't stay the same, so why should your surroundings? Or why should the fact that you fit or don't fit in a place remain the same over the years? Maybe there was a time when she was in the right place at the right time over there, at the University of Saskatchewan, but that had not been the case for several years now and it was time to go long before she went. Sometimes it even takes courage to go. More courage to go than it does to stay. To stay on in a place where things have solidified for you—where you are no longer growing and learning—is just plain cowardice. She knew that, and she was not a coward. She moved to White Rock, British Columbia. It was a simple thing to do.

Yesterday she bought and planted her first apple tree. It was called Scarlet Sentinel. She didn't know why she had not planted a fruit tree in her tree patch before. The kind that blossoms in late April and early May, and bears fruit to be harvested in October. This type of tree, the gardener told her, won't spread out all over, but it will have lots of apples. Élise was only thinking of the blossoms that come and go so quickly in the spring; how lovely they are to look at, and how precious because they are the first real flowering activity of early May. Only after it was in the ground and she had poured water over it and tamped down the dirt around the roots did she think of the fruit as well. Instead of going back to work in September, like she always did, she would be collecting red and gold apples. Now she thought she would get more fruit trees, a Golden Sentinel, and maybe a willow tree as well. Trees everywhere. And roses: she was now going to fill the rose plot as well. She wanted the smell of roses when she stepped out: pepper, clover, anise—summer-long scents.

Daily life was in and of itself a busy thing. There was not only the area where she grew hydrangeas and azaleas and lilacs, and now roses and fruit trees. There was grass that kept the jungle away— grass to cut and rake. There were decks to sweep and deck tables to wipe clear every morning because overnight their surfaces became layered with green detritus from the forests all around. Viridian seedlings flying in the air. There were windowsills to wipe and wash because the condensation of the damp atmosphere in this climate created pools of water that became pockets of mold if they weren't cleared. And then, all the usual daily stuff everyone has: laundry to soak, clothes to press, floors to sweep, dishes to wash. Daily things people did not enjoy, usually. But Élise enjoyed puttering, cleaning, working in the house and garden. Because then she could also think. She enjoyed thinking.

She thought back on her days in France, where she came from before transplanting herself whole to Canada. She grew up in the town of Rouen in Normandy. She thought of Rouen more often now, the Place de la Cathédrale, with the cobbled square in front of the ornate pale cathedral with its brown doors (and the inside, which she loved: the wooden benches and railings under the gigantic cement-colored pillars and arches); the gardens of the Hotel de

Ville, with its unassuming oval grass and few flowers; and the Sainte-Jeanne d'Arc construction, so modern, gigantic stained glass windows over low-set pews; and the civilized, green Jardin des Plantes, where Sunday walks took place. . . . What she enjoyed was waking up on a Saturday morning and seeing throngs of people on the streets below, milling about with baskets on their arms, chatting, looking. Hunting. The flea market vendors in Vieux Rouen set up their tables so early they seemed to arrive by magic. The Place St-Mare and the Place des Emmurés: full of stuff—brocante, antiques, art. Old coffee mills with brass handles; key chains with dog faces; red dial-telephones; doll-house kitchen utensils; toy Ferraris. Fresh strawberries and eggplants from the farms around. The street markets. It was fun: milling about town on days when everyone was bargain hunting and socializing. It was just plain fun. So why didn't she go back? The answer was not simple: once you move like this, once you reestablish in a new country, it isn't that simple. Not simple at all.

As she got older, Élise's life became quieter. She enjoyed the quiet. Small things became enough in themselves. It was entirely enjoyable to come out in the morning and see how the leaves on the deciduous trees were trembling hard in the light breeze. The energy in all that rustling everywhere impressed her. And the leaves themselves were what they called "spring green"—a bright, lime-colored sunny green. As summer wore on, that verdant luster would darken and turn to something more like pine needles and avocado. The color of watermelon rind. But early spring was a young time, with lilac-pink blossoms on the cherry trees and apple trees, and lemony green-tinted alder leaves and pale young hemlocks just coming up new in odd places along the road. The geraniums in the Mexican clay pots were sprouting their carmine buds in all directions, and the hanging ivy reached out for a place to cling. A happy time of year.

Élise was determined to let the joy of nature seep into her being. And this time it would stay.

Holby's mention of Suzette put Élise back in touch with her graduate student years. What was that now? Twenty-three years had passed. They were already teaching as graduate students then, and the professional scene had in fact begun—not to end until just now, this month, for Élise. Both Suzette and Holby went on to other disciplines, Suzette to law school, Holby to geology. Suzette was, in spite of her girlish French name, not in the least either girlish or French. She was tall and had long straw-colored red hair down to her waist. She towered above everyone and made Élise think of her as a Viking. By contrast, Élise was rather petite, had dark eyes and eyebrows, and mahogany-colored hair, which she sometimes tied up, even though it was not very long. She liked black and dark navy clothing, especially velvets and suedes, and she often wore blanched scarves. She kept her nails painted cherry red and liked to wear nearly orange lipstick. They were all such good friends then, the three of them. Not a day went by that they weren't together; they did everything as a trio. Suzette veered off for a while in an affair with a poet (who prided himself on having slept with over two hundred women) and when that ended, she complained of having lived on Japanese noodle soup for too long. Too much tofu and ginger—she was sick of watercress and pepper flakes. Holby and Élise then cooked her a big batch of dark spaghetti. They drank cloudy Chianti from San Gusto a Rentennano. They laughed and jeered at the world. But now Élise had not heard from Holby since his last letter of about six or eight years ago. And Suzette—she had lost touch with Suzette completely. How did that happen?

We've been drilling in the Bayside area and Mathews County—there's a crater under the bay. Seems like a super hurricane, a "hyper cane," came down there something like thirty-five million years ago after an asteroid. It must have been some explosion: a fireball that broke up the rock as much as seven miles down and eighty-five miles away. There was a comet that landed there sometime. We found the crater center at Cape Charles. Huge tsunamis must have occurred—the impact is estimated to have been a hundred times more powerful than all the nuclear bombs in existence now. Think of that! Seems what we know of as Virginia may have been completely trashed. The comet would have been about two miles wide, and it slammed through thousands of feet of ocean and bedrock, and created blasts of fire and water, burning up and flooding all of Virginia—and then after that, some major hurricanes destroyed whatever was left of the place. "Super hurricanes." I gave a paper on this at a science conference in Chicago recently, so it's all fresh in my mind. We simulated the hyper canes on computer. There was something like it in the Yucatan Peninsula about sixty-five million years ago—that's what they say may have wiped out the dinosaurs. . . .

It was vintage Holby, she could see that. He was enthusiastic about everything. That was his endearing quality. She put the letter aside for a moment and remembered his face: a little pock marked, but that made him look rugged. He was always a natural sort. Loved nature. His hair was pale, almost clay colored, and his eyes were lake-blue, like those lakes in Ontario. She let her gaze wander out over the frilly leaves shivering on their branches. When Élise let the morning dissipate like this without "getting things done," the way you're supposed to accomplish something all the time, she wavered between feeling guilt and relief. She was still tied to the mentality of the clock, but she was also trying to change her mind. She was attempting to be free of the orderliness of time and be more in tune with nature. It all sounded rather kitschy, but it was quite real. She had done her duty by society for twenty-five years. Now she was going to do another sort of duty—to the spiritual side of things, not the material. In a massive metaphor for herself, it seemed as though the earth beneath her feet had crumbled one day, and she never got back on level ground again. Maybe it was two, three or even five years ago now; she no longer remembered (if she ever knew) when it started. But the earth beneath her feet simply caved in. Metaphorically.

But it also did in reality. That was the strange thing. It was a few years ago now, but she was visiting old places and friends in Normandy then. That was the last time she was home. They were at table and heard a sudden mammoth crash outside. Sébastien ran out the door and fell straight into a deep sinkhole. Forty feet, and the corner of the house was hanging over the edge of it. It turned out that craters like that were appearing all over Normandy and also in populated areas (in gardens and roads and even right under houses). It was the *marnières*—chalk quarries that had long since been abandoned and were sinkholes waiting to happen. They were deep below and had been there for several hundred years now. They had been forgotten; the mouths to the quarries were now farmed over and maps disregarded. Then in February and March of that year, there was so much rain that the water seeping into the earth started to dissolve the chalk pillars that held up the caves. The newspapers started saying there were over a hundred and forty thousand caves and tunnels that could cave in all over. The *marnières* were created when people took limestone and chalk from the earth to put on their fields. They dug down as much as fifty yards, and then branched out at that depth. Élise learned a lot about these things quickly. Apparently, in 1997 a whole house vanished in a cave-in. They woke to what sounded like the boom of a cannon. They found cracks in the kitchen that began to spread all over the house. Élise was impressed by the sense that one morning you could wake up and *things could no longer hold.* Sooner or later the past catches up with the present.

What had happened to the three of them—their seemingly indissoluble friendship? Élise took a trip to Maryland to see Holby some years after graduate school. Graduate school days in Toronto were the party days. Parties came easily—the music, the dancing.

One time Élise had a party in her house and was in the kitchen getting soda water for everyone. Holby came in and before they really knew what they were doing, they were kissing madly up against the counter. They never went on to develop a love relationship; they kept on being friends with that evening hovering like a ghost in the corner of their solidarity. Neither of them ever mentioned it again. In the end Holby left the English department and went into geology instead, and later oceanography. He was a student of estuaries, and had been in the Chesapeake Bay region for over nine years now. Suzette moved to the Maritimes and got a job with the government, after which Élise lost touch with her. Élise went on with literature and became a professor of English—"a fate worse than death," she was later to joke to Holby. When she compared their lives now, it seemed Holby had the best deal. Because he got to work with nature and animals—but more, he got to be outside. She had not thought of such a simple thing: the difference between whether you spend your life outdoors or indoors.

While she was in Maryland, on one of the periodic visits with Holby, a controversy was raging about whether to cull the swan population in Chesapeake Bay. There were so many kinds of waterfowl there—egrets, ospreys, ducks—but the mute swans were taking over. Natural resource workers were spraying the eggs with oil so the embryos would die. For Élise, it was a painful thing to see after the romance of *Swan Lake* and *Evening Idyll*, the lovely pale orange and gold Robert Bateman print she had of two mute swans approaching a cluster of swamp grasses, and the ponds with the graceful, long-necked, orange-billed birds on them all over Europe.

Anti-swan people called the mute swans "garbage birds." The bay was host to, they said, two million birds. The problem with mutes, the cullers were saying, is that they don't migrate like the tundra and trumpeter swans. They just stay there and eat away all year round. The grass beds were in danger. The answer they came up with was to pair off same-sex swans. The life-partners solution. Élise read in the *Inside Annapolis Magazine* that the mutes were imported to the bay from Europe and that some of them escaped from a farm in Talbot County in 1962. They were heavy, twenty-five pounds, and had a wingspan of eight feet.

Moreover, since mute swans don't migrate like the tundras, they get bigger (tundras travel over four thousand miles every fall, Holby told her). Mutes eat the bay grasses, ripping up the whole plant, root and all. Élise read that addling eggs meant that the eggs were shaken and then put back. The embryos simply die from the shaking. All this was fairly sad stuff. Perhaps, she thought then, things are better left alone. Don't shake them up because they'll die? She and Holby were exploring the estuary, which fascinated her: fresh water from the rivers mixed with the ocean water—maybe four meters deep at first. The water circulated in stratas, and the fresh and seawaters started to mingle vertically. Élise was comparing this estuary with the Gironde River estuary back home, the sand ridges, the flood channels. They went to the Delaware River, with all the history of ships sailing into Philadelphia. There was the Delaware Canal linking the river to the bay. Holby told her about George Washington leading his troops across the Delaware on December 25, 1776, and fighting the German mercenaries of the British in the Battle of Trenton the next day. He was going on about the oysters and crabs you could get there. They went to Smith Island, a low-lying landscape with dark trees and white houses and deep blue seawater. Holby was explaining how about half of the pollution of the area— red tide, for example—came from the atmosphere.

Élise now remembered that as a very pleasant visit. Holby was living alone at the time, which made it easy to go see him. Perhaps he was lonely? She hadn't thought about that before. He had bought himself a small house in Virginia Beach in the working class part of town. He liked to sit on his screened-in front porch in the mornings and also after work in the summers, surrounded by dogwood trees and climbing yellow jasmines. He read *The Wall Street Journal* on his porch and watched the mailman make his rounds, the clanking of the mailboxes at every front door. There were willows in the yards, their thin branches weeping, trailing leaves against the grass. When Élise visited, she too found it pleasant to converse on Holby's porch. Not until later did she remember what the experience reminded her of: his mother's sunroom in Ontario. Was he reenacting a childhood scene? She hadn't thought about that till this morning. She just remembered the old Baldwin piano Holby had bought, amateur pianist that he was, and put in his small dining room. The antique furniture he had inherited from his mother in the living room—such little pieces for a burly outdoors-type of male was interesting. He simply didn't care what furniture he had, Élise figured. His priorities were elsewhere: his pasta, his beer (his latest enthusiasm was a type of beer Cistercian monks in southern Poland planned to make, based on a seventeenth century recipe, and he intended to order from their first batch) and Napa Valley wine, his Jeep Wrangler, his expeditions to landscapes with seawater and river water and sluicy bays and marshes.

She was thinking about a summer she went up to Holby's mother's cabin at Lac Des Milles Lac in Ontario. Élise and Suzette drove there in her old green station wagon, down the country roads toward Thunder Bay, and into the cabin settlement. They were oddly ramshackle cottages—more like shacks than actual cabins. You entered along a grass plain rather than a road to the pale-gray wood house with a newly built gazebo at the end. A small garage-shack painted tomato red was off to the side, and the lake was out back. Here Holby had come with his family for years during summer vacation. The roads in the settlement were like alleys—narrow gravel paths with large potholes. Holby's mother's cottage lay in the middle of the area, with a screened-in sunroom facing the lake. She loved to sit in her sunroom at all times: having coffee there in the morning, sewing and reading there all day, having tea there in the afternoon. Even though Élise was young then, she instinctively recognized the kind of pleasure the older woman was talking about when she described the life of the sunroom. Now Élise was the age of Holby's mother then—and she understood this perfectly. How life gets circumscribed as the years go by.

Since then, Holby had been through a marriage with Marianne and had one child, a boy named Hart. Élise could not follow what had happened to the boy; time went too fast to keep track of the details. Élise herself had been through two common-law relationships. She had promised herself she would never marry—not after her marriage to Don Carpenter. They even wrote a book together on ghost towns in Saskatchewan, and they visited those places: Fosterton, Shakelton, Cabri . . . which she abandoned when she realized it would be a choice between her own life and someone else's life for her. The least you can do, she told herself when she took the bus to leave Rosetown (where they had decided to buy a place and be "rural") is *live your own life*. Élise had been very friendly with Marianne, but there was something complicated about her. A woman without any career, with no circumference of her own, Marianne was unhappy. She took out her unhappiness on Holby, who was an enthusiastic type and did everything he could think of to please her. But he never did please her. Élise had one memory of Marianne after all these years: her sad face. How she never smiled.

There were times when Élise and Holby ended up talking about Marianne. Élise didn't really want to pursue those conversations because she was uncomfortable with what Holby would eventually say. She knew he would: that Marianne was somehow mentally unwell, if he put it agreeably. Unstable. neurotic, if he put it disagreeably. Élise had no stomach to listen to one of her best friends complain about his wife in that way. She changed the subject, something she routinely did. They always ended up talking about very concrete things that had no personal value. Like the sinkholes in Normandy. Holby would have been fascinated by the collapsing quarries all over, the government scratching its head, saying, "We knew about it but didn't pay attention . . ." *Le phénomène est connu et ne date pas d'hier . . .* and how it is clear that la Haute-Normandie *va être confrontée à une veritable catastrophe tant humaine qu'écologique. . . .* It was just the kind of dramatic story he loved. He was fascinated by the idea, for example, that New Orleans could collapse in the same way, she remembered now. New Orleans could just begin to crumble.

Élise was thinking how the past—your memories, the thoughts you started to have but never finished—come back later in life like the stratifications of water in an estuary. The freshwater from the land and the saltwater from the sea: they meet, they layer themselves, they circulate in levels and wander into each others' territory. When Holby's mother died, he took it hard. But those were the days of Marianne, and Élise didn't see Holby much. With his inheritance, he bought a house in Dundalk, Ontario, about an hour's drive from Brampton, where he was going to write novels. But there never were any novels. Marianne was unhappy there, feeling isolated and alone while Holby went to work in the city. Élise visited them once there. It was a great house: one of those old, wooden residences from the turn of the century, renovated to look gorgeous. All wood floors, oak banisters on the stairs, many rooms on three floors, a wine cellar in the basement—because Holby continued to enjoy drinking wine. He loved to laugh and socialize, but Marianne was never interested in parties. Élise couldn't remember a single occasion when

Marianne had an actual dinner party. At best, it would be Élise and Suzette over for spaghetti. Holby bought a pasta maker and created his own fettuccine and fusilli and lasagna and linguine pasta with it—something he was proud of. Marianne treated the device dismissively. She probably thought it was unnecessary when you could just go to the corner and buy a pack of spaghetti readymade.

Élise turned back to the letter. *This all started when Poag was diverted from his tektites in New Jersey (back in the eighties) and he was asked about the strange and unusual nature of Virginia geology. They figured then, looking at the data available, that the asteroid impacted an area from Hampton to Gloucester County and Norfolk and Virginia Beach. The waves that resulted were probably as high as the Appalachians. I figure the surface of Virginia was wiped out, washed to sea. The drilling in Mathews County, down a couple of thousand feet, makes us think there were those hyper canes. The breccia is a mess of stuff there: microfossils, spores, minerals, tektites, pollen. A real quandary. Doesn't fit with anything else around there. Shows a flow of stuff going in one direction, like a surge. A hyper cane is like a wind over six hundred and fifty miles per hour, ten times more than a regular hurricane, if you can imagine that. The ocean temperature for tens of miles would rise to over a hundred and twenty degrees. Actually, there was a squabble about all this at the conference—made me a little tired. About whether it was a hyper cane or a more regular tsunami that made all that strange layering. . . .*

As Élise read the letter (which was long; she could see at least four tightly handwritten pages), she started thinking of that visit those years ago when he lived in his wooden working-class house. He had a guestroom off the living room, where she stayed. He had a small bedroom upstairs and an even smaller study. The study was no bigger than a closet. She remembered wondering how he ever got work done up there. But he did. Quite a lot, as a matter of fact. And then he had the office at the university. His argument was, that with computerization, you needed less space. He took her to dinner at a place called The Inlet Restaurant on Shore Drive. She remembered it as elegant: seafood on the deck, a waterfront view. Flowers were hanging from the ceiling; a steel drum band played later in the evening, and there was a buffet of fish and eggplant and grapes and oysters. Darkness fell over the calm water, making it glow like molten lava encased in a slow flow of thick tar. She wore a black silk suit for the occasion—and in fact, she didn't know what the occasion was. She no longer remembered if it was a weeknight or a Saturday night. The evening had receded into a fog and only reappeared now, with this letter.

What had he wanted? She didn't ask him, and he never volunteered. For some reason he invited her, and she figured he would say what it was when he was ready. But he never did. Should she have asked? He was wearing an ivory-colored corduroy shirt—probably the most dressy thing he had. She had never, in all the years she knew him, seen him wear anything other than a faded blue denim shirt and jeans. His hair usually just fell over his forehead, like he had forgotten to comb it. When he talked, he didn't gesticulate with his hands like so many do: all of the energy of expression was in his face instead. More accurately, in his eyes. His eyes lit up somehow, and he looked intently at people when he spoke. Now that she had a chance to think about it—really think about things that have passed, as if for the first time—it did strike her as unusual in retrospect. That he should call her and ask her to come, and then never say why or broach any subject. At the time, Élise thought he was in need of company. He was new in the place, had just taken the job eight months before. Didn't know too many people, and Marianne was still in Toronto. They had just divorced. . . .

When Élise went to the post office in the afternoon the day before, she got there when it was completely empty. There were no customers waiting in line, as usual, by the counters. In the postbox room, only one other person was getting his mail. He stood in the corner, and Élise couldn't see him well in the shadows. But there was an odd shape to him, so she stopped to take another look. It was a darkly clad man in his forties, she guessed, wearing a dusky baseball cap, a brick-colored leather jacket and baggy sepia-shaded pants. On his shoulder, where some eccentrics allow their parrots to sit, was a small, white, Persian kitten. The kitten was in a slightly nervous position, clinging to the shoulder of its owner, with its big eyes looking out at the entrance where Élise stood. She got her mail—the letter from Virginia and a notice of an auction—and went out again, but when she rounded the corner in her car, she saw the man sitting on a bench in front of the post office. The kitten was still clinging to his chest, just below his neck, with the front paws holding on to the leather shoulder. When she passed, the kitten looked at her again with big anxious eyes, but determined to hang on to what it had.

Élise turned back to Holby's letter, which for some reason she realized she was hesitating to read. Did she think there would be some news in it she would not like? She didn't know until this moment that she actually had "feelings" when it came to him. It seemed impossible because she had forgotten about him so completely for years at a time. Like she had forgotten about everything; everyone and everything. That was part of the problem with the job she had been in for so long. It took not just a certain number of hours every week: it took her whole being. There was no time off. The job defined her, determined her, marked and encompassed her. It was a job that staked out her circumference and created fictions around her that she couldn't figure out. It was like moving in a maze of uncertainties, where everyone lived in his own reality. When your reality is at odds with the world of others, and you see the realities of those around you are also at odds with each other you have a recipe for insanity. The problem is you don't know who the deluded ones are. It could be just you, or it could be *them*. The only consolation for Élise was that she was wondering about it, and being able to question and puzzle over one's hold on reality was the first sign of good health. But the world was at too sharp an angle in all this. It took nerves of steel and a powerful force of will to lumber through the psychological jungle that was work. She would have been better suited to the sciences, she found herself thinking. Like Holby, who made that realization early enough to not go wrong.

After the last conference, she read on, *actually, I figured I had had enough of them for a while. It's got to a point now where I can't seem to give a paper without some controversy developing. There's always someone in the audience who disagrees—doesn't just disagree, but just plain hammers me. There are too many clandestine operations going on that involve basic things like funding. I've been wondering whether working for private corporations is any better. Don't know. I guess I think you're lucky. You escaped! We've always envied you, it seems—that'll strike you as strange, I know. Marianne used to be tormented by you, actually. She was jealous. She thought there was something going on between us dating way back. Did you know that? She was consumed by this. . . .*

No, Élise did not know that. She was surprised, not so much by the fact that Marianne was suspicious like that (she seemed to carry that on her sleeve), but rather that Holby would be telling her this now. In a letter, after so many years. Did he think she was above it all? Beyond everything, now that she was out of the workplace and on her own? What was he thinking? It was a slightly painful thought for her, whenever it did come up, that sometimes it seemed to her that other people thought she had no feelings. It was strange but true. She was often considered to be barricaded against emotions, operating on some level that didn't touch the world. *A level of the angels,* perhaps. She sometimes joked about "the French character" to put people at ease (they keep under wraps—*during the German occupation, you know they learned to hide their wine. . . . Give the French anything and it's an art form a week later. . . .*)

Then she thought: how did Suzette know Élise had resigned her position and moved to the coast? She wasn't in touch with Suzette, and she didn't think they had friends in common. She remembered visiting Suzette about ten years ago, right after Suzette had moved to Victoria. She had taken a job as an information officer with the provincial government, and her portfolio was "Old People." She talked about it without irony, and Élise realized Suzette really cared about her subjects: nursing homes and funding for medical care and geriatrics in general. To top it off, Suzette was living in the house that had been her grandmother's. Suzette grew up in Victoria, and her grandmother had an English-style Tudor house, sitting a bit back from the road in the maple trees. You couldn't see the house until you went through the gate and into the garden. It was what would be described in the English countryside as a cottage and was low-ceilinged, dark oak wood-beamed, small-windowed. There was a faded Persian-style rug on the floor of the big room and a narrow staircase up to the second floor. Élise came for supper, which Suzette cooked in the tiny kitchen—or didn't cook. They had tuna salad in tomato cups with sour cream and dill and baby peas, she remembered that. They ate it on a small cherry-wood table in the too-big room, and Suzette was happily describing her work with problems in geriatrics. Suzette had become somehow pale, lacking vitality, although she was also happy. She looked like someone who had been indoors too long. They spent the evening the way they used to in the old days: gossiping about people, laughing at the past, talking about Holby, whom they were missing. Somehow just the two of them together wasn't quite complete, and they both knew their friendship depended on there being three of them.

After that visit, Élise and Suzette corresponded for a couple of years, but that too dried up. She really had no idea whether Holby and Suzette kept in touch. She just assumed they didn't.

The conference I just came back from was in Chicago, Holby wrote, *but I ran into Suzette again. She was there because it was a seminar on the environment, and she had been sent there by the law firm she works for. We were at a session on waterfowl—the flocks that fly in chevron formation to the breeding grounds in the spring. I love to watch them take off from the water: the way they pound the surface with their feet and their wingtips as they run to take off. Did you know that after waterfowl breed, they can't fly for several weeks? I'm getting good with ducks—mallards, teals, widgeons, pintails, mandarins, wood ducks, and sea ducks like mergansers, and inland ducks like canvasbacks, and divers like ruddy ducks— I'm getting to know them all, watching in various places. Well, maybe it was the conference, the fact that I was getting sick of it, or remembering old times. Whatever it was, Suzette and I had an affair in Chicago. Maybe you'll be surprised at this, but that's the way it is. I don't think we can make anything of it. After all, I'm out here in Chesapeake, she's over there in Vancouver, but things have been a long time coming around. . . .*

So that was why he wrote her all of a sudden. Élise understood now. He was hemming and hawing with all those ducks and swans and geese and asteroids in the bay. What he wanted was her *permission* for this. She felt certain. He wanted her to know about them and write back and say she was happy about it. She put down the letter and looked out at the beautiful sunshine that had permeated the whole world. Her decision to only do things in her own time, to only respond to questions she felt like answering, to not say anything to anyone if she didn't feel like it: suddenly, those decisions were being tested—her past asking her questions, her past wanting her to answer. She was trying to hold back a wave of sadness. Why was she sad? She knew she didn't want Holby for herself anyway. She would never take him if he offered himself. The chemistry wasn't there, as they say, although Suzette knew they had fooled around because she walked in on them in the kitchen those many years ago. But still, perversely, she didn't want Suzette to have him either. She decided not to finish the letter. She folded it up and put it back in the envelope. She would not answer. Not just now. She didn't like the way the past comes and claims you sometimes. How you can walk out your door one morning and end up buried alive in a sinkhole, a cave-in of some kind. A collapse of the stuff you constructed in your youth: the pillars of salt or chalk that don't hold in the effusive rains of later life. . . . She realized, realized without warning: *Soutenez-moi avec des gâteaux de raisins, Fortifiez-moi avec des pommes; car je suis malade d'amour.* . . . Je suis malade d'amour . . . with wine, with apples . . . for I am sick with love, je suis malade d'amour. . . .

It's Raining Gently All Over the World

$\mathcal{T}$he call was for the municipal building downtown, 3rd Avenue North. They wouldn't say exactly—just that they should come down immediately. Adam and the other three officers breezed past the Bayside Mall and the liquor store on Twenty-fourth—a familiar location! There was the City Hall, the Public Library, the Sheraton Cavalier. The South Saskatchewan River and the River Park Promenade down the street. You actually had to enter through a café downstairs. In the back of the café, the "Voodoo Room" it was called, a cobalt blue door. From there, an old stairway lined with linoleum and puddle-colored paint turned grimy, like milk gone sour. Up the stairs to the fourth floor, the cream-colored banisters holding up as if to defy the odds, and the middle of the stairs worn into a groove from decades of use. Through the powdery corridor doors and into a narrow hall where no light shone, walls that looked like somebody's bad suntan. Doors with name tags. It couldn't be, he was thinking as they made their way down the hall that smelled like pumpkin and smoke. It couldn't be. That would be too much of a coincidence. A small group of people—a woman in a blue coat, a man in a short red jacket, a couple of guys in jeans and shirtsleeves, a lady in a tangerine suit, a man in a white lab jacket—had crowded around the door. It was *the* door. The crowd parted as they entered. A grimy office with clutter; a desk, a plastic wastebasket, a tabletop fan, a computer, two empty bottles of water, a poster that said "Moriarti," a swivel chair, and him on it. It was him. He had fallen onto the keyboard, his head unnaturally turned. His eyeballs popping out of his head in what must have been a final moment of terror. His right arm hanging limply down his side, the gun flung way over towards the wall by the radiator. And blood. Blood was everywhere—and brains. A feeling of revulsion, nausea, disgust, panic, sudden grief: a cocktail of emotions that didn't taste any good.

Adam Ainsworth retired early from the force. He had handed in his badge one Friday afternoon at the Saskatoon Police Headquarters, to everyone's surprise. Walked with it gingerly past the teak desks in a row on the eggplant blue broadloom they recently installed in the building, the frosted windows and black chairs, to the chief's office. And to some people's sadness, he realized. He knew that as well as he knew his name was Adam. The women in particular: secretaries and associates, female colleagues. They liked him and he knew why. You could say it was vanity, but what harm is there in a little vanity? He did no wrong. What he did was enjoy the attention. Because he was a handsome man. He was tall and trim, his hair was now elegantly white, he had a tan even in winter, and he had an outgoing, talkative personality. He didn't talk rubbish either. He was so good at his job that people inadvertently confessed their misdeeds to him before their cases got to court. More than once he had to keep what he heard under wraps because it came at inadmissible moments. Sometimes waiting for the court proceedings to unfold was simply tedious because he already knew the story. Everyone loved talking to him, he knew that. During coffee break at the canteen, lunches on the grounds outside or in a diner somewhere, stops on the way, Tim Hortons or The Second Cup—they all wanted to be near him. To be the center of so much pleasant gravity gave Adam Ainsworth confidence and not a little lenience. He would come upon a speeding driver and let him go with a warning instead of a ticket. Things like that. He was a good man—he saw himself as a good man, and that was helped by the feeling others gave him that they thought so too.

So when he announced he was retiring, people were aghast. They thought you only leave your job when something is wrong. Besides, his pension was simply too small to live on. No one would in his right mind go into old age on his pension. "Pensionlette," he joked. Well, they didn't need to bother about his story. They could just let him go and give him a goodbye party. A sendoff—which they did (in the park under ash trees, picnic tables spread with oil-cloth and food, things like potato salad and hot dogs and macaroni salad and iced tea and watermelon—whatever). Truth is, things happen. When you're in the police force especially, things happen. You see it, you're there, you're supposed to take care of it. You go year after year with an accumulation of sad detail, and you still have your summer barbecues with the family and the Christmas get-together with your colleagues and your little two-week vacation at Tobin Lake or Last Mountain Lake. But inside you the sad little details have built from a small pile into a mountain ten years later. You walk around with this mountain inside you, and pretty soon, well, you've gotta let it go.

Adam Ainsworth decided, after moving to the Sunshine Coast because his wife, Kelly, wanted above all else to live there, that he would get a small job to make ends meet. Nothing major—just something to supplement his pensionlette. He sat down at the kitchen table of the new house they bought in Davis Bay, overlooking the great Pacific Ocean with the freighters steaming away from Vancouver, and the cruise ships that always came in threes on their way from Vancouver to Fairbanks, Alaska, with tipsy passengers playing roulette on board. He worked on the answer like a math problem or a budget sheet: What am I good at? What do I enjoy? And the answer he gave himself was that he was good at socializing and talking, and getting people to do what he wanted them to do. And he enjoyed cars. He had always liked cars. He bought a new car every three years, and it was something he looked forward to: going to the dealers and trying out a new vehicle when it was time to renew. The new gadgets every year, new inventions put into these things: brake-park interlock, auto dimming rear view mirror, security alarm, remote keyless entry, cup holders. The obvious answer was that he should go and sell cars for a while at a dealership. He could do that. The customers would trust him, he could talk them into good deals and he would probably make a nice wad of cash on commissions just from being who he was. And besides, when he told them he was a police officer before—done deal! Who wouldn't buy a car from Adam Ainsworth, formerly of the Saskatoon Police Force, now retired in pleasant circumstances on the Costa del Sol?

He and Kelly had a good routine by now: he made breakfast every morning, scrambled eggs and bacon, and served Kelly coffee in bed and her eggs when she came out. In the evening, she made dinner while he puttered in the yard or watched the news or fixed something on the deck, all depending on the weather. A routine that he could see was going to go on—possibly endlessly. . . .

In his new workplace among the shiny cars just out of the factory—Chryslers, Fords, BMWs, and their main line, Chevrolet Trackers and Dodge Dakotas—Adam Ainsworth had a cubicle at the back of the showroom for an office. There were four such cubicles, divided by felt-lined parch-board that could be removed and reassembled easily, for four sales assistants. There was a counter at the end of the cubicles where the secretary sat. Suzy, who was actually a no-nonsense car mechanic down at the Chrysler dealership in Gibsons, who wore coveralls soaked in oil and grease all day long before this and whose short, strawberry hair was grimy from the garage, had freckles and was from Australia, and you didn't mess with her because she just told you off. He guessed she got tired of the garage and wanted something cleaner here, but it was a big change, it was. Suzy had a perch and greeted customers and assigned them to one of the four cubicles. The only actual office, along the other wall, belonged to Belinda, the financial manager. When he was through with a customer, Belinda took him or her over and polished off the car financing. Her office was behind a glass wall, so even there things were transparent. Adam liked that—the transparency. The last thing you want, he knew well from experience, is an office that is dead to the world once you close the door. That's what Georgie's office was. Just one window facing the cruddy downtown Saskatoon street below, the pane already yellow from previous workers smoking all day, every day, for several decades. When the door closed behind him, no one could see what went on back there. You should always be able to see inside a person's office.

Transparency—that was the key. Otherwise it could break your heart. It was Georgie who started this whole retirement thing for

Adam. That was clear as day. Georgie didn't cause it—no one person causes such big changes, and causes don't go back to just one thing. But Adam wasn't so sure that everything in his life didn't simply converge with Georgie. It culminated there. All the sad little details blew up with Georgie's head inside that crusted blood-stained office.

The rest had to do with Les, most likely. Adam and Kelly Ainsworth, parents of Leslie Ainsworth, writer of science fiction. Whatever got into that boy, Adam would never understand. Not that Les—who had become a tall and gangly young man with very pale skin and very auburn hair that fell over his face—couldn't do other things. He just got this fever. That was the best way to describe what happened: a fever to write science fiction. First he went to the U of Saskatchewan and instead of studying something useful, he majored in English. Next thing, he was trying to be an author. He was a serious reader of sci-fi, even as a boy, and Kelly (who wouldn't listen to Adam's warnings about all this) encouraged him. Adam tried to tell her that Les would turn into a pale, ineffectual bookworm, when he should be out there making things better for other people. Kelly disagreed. It was the only thing they argued about—Les and his scribbling and fantasizing. He had rows of science fiction books on his shelves as a kid; it had started with Douglas Adams' *Hitchhiker's Guide to the Galaxy*; after that, Guy Gavriel Kay's *Sailing to Sarantium*, Arthur Clarke's *Rendezvous With Rama*, Robert Heinlein's *Stranger in a Strange Land* and Kate Wilhelm's *Welcome, Chaos* . . . and then instead of growing out of them, the boy wanted to go write them. Adam once went into his room just to look at the titles—maybe by looking at them he would figure this fantasy thing out: *The Blue Sword, The Tranquility Alternative, Doomsday, Rising of the Moon, Seventh Son, Dreams Underfoot*—and truth was Adam was more disturbed instead of less.

"Isn't this world good enough for you?" Adam shouted to his son in frustration, pinning him against the door to his room (a poster of *The Judas Rose* hanging there perniciously). "Doesn't this world, the real one we're struggling in, interest you enough?" And Les, in defiance, actually looked his dad straight in the eye and shouted back: "No!" and slammed the door at him. Well, let him do it then. Adam renounced all responsibility and simply stopped thinking of him. Kelly, however, was on the phone every day with the boy. (Les was living in Vancouver with a girl he married; they had a baby whom Les was staying home with while his wife, Sandy, was working at a computer firm. A house-husband, that's what he was. Because he was no writer; he had only published two stories in some fantasy magazines. Hardly anything to stake your life and career on! His son Les the housewife with his fantasy life. Why didn't people's kids grow up any more? Well, Kelly could have him. It was a parting of the ways for him and Les.

One good thing about being a car salesman instead of a police officer, it had to be admitted, was that now he could flirt freely. Transparency was good there too. The more openly you flirted with women, the less people believed you were doing it. That was the paradox. He liked to flirt with Belinda in the financial office, and he liked to do it out in the open. They flirted with each other, and it was part of the culture of the whole place by now. Everyone expected them to joke and say insinuating things to each other in front of everybody else. People thought that was all there was to it—well, it was. For now. But for Adam, it was a relief not to have to hide his escapading behind emergency calls from Georgie. He and Georgie had a good thing going for a long while. They helped each other: Georgie called Adam's house at appointed times to get him out. Adam made sure Kelly answered the phone so it looked legit, and then Adam threw on his civilian Davis Classic Biker jacket and off he went for a tryst with

Mary or Hilda or Sherry. In return, Adam helped Georgie with the money thing (it was a little complicated with the setting up a new account at the Saskatoon Credit Union that he could draw on and hand over to Georgie). Georgie wanted to send sums of money home to San Salvador, to his aging mother, he said, whom he hadn't seen in forty years. It may have been his mother, it may have been something else, but he didn't inquire too eagerly into the details. Georgie usually didn't know where Adam went when he went out, and Adam didn't exactly know where the money went. But they both knew that the less they knew the better it would be in the end. They couldn't be questioned and wouldn't have to lie.

No, everything was a paradox. That was the only sure thing you could say. The accumulation of sad detail that caused Adam Ainsworth to want to leave the force and move to another province was not, in fact, about what happened. It was about all the things that *did not happen.* What bothered him was not that there were crimes he couldn't handle (there were crimes he found hard to take: girl-pimps too young to charge; telemarketing scams that gobbled up naïve old-age pensioners; that young woman found dead in the bush after God knows what . . .). It was not that the police of Saskatoon were crooked in some way. After all the media about bad policing (officers leaving native people out in the country on winter nights was one thing they never got tired of writing about in the press) the fact was that policing in Saskatoon was good. Officers were law-abiding themselves—of course they were! Adam had always been strict about enforcing the law on himself. Especially now that he was a regular civilian all day, every day, the last thing he wanted was to get caught with anything. Even a traffic violation or a speeding ticket would be too much. He drove to work this morning at exactly sixty kilometers per hour where the sign said sixty. No more, no less. There were always some punks who wanted to go fast, maybe eighty or even a hundred on that crooked highway. This morning this guy in a white sports coupe was on his tail like a sniffing dog, then he passed and as he did he stuck his arm into the air with the finger up. Adam found his fury rising like blood-thirst: he stuck his finger into the windshield of his yellow Fiat in return and honked his horn in a long wailing siren at the punk up ahead, and he kept at it for ten minutes—ten whole minutes! Adam would have to see about that in himself . . . he only stopped because he had reached the turnoff to his car dealership.

No, it wasn't that the Saskatoon police weren't law abiding. (They were allowed to have a temper, weren't they?) What was really getting to Adam was *the presumption of crookedness.* Not that you were, but that you were presumed to be crooked in some way. Because you carried a gun. Because you spent your time with the dregs of society. Because you were tainted by all that. How public fear turned into public suspicion. Because you were businesslike when you had to deal with people at the peak of their emotions all the time. That created mistrust and fear, and the presumption of guilt where there was none. How do you get back from that? How do you unconvince those who are sure they have a handle on you? You can't. You just plain can't change minds that have been made up. Such invisible things can be what take you down. What makes you depressed and then suicidal. (Fact is, Adam learned from associating with Georgie in his new line of work dealing with domestic problems that the highest rate of suicide happens to be among white males over sixty.) It's nothing you can point at. Nothing anyone else can see. It's in the air, like invisible radioactivity slowly poisoning your life. Georgie fell into it. He fell into the bottomless hole of public suspicion and didn't know how to get out of it.

Happily, everything out here on the Costa del Sol is clean, Adam thought to himself as he twirled his ballpoint pen in his hand between his fingers at his oak-veneered desk behind the partition lined with gray felt. The slate is empty. No one, absolutely no one, thinks such thoughts out here. No one is under suspicion for anything. People drive down the road with their tops down and wave broadly at each other, calling out neighborly comments, joking over their dashboards, chatting loudly on the bus, chirping like birds in the grocery aisles, gossiping in the small stores and businesses dotting the coastline. People here have all the time in the world, and they don't use it to think ill of each other. The pen he was folding between his fingers had written on it "Sunshine GM." Sunshine indeed, he thought. This was a sunshiny place, and he was happy as a clam to be out here and away from the dusty town of Saskatoon, where you either got frozen to death by frost or bitten to death by mosquitoes. And when you were indoors, it was gossip and rumor. No thanks, he thought again. No, thank you! This incident on the road this morning—well, that was an aberration. It was Adam Ainsworth still wearing the toxic armor of his former life. It was going to fall off, chip by chip, he knew that, and in the end he too would be clean as a whistle.

From his veneered desk, where he sat in his chrome-and-felt chair, Adam could see out into the dealership parking lot. It was a big lot, with at least two hundred cars gleaming in the sun: Chevrolet Cavalier, Pontiac Grand Prix, Buick Century, Chevy Trailblazer. . . . And behind that there was the ocean with its whitecaps when the wind blew. Adam could sit at his desk with papers in front of him, pretending to be working, while twirling his pen and looking at his computer screen (no porno there, not in this place where everyone could see!), and at the same time he could cast a glance out to the lot and follow what went on there. And right now he was seeing something. He was eyeing something very fine out there: a woman in her mid-forties, most likely; tall, very slender, short blonde hair in well-done waves; a natural-looking lady in jeans and a cardigan and sandals. And alone. He immediately rose to make his way down to where she was peering at the sheets on various car windows. A lady in the market for a car. He paced down the steps and into the lot, winding his way between parked Trackers and Jimmys. The woman looked familiar. Wasn't it the newly divorced wife of the Gibson's mayor? Yes it was. He greeted her as she stood next to a Chevy Silverado.

"Good afternoon!" he enthused with a broad smile. "Nice day for car shopping, isn't it?" She looked up at him with a mild, gentle-looking face, but a bit stern too. She had a thin nose and high-set, hazel eyes. A little bit of Fuchsia lipstick, nothing else.

"Very nice indeed," she answered. She had an accent, she did. He held out his hand for a handshake. German, that's what she was.

"Hi, I'm Adam. Can I help you find what you need?" She shook hands with him.

"I'm Eva."

"Eva! That's a good one!" He couldn't help himself laughing. A great connecting device, that was. Adam and Eva. She laughed too.

"I'm just browsing actually," she explained. "I wanted a new car but don't know what I want yet, so I thought I would look around first. I'm not at any buying stage yet, so you don't have to trouble yourself."

"Oh, but I'd be happy to give you information on any of these. I see you're looking at a truck—could that be?" She laughed again. It was a very controlled and elegant laugh. This was a classy woman, he could see that, unlike the Marys and Sherrys of Saskatoon, who more often than not were on social assistance, poor things. But that's what made them so enamored of him, Adam Ainsworth, police officer: someone who might be able to protect them. And he would, could and did, more than once, save a girl's skin, for which she was grateful in many ways. But here he knew he would have more of an uphill climb, a challenge he was looking forward to, if he got the chance.

"Oh I'm not seriously looking for a truck!" she said dismissively. "But I am looking at the prices of everything here. Just for comparison."

"You'd look good in one of our soft-topped Sebrings," Adam said assuringly. He was careful not to misspeak and say "topless Sebrings," although he almost did. His mind was racing.

"I love those," she agreed. "That would be great—but they're also expensive."

"We have many payment plans to make these products affordable," he quickly responded. But he didn't like the sound of himself— he sounded like a paid advertisement. He'd have to work on that.

"That doesn't alter the cost of things," she argued with impeccable logic. He realized he would have to let her do her browsing by herself for a bit.

"Here is my card," he said offering her a business card. "You let me know when you're ready to inquire about one of our vehicles, and I'd be more than happy to take it out with you for a test drive." She took the card and thanked him. She smiled favorably. Adam liked the idea of not being aggressive—he knew a woman was more enticed by reticence than by aggressive behavior. Psychology, that's what. He slowly meandered back to the showroom, leaving Eva to wander on her own, but now he had her in his net. If she was buying here, she was buying from him.

Adam Ainsworth kept it all to himself. All the feelings that boiled just below the surface: a sense of sorrow, a bit of rage, some bitterness, gratitude. He was not sure why gratitude, but it must be the fact that he had a job at all and he retired from it and everything went smoothly. But there was Georgie: his dark, curly hair, graying just above the ears, his small brown moustache and favorite Polo shirt and slightly round face. So long as he was there, with his story, his life, then the rest was insignificant. Adam didn't share his thoughts with his so-called friends. His friendships didn't go that deep. Georgie was his only real friend. Not even Kelly had heard his tale. She was to be kept out of it. Her reaction to Georgie was simply incomprehension. His real name was Jorge Gabriel Garcia-Ramirez. They called him Georgie as soon as he entered the force. He had an accent; he was from somewhere else; no one could picture his background. There was a whole portion of Georgie's life no one knew anything about. Maybe for all those reasons, maybe for none of them, he didn't seem to fit in with the rest of them. He didn't enjoy bowling nights, wouldn't take to the curling matches they had twice a year, didn't have much energy for picnic baseball or late-night poker or just plain beer. It seemed that what people didn't know they simply made up. Rumors circulated about Georgie—unstoppable rumors, and when they got back to him he felt betrayed but didn't know whom to blame. So he turned them inside. Eventually, he left the force altogether and took a job with Social Services. He had a social work degree that he took up, polished off, and started to work for the office of child welfare. Pretty soon he was dealing with domestic violence issues almost full time. But it was deskwork. They seemed to like him there. He was put into one of their downtown offices, where it was easier for people on welfare to go see him. He got along there. They called him Georgie there too, but unlike the police crowd, who were belittling him in their own underhanded way, the government bunch used the appellation as a term of affection.

Georgie started out on the force being happy and sociable. In fact, they couldn't stop him—joking, teasing, saying funny things off the cuff. But over time, he grew quieter, stopped joking altogether and his face took on a grim aspect. What was the matter?

Adam didn't know, and if he didn't, no one did. But Adam realized he was possibly the only one who cared. The others didn't seem to give it a thought. And Adam—why did he care? He remembered bumping into Georgie in the mailroom shortly before his exit to Social Services. Adam was pulling out his mail from the slot with his name on it, Georgie came in wearing that black and white striped Polo shirt, off duty, and seated himself on the corner of the table where they dumped the junk mail.

"What's this with the 'Starlight Tours'?" Georgie was saying, with disbelief and scorn in his voice.

"Oh, it's just a joke, really," Adam said. "They wanted to send the Chief of Police on one of those 'Starlight Tours' for the fun of it. Or to say they did."

"What is it? I mean, what is it really?" Georgie's mouth was open, his teeth were showing in a smile that wasn't really a smile.

"They take the Chief of Police out to some godforsaken spot in the countryside, where there aren't any farms or cottages or anything, and leave him there to find his way back. If he isn't back in civilization in three days, they wait until somebody accidentally finds him because it's too expensive to send the force out." Georgie was laughing soundlessly, as if he were trying to make himself part of the game. The way you do when you don't get the joke, but you make yourself laugh anyway to seem like you're in on it. Adam shook his head in front of his friend perched on the table. "It's a sick joke, that's all. These guys— they're sick sometimes. You gotta know that. Letting off steam."

"I feel so isolated." That came unexpected, unasked for. Straight out of the blue, a confession. The kind of comment no one actually made around there. Adam nodded in assent, just to indicate he understood. Even though he didn't really.

Adam walked straight back to his office behind the half-partition at the back of the dealership showroom and sat down at his desk again. He was sitting where he could keep an eye on Eva. She was wending her way between the different sedans and trucks and off-roaders. He was playing with his pen and thinking about her out there. There was something about her bearing, her attitude, that he didn't like. She seemed incredibly composed. Too composed. A woman should be a little nervous in front of a man. He didn't like that self-confidence. But it was also something to conquer. He found himself wanting to set her straight; give her something to think about. Something she wouldn't be so composed over. He wanted to break that veneer, that's what. He also realized what he was thinking as he thought it. It couldn't be good to think this way, but then again, it wasn't good to be so arrogant as Eva out there. He started to fantasize: how she would look without her clothes on. She had a slim waist, long, slender legs, rather low buttocks, shapely shoulders. She would be a sight to see. He hadn't got a look at her breasts under that silk cardigan, but they were probably moderate breasts. Like medium-sized pears on a pale white body, with nipples the color of café latté. Her bodily juices would taste like Crown Royal whiskey, and in some places like rare Cointreau. . . . His mind was wandering, and he didn't even notice that she had come in. Adam was pounding the tip of the ballpoint pen into the palm of his left hand and staring at the floor when he noticed the tapping on the partition. He looked up and she was there.

"I thought I would pick up a brochure for the Sebring," she said. He burst into his daytime smile and jumped up from his seat, leading the way to the display case where he pulled out a leaflet for her.

"You can read all about it here, but you won't know the car really until you've taken it for a test drive. We can do that any time you like. Now if you want. I can just get the key, and you can try it out!"

"I'll wait until I've looked into it a bit more," Eva said definitively. Adam was again a bit taken aback by her certitude. The feeling that she seemed to know her own mind far too well. "Let me know if or when," he added. He was not going to beg. Not him. She could beg him for a ride in a car, not the other way around. She nodded and smiled courteously. Then she was gone.

By the end of the day, Adam Ainsworth had not sold a single car. He was packing up to leave for home. Another salmon barbecue with Kelly out on the windy deck. They had a couple of oversized salmon in the fridge and were eating the first of them today. Spring potatoes, fresh dill, melted butter and barbecued salmon. Good fare. Kelly got this electric barbecue she wanted to use all the time—one of her pet peeves, it was. But that was all right. Kelly deserved to have a little fun. She was good enough to stay in Saskatoon all those years with him, and he was returning the favor. Why not? Maybe she was a little boring, he admitted that (he once even told Georgie that, when they were having a rare conversation about spousal life; Georgie and his petite wife, Sylvia, whom no one ever knew because she never came out with him, were having some trouble. Adam didn't want to inquire about what). The only time he saw Sylvia was at Georgie's funeral, after the service at the Holy Spirit Church on Kingsmere, where they had that shrine to Mary, Our Lady of the Prairies, (a permanent pilgrim holding her sheaf of wheat and her infant, all that wheat the bread of life, and a mantle cloaking her head when the prairie winds flared through). He went along to the Woodlawn Cemetery, the mowed grass and headstones and that hole in the ground with the mound of dirt beside it and the crass way they lowered the casket with a truck because there weren't enough men willing to hold it up, such a pitiful showing at the funeral, and Sylvia standing there in a black and white checkered skirt and a black turtleneck with a huge brass necklace made of big medallions on two chains, her hair tied up on the top of her head, with their five kids around, something like five years old to fifteen, and she had a bruise on her neck. Adam was trained to notice these things, and he distinctly noticed the bruise the size of a grapefruit even though she was trying to hide it with her turtle-neck sweater, and the priest was uttering a graveside reading that Adam was only half-listening to: *For if we have been planted together in the likeness of his death, we shall be also in the likeness of his resurrection,* and he had this feeling of hopelessness throughout the whole service at the graveside, a sinking, depressed feeling he knew he was not going to get rid of unless he forced the issue somehow, just forced it out of himself like a camel through a keyhole. . . .

Adam put his steel thermos into his canvas bag, the one he took to work every day. His paperback—Robert Ludlum, *Road to Omaha*—to have some sort of backup in order to appear to be doing something if it was a very slow day. Belinda from the financial office came into his cubicle. She had a rose-colored linen jacket on over a tight, frosted tank top, and black skin-tight jeans.

"Sold any cars today?" she teased and sat herself on the edge of his desk. Her thighs were at exact eye level with him as he bent to put the book in his bag on the floor.

"What goes around comes around," he teased back. He had no idea why he was saying that. He stood up with his beaming daytime smile. She stayed put. She was too easy, that girl, Adam thought. Displaying herself like that all over his desk. Her hair was straight, long and the color of dry hay. Thin lips, thin shoulders, a rather defenseless appearance. Inside there, though, she had a good head for figures. He clicked his tongue and poked her in the ribs. She giggled like a schoolgirl. Maybe someday, Adam thought, before he left the place finally, he might take her up on this. They could go to her place, once she got rid of that cigarette-smoking, straggle-haired boyfriend of hers named Barry, whom Adam could do without. (Last time Barry came around he was going on about filing income tax for over a million bucks and collecting a tax refund—some harebrained scheme he and Belinda had heard about another unemployed person trying to get away with in the States). They didn't want him near the place. He lent an air of decrepidation to this otherwise spick-and-span establishment. Why do girls like that get involved with scummy men? Just plain scum. He looked at her sitting there, her legs slightly spread on his desk, giggling, her sandal perched on her foot as if about to fall off. Must be because these girls just aren't that good with their emotions. Heaven knows, it's hard enough for a man like me, Adam assured himself, trying to curb wayward thoughts and feelings. But she—this little head of figures here—she probably had no emotional self-discipline, and guys like Barry were able to walk all over her. Adam slung the bag over his shoulder, got out his car key, and said—by way of dismissing her—"Time to go home."

He had a ten-minute drive to get home. No more. It was a short drive across a bridge where Chapman Creek rustled its way to the shore from the hills and mountains inland. Just before he got to the bridge, he saw a smallish white poodle standing by the road. The dog looked a little lost, as if it couldn't decide whether to cross the road or not. The small ears pointed straight up, the little pink mouth was frantically open, the beady eyes glued to a place on the other side of the road. It was standing very close to the edge of the road. There were no other cars just then. Adam wished the dog would just go. Cross! Get it over with before I get there! Still the dog stood with front paws on the asphalt. Adam suddenly decided, without knowing why, that he would make up the dog's mind for it. Have done with it. He turned his steering wheel a little bit to the right, swerved onto the shoulder of the road, and hit the dog smack in the middle. He couldn't see it, but he could feel the bump as he drove over it. A soft, not very big bump. That was all. He kept driving without looking at the rear-view mirror. Just one of those things, he said to himself. Just one of those road accidents. Happens all the time.

He was feeling a little cross with himself for running over the dog as he turned up the road to his house at the top of the hill. But he was used to having to get over things. Corpses—you get used to them. He turned into his clean driveway by the well-mowed lawn and parked the car, stopped the engine, and pulled out the key. Before he opened the door of his yellow Fiat to get out and walk in, he pictured Kelly piddling in the kitchen upstairs, wearing some loose and slinky ultramarine acetate pants and snowy rayon shirt, not a single hair of her well-groomed, meek head out of place. He noticed it had started to rain. Tiny, ethereal drops, more like a drizzling mist, were beginning to cover the windshield and the hood of the car. There was no sound to this display of small rain: it dropped feather-light out of the sky and eased down on diminutive angel-feet to the ground, a little unreal and maybe the kind of thing Les would get carried away by, the way he got swept away by small things like a soft, gentle rain when no one else noticed it. . . . Adam Ainsworth put a stop to his wandering mind and got on with things, like always. He got out, slammed the car door behind him and went in the front entry of his newly built beige, vinyl-sided bungalow overlooking the white-capped sea.

What is Had and Had Not

"What I love about you is your smile, Karen Brown," Magnus said when they were at the mineshaft. That was twenty-five years ago now. . . . "You smile as though you just heard you've won the Miss Congeniality Award. Or the Miss Canada Crown. It's such a happy smile!" They were with five other people being taken into the mine at Crows Nest Pass. The guide, a Mr. Dawson, who looked like a miner himself, was reciting the background of the Frank slide disaster: "April 29, 1903, Turtle Mountain here completely collapsed, and we had the biggest landslide in North American history. It took only a hundred seconds; seventy-six people were buried under the huge limestone boulders, and nearly all of the homes in Frank were smashed. On top of that, the Canadian Pacific Railroad tracks were destroyed for over a mile, and we had a flood here." As Mr. Dawson was speaking, they were making their way into the mineshaft, where they were given helmets with lights and told to wear them. It was very dark in there. It was the definition of gloom. They were told that when they got into the interior of the mine, the guide would have them turn off the lights. They would be able to experience complete mineshaft blackout. Mr. Dawson continued his lecture: "This all started in 1901 when they began to excavate and sunk a drift mine into Turtle Mountain. They wanted to mine the coal deposits on the eastern side. The mine was made of big stopes, and between them big twelve-meter pillars and chutes and walkways. By about a year later, they had stopes as far as seven hundred meters in the eastern coal vein. There were frequent tremors, and the miners were used to them. The shaking earth actually loosened the coal and the miners just had to shovel it up!"

Karen was keenly aware of how dark it had become as they made their way deeper into the mineshaft. The absence of all light. But if they freaked out when they shut off the helmet lights, they knew they were only a click away from turning them back on. As Mr. Dawson was going on, Karen only half-listened. She was basking in the comment Magnus had made about her smile and was keeping close to him in the helmet-lit darkness. She had to admit to herself she was *not* Miss Canada material; she was too short and too fat. But congenial—that she was. She had a happy disposition. Or seemed to. It was what she had taught herself. There were all sorts of ways of compensating for her unmanageable anatomy. Mr. Dawson started up again: "Outside the entrance, the Old Man River was winding at the base of the mountain, and then the town of Frank, with Gold Creek, which flowed into the river. The CPR ran alongside the river on the east side of Frank; the mine spur line ran to the west of Frank, so a triangle of rail line, river and mineshaft surrounded the town. We also had the Frank Grassy Mountain Railroad down the valley. Thing is, native legend called Turtle Mountain the Mountain That Walked. How right they were!"

In the mineshaft darkness, Karen felt comforted by the presence of Magnus—his solid being, his human warmth. She did not like this excursion at all. Mr. Dawson was talking, and she was sidling up to Magnus in a growing feeling of panic. "The miners were in here," Dawson was saying, "and heard a sound that was like thousands of thunderclaps. As the mountain wedge broke off and fell down, they felt a rush of icy air before it. The mine entrance was suddenly gone, and the coal car was blown three kilometers away across the valley. The wall of air flashed across the valley, tearing up houses and tents and people, and throwing them huge distances, where they were buried under a mass of limestone. Statistically, the bulk of mountain that broke away and crashed down here was six hundred and forty meters high, nine hundred and fifteen meters wide, and a hundred and fifty-two meters thick. The slope fell seven hundred meters."

Karen was terrified. Not just the idea that a mineshaft could suddenly, in a hundred seconds, cave in violently. No, the darkness alone frightened her. Magnus noticed how she kept close to him.

"Are you afraid in here?" he said half-jokingly, but also affectionately.

"Terrified," she admitted. He chuckled. That friendly chuckle—how it would accompany her for the next quarter century. . . .

"Well," he said half-mockingly, "we can recite the final words from Conrad's *Heart of Darkness* right now. Shall we do that?"

"By all means," she joked along, trying to sound composed.

"The very last words of Kurtz: 'The horror! The horror!'"

"Oh, go on!" Karen retorted.

"'The dusk was repeating those words in a persistent whisper all around us, in a whisper that seemed to swell menacingly like the first whisper of a rising wind. . . .'" Magnus was teasing her, and she knew it. Now, twenty-five years later, she recognized that as a form of courtship. "Reciting things when you're in a mineshaft always helps, you know," he said.

"I would prefer something from the Bible rather than Conrad," she said. "Something a little more comforting, like Psalm 18, 'For thou wilt light my candle: the LORD my God will enlighten my darkness. . . .'"

"Good lord, you know these psalms by heart!" He was genuinely surprised, but also making fun.

"I do. I had them repeated to me when I was a kid."

"Oh. Well, I have to tell you," he addressed her with mock courtesy, "I come from the north of Norway. Jesus never made it that far north!" He laughed heartily at that. A deep, comforting laughter. She laughed too.

It was almost inevitable that Karen should be thinking of that comment right then in her emerald blue Festiva, driving up Highway 101 to Pender Harbor. Her brother owned a cottage on Frances Peninsula Road, and she was going to stay there until after Christmas. It was November 18; she came off the three-thirty ferry from Horseshoe Bay, and it was now five. Already dark, it was raining profusely. The wipers were flopping full speed, back and forth, back and forth, trying to keep up with the deluge on the windshield. She couldn't see anything beyond the headlights, and all around was nothing but pitch-black night. No lights, no signals and no other vehicles on the road. What a desolate place! She had the instructions her brother Stan had given her: "Go on the highway till you get to Frances Peninsula Road. Turn left and find house Number 4937.

That's the place. The key is under the Grecian urn. Go to the side of the cottage, lift the lid on the wooden box in the ground, and crank the handle to turn on the water. The knob for the heat is in the front hall. Good luck!" he then wrote in his email note. Good luck, all right. He often said that—his mantra when they were kids. When she went to the Dinosaur Safari and the Insect Mania and the Meet the Pipe Organ programs at the children's circus in Powell River, when it came up from Indianapolis, Stan used to shout after her, *Good Luck!*

There were also the Cranberry Days in Powell River. She started thinking about the outings to Cranberry Lake. They tried to mine up there too, but all they found was mica, and it wasn't good for making glass anyway. Instead they created orchards and pig farms and dairies. There was a shingle mill and then a sawmill and pulp mill. It wasn't that long ago that people walked to work or rode bikes; they had to cart in their water and use oil lamps for light and wood stoves for heat. She remembered a Sunday meeting she once went to with her Aunt Hazel in Powell River when she was ten. Why she started thinking about that, she didn't know, but it was a Kingdom Hall meeting that she had to sneak into because her parents were against it. The Hall was a very plain white building with a blue roof. It had an auditorium with rows of pale blue seats. The carpet on the floor was seaweed green with plum-colored flowers and a purple line along the chairs. In the kitchen were tiles of the same colors, with salmon and coral. The baptism area was especially impressive to her back then with the tiles on the wall and decorative urnlike protrusions high up. Lots of people came wearing light suits and nice white coats, and the women had heels and men had ties.

The speaker was saying things she was attentive to, just because it was so *curious* to her and because she knew it was somehow *illegitimate* for her to be there: "What if Jesus had not come to this earth?" he was saying. "Let us try to imagine a world without Him. Have you ever thought what our Earth would be like without Christ. . . ?" The days of Powell River had receded into the blur of a forgotten past, but now that she was headed in that direction again, the memories slid into her consciousness uninvited. Even Magnus never heard all her stories of the pulp mill smell and the ocean swims and the Kingdom Hall of Aunt Hazel. It was her private life—even more it was somehow embarrassing. Magnus was so secular; she didn't want him to think she had the background of a kook. And she didn't. It was just her Aunt Hazel. Aunt Hazel was a bit of a black sheep in the family—ironically because she was a Jehovah's Witness and went to the Kingdom Hall. She took Karen along a few times, and it was their little secret. The mural in the entryway of the Kingdom Hall—she loved looking at that. The mural depicted a peaceful scene on a wide river with lotus flowers and a swan, large rhododendron-like flowers on the banks, pearly white sheep grazing and drinking from the water, deer looking on and a mountain going up high in the middle of it all, with a peaceful waterfall coming down.

Karen Brown and Magnus Heyerdahl were both twenty-five that long ago day at Crows Nest Pass. They were students of history at Calgary, and this was a field trip. Magnus had shown her a picture of his mother in the Telemark costume: the folk *bunad* of East Telemark, where she came from. It was black with a wide, maroon belt and two large rope tassels down the front. The blouse was dark lilac with a gold brooch right in the front of her chest. The skirt was embroidered at the bottom with big reddish-blue designs. Karen remembered thinking the costume was something extraordinarily *different*. Magnus was tall, had brown hair and always wore a blue parka—*anorak*, he called it. He told her he was from the town of Tromso in northern Norway. He had described the place. The town square had cobblestones and benches where old men sat, and an open-air market. There was an "Arctic Sea Cathedral" right at the base of a black, looming mountain, which he liked to talk about. And the boats in the harbor, the white lighthouse. He said the sun hardly ever came up in the winter. In January it just showed itself like a raw wound on top of the mountain and then disappeared again. The downtown was deserted most of the time. People didn't have much of a street culture, he liked to call it, in the wintertime. He was very fond of summer at a lake he called Prestvannet. He talked about the midnight sun as if it were a close friend. He even said the girls were pretty—maybe to tease her? He talked about the fog sliding down from the mountain, filling his childhood world with darkness. But Karen didn't spend much time, then or later, asking about that place. It didn't interest her.

Magnus was used to the darkness they experienced in that mine, but it was new to Karen. In fact, the whole area around Frank, Alberta, was marked, it seemed, with one dark disaster after another. Another big slide was waiting to happen, and still people lived there. Karen had to wonder: what is it about the human mind that enables you to not think about the possibility of a slide or an earthquake or a tornado, even though both science and the news tell you otherwise? Is there a rift between the rational and the emotional part of the human brain—so much of a gap that the two don't communicate? Or worse, the two sides are in contradistinction, in opposition to each other? A running quarrel? You know something rationally but refuse to know it emotionally at the same time? You carry on in spite of things? In spite of your better logic?

As they were escorted deeper and deeper into the mineshaft by the guide, all the light from the entrance disappeared. Karen felt her rib muscles tense. She almost felt like she couldn't breathe. She imagined with longing the white daisies outside, nodding in the breeze, the alpine flowers. . . . She was thinking of the story of Proserpine: how the giants were buried under Mount Aetna and when they struggled to escape, the earth shook. The air rushing up is really their breath. Karen kept walking into the mountain, and after about fifteen or twenty minutes, the guide made them stop and turn off the safety lights on their helmets. It was not only just too dark in there, but freezing cold. Outside it was a hot day, but inside the mountain, it was icy. They all turned off their lights. Magnus was standing next to her. She suddenly became petrified, paralyzed. Too embarrassed to say anything, she stood in the darkness completely numb with fear. She clutched Magnus's hand and held on tight. When the lights went back on, she let go and acted as if nothing had happened.

"Perhaps you like Emily Dickinson better than Joseph Conrad, then?" Magnus said on their way back out. "I think I remember a good passage there too: 'I fit for them,/ I seek the dark till I am thorough fit./ The labour is a solemn one. . . .'" Then she realized Magnus had taken her hand again, and they were actually walking out of the mine hand in hand. She was transported . . . she was happy.

Karen had never been to her brother's cottage before. Stan lived in Toronto and kept a cottage at Pender Harbor in B.C. for summer vacations. Why he didn't find something closer, Karen never knew, but it must have something to do with reconnecting with childhood. They spent part of their childhood out here, during their dad's stint as economic consultant to the pulp mill industry. They lived in Powell River, which she remembered not so fondly now as being inundated with the stench of pulp mills. Some days were worse than others, but there also were times when the town was free of it. But when there was a cloud of pulp-mill toxins, the smell of rotten eggs and decaying cabbage (she had heard somewhere the toxins from that stench included formaldehyde and methanol) settled into everything: the clothes, the furniture, the forest. You couldn't get away. But here in Pender Harbor there were no pulp mills and all you had was open beauty everywhere, fresh air, the heavenly odor of British Columbia rainforest. That's what Stan Brown had said, and she would find out. She remembered Magnus telling her the chlorine bleaching at pulp and paper mills affected the ability of bald eagles, mink and river otters to reproduce. It struck her now: maybe that was why they never had children? Because they didn't—there was a failure there somewhere. . . . At one time several grade-school students in Powell River got sick from an accidental release of pulp-mill toxins into the air. This was heavy-duty pollution. Yet people stayed. People stay, that's the thing, Karen was thinking.

She drove on for another hour, and the road began to wind excessively. There were very sharp turns suddenly, and huge gaps in the pavement. Occasionally, the Festiva bumped loudly on a pothole, jumped and rattled. It was slightly frightening because she couldn't see the holes in the road until it was too late. There were sharp rock faces that suddenly came into view on the right-hand side and steep drops on the left. Suddenly, the headlights revealed a crooked arbutus tree leaning over a precipice, and next thing you saw was a driveway to someone's house. Stan told her it would be dark and she should bring a flashlight or she wouldn't be able to find her way to the door and let herself in. The flashlight lay dutifully on the passenger seat. The description of the cottage (it was blue with white trim, he said, with a small deck on the side and a driveway by the front door) would have no meaning on a night like this. She could hardly see the tip of the hood of her car with the furious rain pelting down on it loudly. She saw a turnoff up ahead under a streetlight, and a sign that was illuminated as she drove by: FRANCES

PENINSULA ROAD, with an arrow. So far so good, she thought, and felt vaguely proud of herself for finding her way so easily. When she got to the junction, she turned left and drove in toward the bay. The road here wound and turned dizzyingly, but she had the house number memorized: 4937. There was logic to this. She just had to find the house with that number.

After at least forty minutes of driving around, however, Karen realized there was no house on Frances Peninsula Road that had the number 4937. This was disconcerting. She would have to be inventive now. There were no hotels in sight, no towns or villages. If she tried to get back to Gibsons to find a place to stay, she would be driving for another two hours at least, and even then she could not be sure she would find a place. She berated herself: she should have come earlier, at least during daylight. Right now, at seven in the evening, it was as dark as the inside of a tunnel. She stopped the car by the road and decided to have a think. "Having a think" was her standard response to unexpected difficulty. Magnus used to joke about her "think-it-through" method of dealing with problems. Karen had a rule that when something came up that couldn't be dealt with or that was disturbing in some way, she would sit down and not get up until she had thought it through. Magnus complained that this method was too intellectual and that sometimes problems were emotional and couldn't simply be dealt with by logic. Sometimes time, memory, feelings and chance all entered the picture and had to be allowed in. They disagreed on this. Karen was a no-nonsense fix-it type, and nothing could change her. Magnus was a let-the-wind-blow-where-it-may type. He loved the feeling of being guided by "synchronicity" and chance, cosmic events for which Karen Brown had no respect. No respect whatsoever: she argued that "waiting for a sign" was simply a cop-out. A way of not dealing with anything.

"I'm tired of being an enabler for you," Magnus had once said during lunch on their tiny patio at the back of the kitchen. The walls were so high that no one could see into their garden spot, and Karen liked it there. They had been talking about her restless desire to get everything fixed as soon as it appeared broken.

"What do you mean? What are you enabling, exactly?" She was stunned by the remark—and stung.

"It's the way you think you can cover everything. All eventualities. You can handle it all. Sometimes life isn't fixable. Sometimes there is tragedy. Then you just have to let go. Imperfection can be good. . . ."

"Well, so can enabling!"

"Oh? How so?"

"In the church they say that enablers are resource persons. They get people to do things. They apply their faith to life. They take care of creation. . . ."

"It's a different subject, that."

"They are God's workers, that's what." Her final declaration on this issue. She was not going to agree to any kind of psycho-babble in her house. Magnus knew that. He could never bend her to start talking about their issues as if they were problems, Karen insisted. There were no *problems*. Only eventualities. She put down her spoke of chicken souvlaki that they had made for lunch on the grill outside and looked at Magnus straight in the face. "I'm sorry Magnus," she asserted, "but if you think I want to live like those people in Ingmar Bergman movies, you're wrong!" He started laughing then. He laughed heartily, the chortle coming from deep in his chest, his head cocked sideways and his eyes crinkled. She loved it when he cracked-up like that. It was full of affection. She loved him then, even when the reason for his laughing was bizarre. She remembered how he once said to her, "Darkness is not the enemy; living in constant fear of it is." She made an effort to remember that. One good thing he had to say, anyway.

As she sat in her car, the motor humming, the gear in park and the emergency break on, the rain pelting on the hood like loud clashes of a tin drum, she found herself thinking: was this the parting of the ways that did them in? Was it a philosophical difference, after all? That they had become increasingly irritated with each other's way of handling life's situations? Meanwhile, she reasoned that perhaps one of the side routes would have a house with the right number on it, and maybe Stan had something wrong in his instructions—some minor glitch in his description. She decided to check the lanes off the main drive, starting with the first one, called Martin Road. Sure enough, here, right on the corner of Martin and Frances Peninsula Roads, was a cottage marked 4937. A minor triumph for Karen Brown, she thought a little proudly to herself. One little win for her in the long-standing argument with Magnus Heyerdahl and another reason for him not to leave her. Because leave her he did. But he could have—should have—trusted her. Seen her side of things. She drove into the driveway of a bungalow-style cottage and saw a path of flagstones leading to the front door, and the railings of a terrace in front. There was a place to park where Stan had said there would be one. Now she just had to look for some sort of Grecian urn to locate the key.

Karen Brown took her flashlight, got out of the car and began wandering about the house to find the urn, and came upon it very quickly. A large clay planter, when overturned in the mulch, revealed a small, tinny key. She opened the front door and found a light switch. What was revealed with the lights on was not what Karen had expected. She thought she would find something neglected and run-down, but instead a lively room opened up before her. The walls were paneled with pine, and the ceiling was exposed in trussed cathedral manner, with the beams in natural wood. In the middle of the room was a blue sofa with three pillows, one bright red. On the side was a large wicker chair and a coffee table with stuff on it. There were bookshelves to the left of the door, full of hardbound books, and a kitchen at the end with a raised counter and blue bar stools. A large window at the end of the room was decorated with all sorts of objects hanging around it, and next to that shelving with upturned glasses. And best of all, which she wasn't expecting, a large brick fireplace. There was a dining table of pine with four chairs and a couple of wicker chairs by the fireplace. Straw hats and other items of clothing hung on pegs on the wall. She was instantly happy with all this. What a great little place! How come Stan didn't describe it to her better?

She got the bags from her car, locked it up, and closed the door of the house behind her It was a Dutch-style entryway, what she knew of as a mortise-and-tenon frame around solid planks. The top half had a porthole-style window bolted down with bronze fasteners, and the top of the door was shaped like an arch. A golden glow emanated from the wood paneling, a honey-colored atmosphere, and the wooden ceiling still had the old seaweed-green paint on it. She looked around the place with an unexpected feeling of excitement. The hall leading to the bedroom had plywood and batten walls painted white, and push-up windows over a long bench that served as a guest-bed. The bedroom itself was very simple. Everything was white—the walls and furniture—except for an olive-green cabinet. The ceiling was also unpainted—it was obviously made of beach-combed lumber. There was only one bedroom, but clearly other people could sleep in the hall bed or on the sofa. It was a small cottage, she saw that now, but plenty big for her. Stan Brown and his family (Stan's wife Marianne and her son Hart from her former marriage) were coming for Christmas, but until then she would have the place to herself. A month before and—how long after? Maybe she would just stay a whole year. Or two, even. She got the water going and unpacked, put some items of food—carrots, bread, milk, green peppers and sausages—in the fridge. She unpacked other stuff she had brought: she actually had over-armed herself, not knowing what it would be like. She had with her a water purifier, insect repellent (even though it was winter), Army-type foot powder, a whistle, survival candles and a GI sewing kit—all of which she put away in the hall, and then she took a bath. She made some Red Rose tea, wrapped herself in a black wool blanket, and curled up on the sofa beside the lamp with her book by V.S. Naipul: *Half a Life*. It was a story about a man who floats from one place to another without plan or intent, who slips into life by accident. She did not like this character and she read with only partial concentration. She was also listening to the rain outside, and she was thinking about where she was in life.

Because there was a breaking point here, that was clear. She was glad she decided to mark this divide in some physical way: by getting out of Vancouver, out of her and Magnus's house, and going somewhere unfamiliar. She was in unfamiliar territory, and she should acknowledge that by being in a place she knew nothing about. She and Magnus had been married since she was twenty-five, and she knew no other life. They had a townhouse on Cambie in southeast Vancouver, and had been in the place for the last nine years. Magnus was an engineer who designed the inner workings of buildings— things like pipes and wires. Karen was an educational consultant and had worked out of the home for over a decade. She specialized in struggling teens—whether they should go to boot camp, get special education, go to wilderness camps or residential treatment centers (like that boy Pete George who kept getting into legal scrapes); she determined whether a teenager was troubled or at risk and what kind of behavior modification should be considered. She got a degree in Social Work and in Education, and she kept a website and wrote a newsletter for schools, all done at home. Maybe that was part of the problem? Magnus used to say when you're not in an office setting with other people, you don't have the pressure on you to keep tabs on yourself. Your eccentricities develop unchecked. What was he talking about? She could never figure that out. But Magnus said she had become strident and inflexible over the years. That was hard to take! But he must have meant it because he didn't like her company any more. He said she was too "rough" and she talked too fast. *Talked too fast?* He actually said she was like an engine that you turn on and can't figure out how to stop again—the machine just keeps going on its own, without responding to the listener. That she had a way of launching into "spiels," he called them, and not paying attention to whatever response she was getting. "Insensitive"—that was the word he used. He thought she had become hard-line, aggressive, intolerant and judgmental. It was a lot to swallow. Karen hardly knew where to begin. It hurt, him saying all that. That was the first thing she had to admit. It just plain hurt.

Karen didn't know that she wanted to make this "reassessment" of herself anyway. Why was she letting *him* decide these things? She was not stupid, she knew that—and on the off chance that he was right. . . . What really bothered her about their separation was not so much that they separated or that they had disagreed, or even that they had become incompatible. What really got to her was that she, Karen Brown, the logician and fact-finder and composed person, found herself losing command of herself. She lost control when they argued. She lost self-discipline even in public. In public! They were walking through the shopping mall downtown, Pacific Centre, and it happened even there. They were at a restaurant and the waiter brought her salad, but it had a dead cockroach in it. A dead cockroach soaked in oily French dressing! That was gross in and of itself, but it started the crack-up. She sent the salad back to the kitchen and they gave her a free meal as an apology. She was nice about it, they were polite about it, Magnus was making a joke of it. But inside her—inside the walls of Karen Brown's being—something was cracking. A slide of some sort was imminent. She could feel it.

"You need to make some adjustments too, Magnus, you know. . . ." she was saying to him while they were going down the Pacific Mall walkway. "It can't just be me. Everyone changes with time. . . ."

"But it's *how* you change, not *that* you change," he argued.

"This is all about something else," Karen then offered. It was what she really thought. Or what she hoped would be the case. "This is about you being restless or it's about someone else! Is there someone else? Are you interested in someone else? 'Cause if you are, tell me now!" She found her voice was rising to an argumentative pitch. She didn't like that but couldn't help it.

"It's so cliché, you thinking that. It's what you always think first. Right off the bat—someone else must be to blame. . . ."

"Well, is there? Just answer the question."

"I wouldn't answer it even if it were true. It's not the point. It's not what we're talking about."

"What are we talking about, then?" She found a feeling of fury rising up in her like an earthquake, coming from far below the surface, rumbling toward the crust of the earth of her being.

"We're talking about you and me and how we relate. That's what the subject is."

"If you don't answer my straightforward question, and give me a straight answer, I'm going to believe that's what's happening. You've found someone else and you're too cowardly to admit it!" She was yelling now. Almost screaming. Magnus was taken aback, obviously. He wasn't used to this side of her at all. He was trying to stay calm. "Answer me!" she screamed then. She was mortified at herself at the same time. There were cameras everywhere in shopping malls, she knew that. Her out-of-control manic behavior was now recorded on some video forever with the display windows of Holt Renfrew and the Gap and Banana Republic and Sport Chek as background. It was humiliating. Even so much later, in the privacy of her brother's cottage, by the lamp with her innocuous novel—even here, she could still feel the embarrassment like a heat wave over her whole body.

Suddenly, the lights went out. Power failure. It was unexpected and without warning. Karen Brown found herself sitting in the corner of the sofa in complete and utter darkness. She hadn't realized how dark it would be in an event like this. There were no lights anywhere at all. The sky was overcast with no stars or moon from above, and rain was falling. It was as inky black everywhere as the darkest tunnel. Like the inside of the mountain at Crows Nest Pass. She realized just as suddenly that it was the only other time she had experienced such darkness. She always had lights on and always lived in the city, where you got light emanating from outside—all the cars and streetlights and signs on shop fronts. They had even lived across the street from the Oakridge Shopping Center, and there was always activity and light across the street. That's what she wanted. She forgot to think about how it might get dark out in the country like this. How the power might go out. She sat completely stiff with her eyes wide open, unable to think straight. Magnus used to laugh at this side of her—but he laughed affectionately. It was different. He used to compare her to a deer. "You're the opposite of a deer," he said. "Deer go into a numb stare when they're faced with sudden light. You go into a numb stare when you're suddenly in the dark." He then put his hand on her cheek affectionately and chuckled. She basked in that kind of affection. She purred like a kitten. Right now, she missed him. She had to admit that right off the bat. She missed him—and she had probably been clinging to him ever since that moment of blackness inside the mountain at Frank, Alberta. Without her eyesight, Karen noticed the smells of the unfamiliar cottage. The smell of wet wood. Of old paper and wool. The scent of pine. The slight tinge of wood-rot. The smell of her own body, emanating heat in her fear of the darkness: it was like cinnamon and vanilla. She heard the sounds more clearly: the noisy rain on the windows and roof, the creaking of wood panels, a scratch somewhere—hopefully not a mouse. She sat there thinking and not thinking, sensations flooding through her: fear. That's what it was. Paralyzing dread. Her heart was pounding and she felt hot; buds of sweat had broken out on her face and neck; her hands felt numb.

Suddenly, the lights came on again, a sharp sensation that assaulted the eyes. Karen Brown was washed in a sensation of relief. She could see again. She looked around a little anxiously but more attentively. The books in the bookshelves: the actual titles. A complete set of encyclopedias on ships of all kinds: frigates, sailboats, steamships, passenger liners, ferries. The stuff hanging around the windows: the many-colored baseball caps perched with their visors down. The pillows on the couches: they were striped wool in lilac, rose and white. The glasses on the kitchen shelving: they were brown and clear tumblers for beer and glasses for scotch and wine and martinis. The rug in front of the fireplace was Mexican, the kind you can buy cheaply in furniture stores. And above her head she noticed for the first time a carved wooden fish, hanging from the ceiling, colorless with age, but with big lettering on it that said: BAIT. She was rapidly going through an emergency list. If the lights went out again, it would not only be dark, but it would be cold. The electric heating would remain off. She would have to get several things in order: one, the flashlight; two, extra blankets for the bed. She got up and fetched the flashlight, which she should have with her at all times. Then she found three old Hudson's Bay blankets under the bench-bed in the hall, which was used as a storage chest, and she piled them on the cold wood floor beside the bed. In the bedroom was a high window with no curtains right over the pillows, and two reading lamps plus an old dial telephone. She checked the phone. It was working. This was good. Fears for her security had somehow set in. This she hadn't expected, but it was inevitable. She had no idea what it was like outside the cottage and wouldn't know until morning. She was told there was wildlife (bears and lynxes and raccoons and deer were all she remembered), but only now did it dawn on her that those would also be dangerous. She went back to the sofa, this time holding her flashlight, and sat down with her book next to the lamp again. Her ducks were lined up, as she used to say to Magnus. He thought that was funny. No, he thought it was cute, this saying of hers: "get your ducks lined up." He laughed at that phrase every time.

Now she noticed there were at least eleven big straw hats hanging on the wall around the window left of the fireplace. Straw hats of various sizes and types: some scarlet, some brown, some with ribbons. There were no actual pictures on the walls, just objects of different kinds. A calendar and a dishcloth in the kitchen; a sunflower made of wood in the living room. She guessed it was her sister-in-law, Marianne, Stan's wife, who was in charge of these decorations. She couldn't imagine Stan having a hand in this. It was a nice place. Didn't they miss it when they were away in Ontario? So long at a time? Maybe she would just ask to rent the cottage for a whole year, she thought to herself. She might as well get used to being alone. It was Magnus who had got her through everything: simple things like shopping and driving, and she found it hard to be alone. Now she needed to train herself in the art of solitude. Obviously, judging from how she was feeling now—her stomach cramping and chest constricting—she needed that. She needed to be away from people for a while. The way she was feeling was—what word would she use to describe herself?—in *uproar? Nerves on end?* She was still and quiet on the sofa. The lights had stayed on, but she could sense her anxiety all over her body. She was stiff as a corpse where she sat, but shaking inside. She could feel herself literally *shaking.* Her heart was pounding; the back of her neck felt stiff; her shoulders ached; her legs had begun to tingle all the way into her toes. Would she ever be able to sleep? Perhaps she would never sleep again. . . .

Just as suddenly the lights went out again. She clutched the flashlight. Clearly, power outages were common around here. Stan never told her that, but she could have reasoned her way to that realization: the ocean with its winter gales, the trees falling down in the forest, the pelting rain—which might turn to heavy, water-laden snow in the winter, weighing down the power lines. Perhaps she should get used to it? The darkness. She forced herself to leave the button on the flashlight alone and sit in the tomblike eclipse a bit longer. Wasn't she like the night birds anyway? she thought to herself. The birds that fly into the light at night and hit the city buildings because they're confused. She read in the *New York Times* once about how they dimmed the lights on the Sears tower in Chicago just to save some of the migrating birds from that kind of death. The John Hancock Center too—they turned those lights off. The Wrigley Building and the Tribune Tower. They said it was the song sparrow and the hermit thrush and the Baltimore oriole—different birds that were migrating north in the spring and south in the fall— that can't tell the difference between a city light and a star. Do they really navigate by the stars? Interesting thought. Somewhere she read that in Chicago alone, thousands of birds die every year after hitting buildings. All over the U.S. it was estimated that a hundred million birds kill themselves every year that way. So they started a "Lights Out" program. Toronto had the "Fatal Lights Awareness Program" too, and the Empire State Building in New York turned off its spire lights when the Audubon Society called. The World Trade Center used to do the same, while it still existed, even putting nets on the windows. Somebody picked up seven hundred dead birds and three hundred injured birds of sixty different species from the World Trade Center in one year alone. The John Hancock Center in Chicago had four hundred dead birds at its feet one morning alone before the awareness program started in 1969. There are six hundred and twenty-four light bulbs in the crown of that building. . . . She was thinking fast, like talking fast to herself.

And she, Karen Brown, flew straight into the artificial light in her life too, didn't she? Instead of navigating by the "stars" of nature, by what was natural and organic, she had been ruled by fear. Was that not her relationship to Magnus after all? He kept her safe from the darkness. Now that he was gone, should she just find someone else to rescue her from the darkness? Why not rescue herself? She was fifty now, and she could look after herself. She sat on the sofa in the emptiness thinking and screwing up her courage to go ahead with it. Some sort of project that required a force of will she knew she had. She could hear the rain banging onto the roof of the cottage. Such violent activity in nature. The wind was blowing as well, and the trees were rustling and grating. She heard them more clearly in the darkness. She let the time pass while she stared into nothing. This was a test of her theory to *think it through*. She should just sit quietly and examine why she was afraid of the dark. Pure and simple. She always had been, ever since the night up in Powell River when she fell off the bunk bed. She was in the top bunk because, even though she was a fat little seven-year-old girl, Stan, who was already nine, was even bigger. So she crawled into the top bunk in the only other bedroom they had then, which she shared with her brother, and fell asleep. But she woke in the night. She remembered clearly how she was both awake and asleep at the same time. She tossed at night, a restless sleeper. In one of her tosses, she rolled out of the bunk and onto the floor with a big thud. Her wrist hurt for days afterward, but that was miraculously all. The real damage, she figured, was in her mind. It was so dark that she couldn't see the edge of the bed and fell down, which frightened her. After that she was unwilling to have the lights off completely, and Stan rebelled against having to share a space with her. He was moved into the corridor onto a camping cot, which suited him fine.

She couldn't sleep as a kid. Night was when things happened: burglaries, muggings, child abductions, fallings down. Her parents were simply annoyed with her, and Stan ridiculed her. But she had her aunt in town then, her Aunt Hazel, who tried to be helpful. Aunt Hazel's advice was to say words. They were "helping words" she could say every evening before bed. They came up with a sentence she said to herself every night: *I am able to go to bed without being afraid. Nothing bad will happen to me. I am smart and can figure out what to do.* This was her mantra, her bedtime prayer, and it actually only stopped when she moved in with Magnus and was too embarrassed to say the words before bedtime. And besides, he was there, protecting her all night long. Aunt Hazel had other techniques too, which she taught her niece. One was what she called "whole body relaxation," which meant she should lie down on her back and be completely at ease, letting all her limbs and her head and shoulders just slip into neutral. The other method was a "visual imagery" program. She was supposed to think of a scene she loved and keep it in her mind. It took her a long time to find the right one, but when she did, it worked well. It was an image of a flat field full of snow and in the middle of it, a small stone house, its roof covered with snow. Little windows and a fading sun low in the sky. That was the image. She had no idea where it came from, but it soothed her.

In fact, Aunt Hazel was a smart woman, but since she was also a Jehovah's Witness, she was not so welcome in the Browns' household. Karen and Stan's parents were anti-Christian, not just atheists—plain anti-Witness and would have nothing to do with the stuff. Karen had to sneak over to Hazel's house in secret. She liked her aunt, and she put up with her mini-lectures. It was nice: they would spend time in Hazel's orchard, under the apple trees, and Karen got scones and pickled range eggs there. After telling her what to do about her night fears, she remembered her aunt saying, "You have a choice, Karen. You can stay awake at night and wait for disaster to strike, or you can hang up your fears with your clothes at night. Go to bed, close your eyes and trust your Heavenly Father who's always watching over you." *Hang up your fears with your clothes at night.* Karen always remembered that line. But now, as she thought about it in the complete darkness of her brother Stan's country cottage, so much later in life, she remembered the newspaper articles about those dead birds flying into the artificial lights and killing themselves. What if, she suddenly thought out loud. *what if the very thing you reach for to save you is the one thing that will destroy you?* Maybe, after all that, it was the darkness that was her friend. Maybe the night itself was what would rescue her. The dark: what if she went into it? Stayed in it? Walked right through it to the other side?

Aunt Hazel. Why was she remembering her so vividly now? With her mahogany brown ponytail and her sharp, angular features, her slenderness—the one thing she envied about Hazel.

Hazel would be talking about "The Presence of God" as if she had special license to set little Karen free of her burden of being chubby and thinking maybe she could be slender too if she went to the Kingdom Hall. She could still hear her aunt's comforting, mellow voice, like silk with a stone wrapped into it: *The darkness hideth not from thee; but the night shineth as the day: the darkness and the light are both alike to thee.* . . . She told Karen out in the flowery front yard of her small house by the highway: "There is no such thing as darkness, Karen. Dark is just when light goes away, nothing else. The light of everything is God's Truth, and Truth is never gone away." Aunt Hazel was a staunch person, Karen was aware of that very early. There was a story about Hazel walking through the city park in Vancouver—maybe it was Stanley Park?—in the middle of the night, not at all apprehensive because "she trusted in the Lord," as she said. When Karen was small she was afraid for Aunt Hazel when she heard that story. She knew her aunt should not have done that. It was a foolhardy thing to go walking in the city park at night. Daring everybody. Like walking barefoot on hot coals! As the image of hot coals smoldering appeared in her mind, the lights on Martin Road came back on again. There was a flicker of the light bulb in the lamp beside her, and the refrigerator started humming again. Karen still held the flashlight in her hand, which she had not turned on this time. A sense of triumph again. That would show Magnus. She could see clearly too that her Aunt Hazel had the appearance of being somehow *protected,* and Karen would be safe if she just stuck close. First Hazel and then Magnus took over that function. Magnus too had an air of being safe everywhere he went: safe *in himself.*

"What are you doing up at this hour, Karen?" Magnus half-whispered when he came down to look for her in the night just three months ago. He was barefoot and had thrown on his pajama and T-shirt set a little crookedly, his straight hair all messed up. It was after two in the morning and she was in the living room by the window, looking out at the empty street with its streetlights and the shops across on the other side. She was combing her small fingers through her thick, short hair. It was one of those late summer nights when she was unable to sleep. She gravitated to the living room window: the one facing the traffic and the lights. The other side of the house actually faced a public park, and she was apprehensive about that side. Usually, Magnus didn't wake up when she left the bedroom. But they were having their arguments then—they argued about everything, it seemed, by the end.

"I'm just looking out the window," she informed him, a little annoyed that he was coming to break her reverie, her attempt to stabilize herself.

"What are you afraid of?" he insisted then. "What is it?"

"I don't know!" He had asked this a thousand times, and she only had this one answer. So what? "So what if I don't know?" she muttered. Magnus sat down in the leather lounge chair on the other side of the room and seemed to be waiting.

"What do you think they did in preindustrial times, Karen?" he then asked her. He had started to talk as if she were unreasonably apprehensive, not just apprehensive. *Unreasonable.* That kind of appellation was so hard to live with!

"I think they had a way of supporting each other before light bulbs, Magnus," she echoed his half-mocking tone.

"I'm not criticizing you," he broke in. "I'm asking what you think life was like before people could turn on the lights whenever they wanted to." He *would* ask that—seeing as how he designed the wiring in people's houses for a living, she thought.

"What am I afraid of?" she answered his former question, loudly, hoping no neighbors could hear her high-pitched voice. "Okay,

I'll tell you," she challenged him. She turned around and sat down on the sofa facing him then. "I'm afraid you'll leave me! I'm afraid of being abandoned—by you, by anyone! It's perfectly reasonable to be afraid of the dark—have you ever thought of that?" He looked a little startled at her outburst, like he always did when she busted out like that. But he brought it on, he did. He should just get what he taunted out of her. She raised her voice even higher. "At night, when it's dark, people fall into ditches and off bridges and into harbors."

"Don't be silly," he retorted.

She was building up steam. "Stop saying I'm silly! All sorts of unsavory things go on at night, have you thought of that? Garbage collectors and cesspool emptiers work at night. People in iron forges and heavy industries work at night." She paused, then started up again. "Preindustrial times? Did you know they carried the bodies of those who died of the plague away at night?"

"Okay, okay," he said as soothingly as he could, his palms raised to face her in a gesture of conciliation. But she was just getting started.

"At night the whole social order is upside down. Did you know that?" she went on with a rising ebb of fury. "There are whole gangs roaming the streets; people put on the wrong clothes and you can't tell who's who any more; there are robberies and burglaries at night. The poor and miserable go out at night and get back at the rest— back at people like us! They're out there smuggling and stealing. Cutting down trees and robbing orchards and escaping from prisons. Out on the streets slumming—there are streetwalkers and arsonists starting fires and rapists looking for solitary women. . . ." By this time she was crying, half-hysterical. Magnus had gotten up in a mild panic and was by her side, trying to soothe her. She started to cry like a kid. He folded his arms around her and tried to comfort her, as if he were her father, not her husband. She was sobbing. She hadn't sobbed like that for decades. She had no idea what got into her.

"You're going to leave me, aren't you?" she whispered through her sobs, her big tears staining his T-shirt.

"Yes, Karen." That was all he said. He said it as if he was delivering a tragic bit of news from the army about their son. They sat in silence in the half-dark. He was rocking her gently, and she was sobbing quietly with a load of silent tears flowing down her round cheeks.

Karen knew this scene, this moment in her history was going to replay in her tired brain X number of times now. She began to call it the annunciation scene when she found out for sure it was all over with Magnus. But it had never occurred to her until this moment—this very split-second as she sat in her brother's cottage on the sofa, the flickering light beside her, the unlit flashlight in her left hand—that Magnus, the man she had married and spent twenty-five years of her Only One life with, had spent his entire childhood in the dark. He must have. They say the town where he grew up in Norway, Tromso, is the most northerly city in the world that can still be called part of civilization. In Tromso the sun left the earth for six or seven months at a time, and Magnus and everyone else up there did everything in the dark. He went to school in the morning with his backpack on in the pitch black of night and he came home in the same blackness. He did his homework in the dark, played soccer in the dark, went to the kiosk to buy candy in the dark. He was friendly with the night. He lived it, breathed it, was at peace with it. Now that she thought of it, he was a creature of the night. *A creature of the night.*

In a very strange way, Karen saw in a flash of insight, she had married the night. The one person in her life who would be unable to understand what she was afraid of. She was always striving for the light, always looking for consolation when the light dimmed, always seeking answers and solutions to the unknown and its chaos, always putting things into order and "lining up her ducks." She had never visited that town in Norway where Magnus grew up. Maybe she should have. Maybe that was the problem: she didn't understand him. She didn't know what it was like to be a person coming out of the dark. Maybe it was not he who did not understand her, but the other way around. Perhaps the whole problem here, she was beginning to think, was that she should have gone there with him. In the middle of the winter, like December, when they huddle in the dark room with their candles and celebrate Christmas, the feast of light. She had never known the meaning of all that, really, when she thought about it. . . .

She got up from the sofa and decided to put herself to bed. She would keep the lamp on in the living room, and there would be a faint glow from it into the bedroom. But she had the flashlight with her, just in case. She got a glass of water for when she got thirsty, and took her book in case she couldn't sleep. The door was locked, everything was in its place. Tomorrow she would explore the area and see what was around the cottage. That way she would be less apprehensive. The whole business depended on knowing where everything was. She had lots of time for that because Marianne and Stan wouldn't arrive for another month. And if she liked it, if she could handle being here by herself with the intermittent power failures, she would ask him to rent it to her for longer. She would set up her computer and get a postbox and start up her business from this place. A small surge of confidence went through her. As she leaned across the fireplace to turn off the floor lamp beside it, she saw an old book on the lintel. It was rather small, faded blue with almost indistinguishable gold lettering on the cover. The corners were worn to tatters. Obviously, the book was either very old or much used. She picked it up and opened it. There was a signature on the frontispiece in blue ink: it said *Hazel Brown.* Karen saw it was an old copy of the King

James Bible. She didn't know Stan had Hazel's Bible. What a surprise! What was it doing here? She opened it up and leafed through the onion-thin pages. She was reading at random, flipping forward with her fingers, going to put the book back on the shelf any minute. Job 18:18: *He shall be driven from light into darkness, and chased out of the world.* . . . Job 19:8: *He hath fenced up my way that I cannot pass, and he hath set darkness in my paths.* . . . Psalm 139:11: *If I say, Surely the darkness shall cover me; even the night shall be light around me.* . . . Any second now, she was going to shut the book and put it back in its place. . . .

Pleasures Liberty Cannot Know

*W*hen Carla George was five years old, she played on the sidewalk outside her mother's house on Cumberland Street in Burnaby. There were several bungalows in a row, all alike, and they called them cottages, but they were just regular houses with stucco on the outside. The sidewalk was old and had cracks in it. In some places the concrete sections were at an angle, and sometimes the angles didn't meet. Grass grew in those places, and frequently dandelions. Where the incline was too steep (vertical displacement is what it was), the concrete had broken and there were cracks running clear across. It was on one of those fractures that Carla fell while playing hopscotch with her friends (Maurice called it *marelles*). She had fallen several times before. Once she scraped the palm of her hand, the one she used to stop the fall. Another time she cracked her front tooth. But on this occasion, it was her whole upper arm because she landed while flying forward, and the concrete—lumpy and gritty as it was—gave her arm a thorough going over. She came home crying with streaks of blood-soaked tender skin on her right arm, stomped up the steps from the sidewalk and into the front door, showed it to her mother and said she had had enough.

"Enough of what, dear?" said her mother Aruna. "Enough of playing or enough of crying?"

"I've had enough of that sidewalk. The sidewalk needs to be fixed in that spot!"

"We can't fix it, Carla, dear. The mayor is in charge of that, not us."

"Then I want to talk to the mayor!"

"We don't just go talk to the mayor, dear, do we? Important people talk to the mayor, and they always talk in meetings."

"Then I'm going to ask the mayor to have a meeting with me!"

"All right, dear. You do that." Carla's mother just said that because she didn't think there would be anything more to it. But after the girl had been cleaned up and Aruna had returned to her place in the living room—an ornately carved oak rocking chair that Carla really liked—where Aruna had become used to spending most of her time, the girl came tramping in determinedly, wearing her newly laundered shirt.

"I want to call the mayor!" she announced.

"All right, dear."

"What's his number?"

"We need the phone book to figure that out." Carla got the phone book, handed it to her mother and waited while she looked up the number. Aruna turned to the blue pages for government to pacify her daughter and found what looked like a number for the mayor's office. She wrote it down on a sheet of paper and handed it to Carla.

"You dial the number, Mom."

"All right, all right." And Aruna dialed the number. Ordinarily, Aruna would not have indulged her daughter this far, but in reality, she was what you might call *inebriated* by now. Aruna was fond of Islay whiskey. As a matter of fact, on days like this when she had nowhere to go and only Carla to look after through the front window of the small bungalow, where the kids were jumping on the sidewalk and pushing one another, she helped herself to a little bit. No one was there to comment on the matter. No one ever came to visit, and Artie George, her husband of a few years, was now a husband of a few years past. So the whiskey made her a bit sleepy, and she didn't want Carla in her hair.

Carla ended up talking with a secretary in the mayor's office, who felt like indulging the little girl on the phone. Carla demanded a meeting with the mayor because she had very important business to discuss with him. The secretary went away for a while to check and came back to say to Carla that she could come to the mayor's office on Canada Way tomorrow at three in the afternoon.

"I'm going to bring my brother Pete too," Carla said, suddenly feeling insecure.

"Pete will be welcome too," said the secretary.

"And my mom too."

"By all means. Tomorrow at three. Do you know where to go?"

"My mom will show me." And they said goodbye. Carla hung up the phone. Then she went and told her mother they had a meeting next day at three in the afternoon with the mayor.

"What?" said Aruna, not having followed the conversation at all. When she realized this was for real, she looked at her daughter.

"Well, I'll be darned!" she mumbled, more to herself than to Carla. "Well, I'll be darned."

Carla remembered the incident well. Even now, thirty years later, she could recall those two days almost word for word. Must have made an impression on her! she thought. Actually, it was just one of those funny ideas she had as a kid. She went with her mother and brother Pete on the bus next day, down the Trans-Canada Highway and into the nice-looking, concrete four-story municipal building and had her meeting with the mayor. In fact, the mayor was about to step down, Carla knew that now, and he decided on the spur of the moment to use her visit as a public relations human interest story for the press, a kind of last symbolic gesture. (Carla heard a lot about him in the next few days because then people started talking: he had asthma and his mother made him drink *goat's milk*, and he went to Japantown to get a chest poultice that completely cured him. That's what they said, and they said he was *color blind*, which Carla didn't know, and she didn't know he was a champion of *contraception*, trying to get the feds to legalize planned families, and they said he ran a good *shoe-leather campaign*, something Carla didn't understand at all.) For that reason, not only was the mayor there when they arrived at three in the afternoon, but people from the press too. A journalist and a photographer who took pictures. First the photographer took a picture of Carla and Pete sitting on the mayor's sofa in his office. Then he took a snapshot of Carla showing the mayor a crack in her front tooth. In that picture, she stood with her mouth open next to the mayor in his mayoral chair and her finger pointing at her front tooth. The mayor, wearing his dark gray suit, was leaning over, one hand gently touching Carla's left shoulder, and he was investigating the crack in her tooth, which she had sustained on a previous fall on that same spot on the sidewalk. He was a pretty nice man, she seemed to remember. He was starting to lose his light brown hair, though, and some of the top of his head was balding. In one part of their conversation, the mayor asked her, "What should we do about this situation, Carla George?"

"We have to call the workers to work on the sidewalk. I'll tell you exactly where they should go. I'll draw it for you if you give me paper and a pencil."

The mayor handed her a piece of paper and a pencil, and she drew a map of the sidewalk, complete with curb and concrete sections and cracks in the bad one. When she showed the mayor the map, the photographer was there with yet another picture and the flash went off.

"I guess we'll have to call the workmen, then," the mayor said and picked up his telephone and dialed a number. The photographer took a picture of the mayor talking on the phone, ordering the workers to fix the sidewalk exactly according to Carla George's directions.

When they got home again and the *Vancouver Sun* (it wasn't just the *New Westminster Columbian* or the *Burnaby News Leader*—it was the big city newspaper) came out a couple of days later with Carla's picture inside and the mayor on the telephone and Carla pointing at her tooth, everyone congratulated her. The other kids were envious, she remembered that, but the adults—her friends' parents and her kindergarten teachers—smiled very nicely and many of them said, "You'll go far, Carla!" They nodded their heads with approval and said, "You'll go far."

But Carla, as it turned out, did not go far. In fact, she only got as far as the Sunshine Coast, and to get there all you had to do was take a ferry. She didn't end up in Ottawa or even Toronto or Quebec City with some company logo on her letterhead or some government department nametag for a lot of important seminars and meetings. No, Carla simply ended up making ends meet, going from one job to another, one boyfriend to another, and now she was nearing forty

and was on her seventh relationship: Don. Don Dundas and Carla
George had just moved in together, into a house by the highway in
Robert's Creek. Don had built the house and had a workshop to the
side of it, half of which was full of carpentry tools and machinery:
sanders, electric saws, electric drills. Carla got to have the other half
of the workshop for her stuff—she had a lot of stuff, she did—and
she was going to make something of this situation now. She was
going to do her art: pastel drawings, rough-looking and colorful, of
mythical subjects, bulls and trolls and strange creatures. Maurice
once called them *naif*, but they were really *dreamscapes*, the kind of
imagery you have in your dreams. . . . This time she would really do
it because now Don was there to help pay the bills; she wasn't going
to worry herself sick about meeting those every month. And on this
particular Sunday, the day before Canada Day, she was unpacking
her stuff.

She was a doer. She prided herself on that. No one was going
to find her feeling sorry for herself that getting on in this life is
difficult. You don't just walk into law school and into government
and through university and all that without background. People who
did those things had parents with money to support them. What did
Carla have? She had a mother who was an alcoholic. No one even
bothered to cover that up any more. Her mother had pine-colored,
long hair and became very passive when she had been drinking.
Normally, when she looked at you, she looked directly into your
eyes. At one time her mother thought she was a channeler because
she could sense people's inner lives so easily, but she did nothing
about it. "I didn't want to go there," she later told Carla. But she had
met an Indian sage who gave Raga singing lessons on the floor of his
home and advised her mother on spiritual matters. She had renamed
herself Aruna from her original name "Bea" or Beatrice. His daughter Saida was working at an accounting firm in Metrotown, right

here in Burnaby. (She had met her—intimidatingly good looking, nothing like what you'd expect from her father.) Carla never got the whole of her mother's philosophy, just bits and pieces scattered across the years (*. . . embrace your fears, don't avoid them or deny them . . . your fears are just costumes you can put on and take off . . . you don't have to believe anything . . . you don't have to achieve anything . . . don't behave automatically— behave authentically . . .*). Carla went through a learning curve about the alcohol; it was as if everything just pressed down on her mother and finally she got squashed, and Carla had to find a way to leave her alone, learning about Western "boundaries": to know what you deserve and don't, what you need and don't, what you like and dis- like; to know your rights—your right to be yourself!—to know how to be responsible for yourself, take care of yourself. . . .

And Carla had a father, Artie, who was just a fool. (Her dad married another woman after divorcing her mom—that woman, Dorothy from Abbottsford, who used to be married to an even older man, some harmonica buff named Nick of all things, who managed to stay married to Artie for four months before she divorced him and took everything he owned with her. Turned out to be a gold-dig- ger! She took his house in Abbottsford—she could have it as far as Carla was concerned. It was right next to the highway—no privacy and a shop right next door that sold hundreds of Saris: petticoats, blouses, nine-yard-long Saris in a hundred color combinations of silk and cotton embroidered with gold thread and tassels hanging on the ends. "It is the shimmer of a woman's tears and the falling of her crests of hair and the colors of her many moods and the softness of her skin all woven together," the salesman said to Carla once when she entered the shop and asked what all that stuff was. Dorothy took all of Artie's savings, everything her mom ought to have got. Dorothy even went to court and charged Artie with physical violence so she would get the stuff. It wasn't physical violence at all, Carla knew for sure. Just a fist in the face, which Dorothy deserved! Because Dorothy was one messed-up woman. But the judge is always on the side of women who weep and mush in front of them and claim they've been beaten up by their husbands, so there you are. Artie George lost everything to Dorothy, and Aruna got nothing, and in that case how was Carla George supposed to go to university and get a law degree or whatever you get in those places? That's what she wanted to know!

Then Carla had her brother Pete, who was in jail. Yes, he was. He was a fool like his dad. He was not a wicked man, just a foolish man, making mistakes all over the place. He still had his red hair, but it was longer on one side than the other now, and he had a dark goatee, which is so popular among the boys, and he liked his upturned collars and moody look, he did. James Dean with a twist. Carla had to sit through his court case because their mom wasn't able to do it. Just too much for her, it was.

Carla was unpacking in the workshop. Don was at his workbench. She could hear him sanding away. He restored furniture and things for people—sanded the wood and stained it, and it came out looking pretty good. Carla was playing a CD and the music floated around the place, all over the house and the yard outside and the birds were listening—the robins, widgeons, sparrows, thrushes, Stellar's Jays—so many, and such fun, like a permanent aviary out here. She knew they were listening. (There was good music everywhere, not just the birds; for example, that nice long-haired guitarist by the liquor store in the village, the way he played those complicated tunes. Carla could go there and pretend to be shopping, but it was really to hear him play; when she was upset, she went there and it soothed her, it really did!). The CD she was playing was Natalie Choquette singing with the Orchestra de La Scala de Montréal. She was singing "Caro nome" from Verdi's *Rigoletto*, and Carla always loved to hear those high notes suspended in midair and then come down like a flock of swallows swooping and turning. It was such a theatrical song. Carla had learned to appreciate operatic theater from her Quebecois ex-boyfriend, Maurice Allard—a music aficionado, he called himself. Those were fun times. It was the closest Carla had come to that other world: the life the other half lives, they say. Opera. Fancy dress. Banquets and all that. You'd get tired of it, pretty stressful stuff, but once in a while it was just plain fun. Maurice was not a fool. He was just too French. He couldn't live anywhere except Montréal and didn't take to the West. What are you supposed to do? Go to Quebec? That just wasn't Carla's style. She did what she did, and moving to Quebec wasn't one of them.

She took out a screen she had no use for but had kept because she loved it. It was a half-screen made of plain old plywood, about eight panels put together with hinges. Maybe it was meant to be in front of a fireplace in somebody's cozy home. What was nice about it was that it was painted in folk-art style. There was a person on each panel, standing in blue and lilac and red water, and looking sideways at a figure in white, and a figure in blue, red and black, half-immersed in the river, with two angels above and one angel on the banks of the water. The baptism of Jesus—Maurice said he was sure that's what it showed, painted just two-dimensionally, very flat and shallow. But the whole thing was really colorful: deep cherry reds and violet blues and bright, sunny yellow in small dashes. Where would she put this thing? Don didn't seem to have the house for it. But Carla was inventive. If she was nothing else, she was inventive. This was a happy day for her. A good relationship, a good home, a promising future here. Don Dundas was a good man. What more do you want? He was a bit older than Carla—fifteen years older to be exact—and Carla had never done that before. Crossed such a big age gap. But older men are more stable, she could see that now. He had a trade and a home and had been in one place for so long you knew he was going to stay. He wasn't just going to fly back to some eastern city on Air Canada now, was he? Not Don. (He had a square face and wore big black glasses and a mask over his mouth and nose when he was sanding, and he made rustic furniture when there was nothing to refurbish: picture frames and doors and benches to sit on and tables with legs made of tree roots. Sometimes he designed whole interiors and built them for people, like he did for his sister Doreen when she and her husband Bob moved to the west village—too bad they didn't get to enjoy it very long! They died young, and that goes to show you don't last forever, do you?).

Still, something was nagging in Carla's chest. She had the kind of heartburn feeling people do on television when they advertise acid reflux disease, where there is a bright red searing hot line going down the throat all the way to the stomach. She had that because of Pete. She was pretty sure it was because of Pete. It was only four weeks ago this court thing ended, and it all went so fast, and it felt pretty bad. It made her feel a bit sick, she had to admit it, even though it wasn't intended. Pete hadn't planned to do what he ended up doing. But the law didn't see it that way, apparently. Intention isn't it. It's just what you do and what people can make of it. Like a story. Whatever story people can come up with. The best spiel wins. Lawyers are really storytellers. They make up stories and test them out on juries, and the best fabrication gets the cake. She thought of the eerie beauty of the law courts in Vancouver with all the mixed feelings of a changeable sky. The waterfall outside, the way the water trickles down over the concrete. The slanted glass roof of the futuristic Arthur Erickson building that Maurice was fond of looking at, with all the greenery attached to it in steps. He had theories of "the beauty of confinement" and "the laws of constraint that made freedom possible" that were mirrored in the architecture, "the grandeur of order"—things Carla neither wanted to nor needed to understand. It wasn't real life for him, the law. He didn't know!

Carla pulled out of the cardboard box a picture she had wrapped in a linen cloth. It was large and in a rather heavy wood frame that looked a bit clumsy. But it was a nice looking frame. The work was an engraving she found in an antique shop in Gastown. It was engraved by William Wollett in 1767 of a picture by Cornelius Dusart. When she bought the picture, it was also the day before Canada Day. She was with Maurice back then, who was an art collector and sometimes an art dealer, so she went with him to places where art could be found. She knew very little about these things, but you learn. You sure learn. And if you're clever, which Carla was, admittedly, you learn fast. It was something she said to her girlfriends when they got together for jam sessions of tea and scones and gossip (it used to be stronger stuff, but Carla was very shy of alcohol, and didn't want to be like her mother. No, sir. She did not.) that one good thing about boyfriends, whatever else you might say, is that you learn something new with every new one. They all have something they know about, and you learn it from them. Boyfriend-school. That was her alma mater. Some people go to university; some people learn from "the hard knocks of life," but Carla George had been going to boyfriend-school since she was seventeen, and she had quite an education.

Maurice was a slight man by comparison with Don; he had a high forehead and sensitive lips, and a permanent shadow on his face. But he dressed casually—usually wearing just a red checkered shirt over a black T-shirt and blue jeans—and he liked everything abstract and crazy; and he wore leather hiking boots in the middle of the day. She and Maurice were in this antique shop on Hastings near Gastown. Carla immediately noticed the engraving hanging there. It was very dark. Brown with age. The picture showed a whole bunch of peasants having a rollicking time outside an inn. The inn had a straw-thatched roof and wooden benches and tables in the yard. They were drinking ale out of big mugs; some were standing, some sitting. There were women there, all wearing peasant costumes. There were trees around in full leaf and mountains in the back. A very nice picture, and it had *atmosphere.* She pointed it out to Maurice and said she liked it. He looked at it closely with his loop—a funny thing he had in his pocket all the time, which wasn't like a magnifying glass because you had to put it right up against the thing you were looking at.

"I'm not sure this isn't the real thing," Maurice said.

"What else could it be?" Carla answered. "I mean, do you mean a reproduction of an engraving? If it's a reproduction, then why is it so old and dark?"

"Exactly. And it's quite large." He kept looking, then said: "Do you want it?"

"Do I want it?" she repeated, flabbergasted. "Well, like, yeah!" And he bought it. Just like that. He bargained with the antiquarian and ended up getting the whole thing, frame and all, for seventy-five dollars. When they got back to his apartment in Yaletown, he went on the Net and found another William Wollett engraving at an auction in Holland, selling for twelve hundred and seventy Euros. He said if they had a real, authentic Wollett engraving, they had just cornered themselves over eleven hundred Euros—and that's almost the same as American dollars. That would be, maybe, a couple of thousand Canadian bucks at the most. But hey, it was a good bargain that day. There were other engraving reproductions on sale out there, he showed her, for a hundred and fifty U.S. or so, but even that made this one a bargain. She liked that. She liked being able to find something and love it. It was Carla's little bit of European history. Her own connection to it. The picture, whatever else it was, had a lot of character and it made her dream.

"What's that crap?" Don broke into Carla's reverie, walking into the room where she was unpacking. He meant the picture she was holding up to the light so she could see the small details better.

"That's not crap!" she turned and protested back. "Sweetie, it's an old engraving. It's valuable."

"Oh, it's probably just junk. You get too many high hopes." He was wearing his blue and white checkered summer shirt and shorts and had his work belt over it at his waist. He was a bit rotund around the midline, but it wasn't all that bad. His hair was mostly sand colored now, but he was in pretty good shape. He had his sanding mask hanging around his neck.

"Oh, come on now. I have it on good authority this is worth as much as a couple of thousand bucks. And besides," she added turning back to the picture, "it's nice to look at, don't you think?" But Don had already lost interest in it and was headed back to his workbench in the other room. Carla was left standing there holding the picture, which was getting heavy so she put it down.

She was suddenly beset by a feeling of insecurity. It came over her sometimes, and she fought it when it happened. She fought tooth and nail, actually. It was alike an enemy. "The beast within," she used to say. All the things she couldn't tell Don, even though she wanted to really share with him. She couldn't tell him that the good authority for this picture, as well as everything else, was actually Maurice Allard. He wouldn't appreciate it. More, he wouldn't like it. To hear about her former love life and how she clung to it through these *things*. But it was her life, wasn't it? It was who she had become, wasn't it? What makes us who we are? Whenever she got this feeling of *malaise*, she couldn't help but think of Pete. Pete started getting into trouble already as a teenager. He stole his first car when he was sixteen (checked a whole line of parked cars till he found one with an unlocked door, jumped in, got it to start, bounced it into a tree, down a hill, made a U-turn and drove back, hit another tree, and crashed it while the owner looked on). He stole another car in his twenties, and that one he got away with. He actually sold it to a used lot and made some money (it was a pretty sleazy lot under the Granville bridge). Then he was emboldened, he was. That's when they should have realized he was developing a way of life. Carla thought she should have been stronger, more effective, in talking him out of it. Aruna sure wouldn't; heck, she didn't even know about it. And their dad Artie had already moved to Yellowknife, where he stayed. She tried talking to Pete, and he didn't steal again for quite a while. But he was laid off from work (at a Petro-Canada Station— couldn't even hold onto that!) and he was angry, so he stole his third car on the spur of the moment. He was walking down the street in Richmond, and there was a car parked in a parking lot with the key in it. The key in the ignition! Some dumb driver! And here Pete walks by and gets tempted to jump in the car and drive away. Just like that. Damn him, he was such a fool! He drove all the way to Steveston before he stopped and turned around to look at the back seat. That's when he noticed there was a baby back there, sucking its thumb quietly and looking out the window in its green baby seat. He panicked. He realized too late he hadn't just stolen a car there—he had kidnapped a baby. Child abduction—now that was a real crime. It wasn't just petty theft. That was a real crime, it was.

It was interesting to Carla, in spite of everything, how she was discovering that the older you get, the harder it is to stay grounded. You'd think it would be the opposite. You'd figure that with age comes self-confidence, and with confidence you get better grounding and certitude. But this didn't seem to be the case. As the years went by, it took less and less for her to feel like she lost her balance. A kind of *vertigo* happened more and more—a life-vertigo. Sometimes it seemed she was standing on a precipice and one inch in front of her was a drop of a mile into some hellish abyss. She didn't know anyone who she thought might understand this feeling. Maybe Aruna could. Maybe she was getting more and more like her mother? (Aruna's answer to everything: *detachment*). No, she didn't talk about it because she had heard once that if you tell someone about something really, really meaningful and something you're truly vulnerable about—if you tell that to a person who doesn't understand or is your enemy, well, then, you could go insane. Maurice talked about that once ("that way lies insanity" was what he actually said). And it was true. If something absolutely important to you is criticized, made light of, dismissed by another person, you get a very deep hurt. That's when you're on the precipice. Keep it to yourself, girl! she told herself. Although sometimes, it had to be admitted, sometimes you wanted to share things like that with your loved one. So you try, and on occasion it works. Carla had already spent a lot of time working out what she called "her private life" and how she could keep it intact. That was the life she had for herself alone, which no one else was part of. Like an interesting room you keep the key to in a hidden place, and no one is allowed in there. Only very special people, who understand the place and who adore it. No, who love it. Someone like Maurice, for example, might get an invite into that room of life. But so far, he was the only one. And in that case, why did the man fly off like that? Wasn't Vancouver good enough? Oh, well—she thought she was well over that. She looked at the engraving again. Funny how certain objects have the power to send your mind off in different directions. These objects carry worlds in them, power they unleash once you open up to them. It's what they called magic—black magic, white magic. The magic in things themselves. . . .

When Pete George realized what he had done, he just sat there in the blue Hyundai he had just stolen, behind the wheel, baby in the backseat, and became completely paralyzed. He had spent half an hour getting as far as Steveston and had parked the car near the Steveston harbor. People were walking on the wharf enjoying themselves: an old man with a cane and a watch chain hanging from his pocket and a white hat on; a man in a red baseball cap; a Chinese couple taking long strides past the Life Ring in a big yellow container; another old man trailing an oxygen tank behind him; boxes of tomatoes displayed for sale, and crab and halibut and shrimp in ice; people having beer at outdoor restaurants on the dock. There were some old buildings being used as shops for tourists: antique bookstores and artisans' shops selling stuff related to fishing and the sea and kites; picnic benches in the middle of the walkway and hanging flower baskets suspended from the streetlamps. There was a bleak sun in the sky, and the air was almost white it was so dry. Pete could feel the heat in the air penetrating his skin and getting inside his body. The baby was quiet as a mouse. Pete didn't move. He couldn't think. He must have sat there for forty minutes, empty-headed as he was. But then he did the only thing he could think of—and that was the right thing for sure, Carla was happy about that at least. He got out of the car, pulled out a quarter from his pocket and headed for the nearest phone booth. Then he called Carla. She answered the phone in the middle of painting her fingernails. Two fingers were done, three more to go, on the left hand.

"Carla, it's Pete."

"Hey, how ya doin?"

"Carla, I'm in deep shit!" At this Carla could feel her spine begin to tingle and her hair—invisible hair—stand on end.

"What is it, Pete?"

"I stole a car. . . ."

"You what? Pete?" A silence of a few minutes while the next thing hung suspended in the air.

"I stole a car."

"Darn it! Why are you doing that? Damn!"

"But that's not the worst of it. . . ." Pete was interjecting.

"Did you crash it? Are you hurt?"

"No, it's worse than that. Listen," and Carla listened carefully. She was making a mental note to remember every word in case it was needed later. "I stole this car, see, I wasn't going to tell you about it or nothing, but when I got to Steveston I found out there's a baby in the back of it. There's a baby in the car!"

"Good God!"

"What'll I do? I don't know what to do!"

"Pete, listen to me. You take that car right back to where you found it. Do it now! Take it back there and park it exactly where you found it and get the hell away from it. Take it back baby and all! Do you hear me?"

"Yea, I hear you."

"I'll meet you there. Where did you find the car?'

"In the Costco parking lot in Richmond."

"Okay, take it back there now. Before the police find you with the child and all. Make sure the child is okay. You got that?"

"Yea, I got that. I'm on my way."

"Oh, Pete. Oh, Pete. . . . Go! Just go!" And they hung up. Carla rushed to grab her car keys and knocked over the nail polish. The cherry red ooze slid out of the bottle slowly and onto the table and a few drops fell onto the floor. But Carla was off, her heart pounding, her adrenaline way up. Why hadn't she talked with him more about all this? How would their mom take it if he got nabbed now? It would destroy her—by now so little was needed to tip her over the brink. . . .

Carla drove like crazy to the Richmond Costco. It was a long drive, all the way from Lonsdale, where she was living then, over the Lion's Gate Bridge to begin with, which was slow, through the incredibly cumbersome downtown and all the way up Granville, but the worst part was that left turn after the Arthur Laing Bridge. You wait there forever. So it was at least an hour before she got there. When she did, she found out that Pete had made it almost all the way back to the parking lot from Steveston, but when he made the left turn onto Bridgeport Road, a siren went on behind him and a police car stopped him. He had to pull up then, and he realized it was all over for him. They would never believe he was taking the car back where he found it. And the parking lot was only five minutes away. Five minutes. God, give me just five minutes! But no. One officer got into the stolen car and the other put Pete in the backseat of the police car, and together they all went the rest of the way to meet the owner of the blue Hyundai and the baby. That's where Carla found them when she arrived. Pete was holed up in the police car, looking out the window. The Hyundai that he stole was in front of the Costco, and two police officers were talking to a man and a woman. The man, a thin guy in a white T-shirt and a black cap, with a small moustache, was holding the baby. Carla parked the car, pretending she was going to shop at Costco, and watched what was going on.

The man (the father, she later learned) was holding the baby and answering the questions of the police, but he looked like someone had just taken all the blood out of his body. He appeared to be completely lost. The woman was older (the baby's grandmother she found out) and was dressed from head to toe on a warm day like this. She wore a long dark skirt like some peasant, a short, wool jacket, a scarf over her head like a Russian babushka and woolen socks under her sandals. Carla later learned the details: the grandmother was shopping at Costco, and the son had come to pick her up. That was all. He stuck the baby in the back and drove over there, parked the car and dashed out to help his mother with the load of groceries.

At Costco you shopped for so much at a time, and it took a little while to get the stuff loaded in carts for transporting to the car. It was in those moments—those five minutes—that Pete came along and gingerly got into the Hyundai and drove away. When these people got back to the spot where the car was supposed to be parked, they went insane. They called the Costco security. They in turn called the police. The police came immediately, and the search was on. All of this before Pete even got to Steveston. The baby's father and grandmother could hardly speak English; they were immigrants from someplace—Iran or something. Instead of talking, the woman was flinging herself on the ground at the police officer's feet, grabbing them, kissing them. Then she threw herself at the baby in its father's embrace and flung her arms up in the air. She was expressing her happiness. She ran over to one of the police officers and put both her hands on his head, one on each side of his face, and clapped his cheeks like crazy. Body language. It was the best she could do. Carla saw right away that this strange woman had been completely desperate and destroyed for two hours and now she was overwhelmed with joy. A feeling of bitterness came over Carla as she stood there watching. It was unfair! This woman only suffered for two hours. Pete was going to suffer the rest of his life. God only knew how he would get out of this one.

As Carla stood there in her tight acid-washed jeans and blood-red tank top, her jean jacket and sandals, her long yellow hair tied back in a ponytail, two fingers painted, eight fingers not, she had the awakening realization that she, Pete—her whole family—were not safe. Something had got hold of them—some frog of bad luck had croaked at them—and they were always in danger. In danger from themselves, even. Especially from themselves. She, Carla George, was the only one in the whole family who kept her head on. And even she needed protection. That was clear as day. She walked past the police car where Pete was, pretending to be just walking down the street, and she surreptitiously gave Pete a sign with her hand to say, "I'm here, I'll try to help, hold on, and I'm not going to stop and talk to you now." Pete nodded from inside the police car, so she knew he understood. They had always been close, she and Pete. He came with her to the mayor's office long long ago. Now she'd go with him to the courthouse. Because this time the judgment would be more severe, seeing as how it was a second offense for the same thing—the same thing PLUS. She got back in her Ford and drove all the way home. She'd have to phone her mom in Burnaby, her dad in Yellowknife, and then go down to the police station to be with Pete while they asked him questions. She drove back slowly. It was already getting into rush hour, and traffic on Georgia Street was just crawling along. When she finally got back to Lonsdale, she didn't phone her mom or her dad first. No. It was time, Carla realized more clearly than ever before, it was time for her to get some real protection. A woman needs protection.

She had met Don a few months earlier at a place downtown that sold interesting refurbished furniture. The shop was on Seymour and it was called Liberty. She was coming out the door and he was backing into it holding something he was moving into the store— one of his refinished antiques, a big dining table they were putting on display with pewter candelabras to make it look like a medieval banquet setting. They collided in the doorway, and she fell down on a huge pile of wicker chairs. It was embarrassing for her, but more so for him. He helped her up and apologized a hundred times. Asked if he could make up for it by taking her for coffee at the Starbucks down the street, which he did, and then one thing after another. He said she was good looking. He lived on the Sunshine Coast. They started going together, and he invited her to move up there with him. She didn't think she wanted to do that. But today, watching Pete's fiasco, thinking *where are we all headed anyway?* she was beginning to change her mind. You can change your mind—you can make up your mind—in an instant. You don't have to think about things for years. Funny, that was what Maurice had said, and he said it as an explanation for when he suddenly decided to go back to Montréal. Without warning. Caught her off guard. Well, she could do that too! She telephoned Don. The phone had to ring eight times before he answered it. When he did, he was obviously in the middle of something and sounded distracted.

"Hi, Don, it's Carla here."

"Carla!" Don had this cracking in his voice that Carla didn't understand; maybe it was from smoking before, but he didn't smoke any more. "Nice to get a call from you. What's the occasion?" A short silence. Ever since she was a little girl, Carla had always believed in getting to the point. You've got a problem, get down and fix it. You've got something to say, say it. Who's going wait for you while you go around in circles?

"It's like this," she began. "I came to the conclusion we should move in together after all, you know? I've been thinking about it, and that's what I've been thinking." Even though it wasn't exactly right— she hadn't been thinking about it at all. But she had a revelation. That was it: a *revelation*. Like that medieval bronze wall sculpture of a king on his throne and many, many bowed heads in a row all around him that Maurice had on his wall with a text that said: . . . *and God will wipe away every tear from their eyes.* . . . And it had been revealed to her suddenly, by some angel magic, that Don was her guy. Finito. *Finis.*

"Hey, well that's my girl! Now you're talkin'! What a surprise— that's a swell surprise!" And pretty soon, within a month of Pete's court case, Don was at her place with his truck; she had given notice, and here she was, unpacking in his workshop. Everything was going to be fine.

It's a funny thing, moving. She was thinking how no matter where you go or how many times you move, there you are with your same old stuff. It's still your same old life. Whatever your life is, wherever you take yourself, it's still you and you're just following a bend in the river. It's nothing really new. You're trapped in your life. Take it or leave it, but that's the one you get to play with. Your own life; your only life. If you were really at liberty, she was thinking, you'd be dead. Life has conditions on it, doesn't it? She pulled out of her box a brass bowl she had used as a planter for years. An Italian clay wine container for the table (Maurice had liked this sort of thing with ice cubes in it and a bottle on top of the ice cubes, and he gave this to her, he did), and an old CD of Mireille Mathieu. She put it on. Mireille Mathieu was singing in her throaty but sweet voice… *les enfants qui dorment/ ne se doutent pas/ qu'une route énorme/ les attend là-bas. . . .* Mireille Mathieu was a *chanteuse* from the sixties, but forty years later she was new to Carla. She had found it in Maurice's collection of oldies and liked to play it. He let her take it home and then she refused to take it back. Now it was hers. It was a nice sound.

Then she pulled out an old scrapbook and there was the clipping from the *Vancouver Sun.* She didn't think she would find it so easily.

"Don!" she called over to the other room, real loud so he could hear over his sander. He turned the device off. "Don, sweetie, I found it."

"What did you find?"

"The clipping! Come here, see. . . ." Don came in and took a look at the scrapbook. He started smiling—took a real interest in this.

"Well, I'll be darned," he said. "Take a look at that." It was a clipping of the article that came out a couple of days after Carla and Pete had visited the mayor's office in Burnaby about the sidewalk, and a big picture of her with her straight, yellow hair tied back with a hairpin, one eye shut against the sun and Pete, who was three years old, standing next to her with his red hair and freckles. Not only did the photographer take pictures in the mayor's office, but he came to her house next day and took more. Aruna seemed a little disturbed by it all. She was cleaning up and making herself presentable but shaking her head in her usual noninvolved way. The same journalist and the same photographer came to the playground and took pictures of her in front of the monkey tree and then a photo on the sidewalk, where the workmen were supposed to come. They conducted an interview and printed it word for word. "Let's read this," Don said. He leaned up against the box and read it out loud while Carla listened to it again with a smile, thinking it was just like yesterday now that Don was sharing the story too. . . .

> *Why did you go to the mayor?*
> *Because I'm always falling down there.*
> *Did you just call and order a meeting?*
> *Yes, and my brother Pete came with me.*
> *Have you fallen down on the sidewalk often?*
> *A few times.*
> *Did you hurt yourself last time?*
> *Yes, a little.*
> *What did the mayor say when you came to his office?*
> *He said he'd fix the sidewalk.*
> *Was he going to fix it right away?*
> *Yes, he called the workmen right away.*
> *Didn't you think that was great?*
> *Yes.*
> *Are you going to follow how they fix the sidewalk when they come?*
> *Yes, if I have time.*

And Don was laughing loudly. "That sounds like my girl!" he said. "If I have time! Ha, she's so busy!" Carla was laughing a little again too. "You haven't changed much, have you?" Don said, shaking her shoulder affectionately. "You sure haven't changed much."

The Secret Source of Tears

*I*t was the middle of the afternoon on a sunny day. The kind of day when families go on picnics and young parents take their kids to the seaside at Ambleside Beach to play ball in the park or watch puppet theater or be in the playhouse; when elderly couples who have been together for fifty years go for slow walks along the seawall between Ambleside and Dundarave, still holding hands. When seagulls swing overhead like trapeze artists over the fishing rods suspended off the pier and ice cream wagons pedaled by teenage boys with fuzz on their cheeks are heard jingling along the walkway by the community center. But John Henry was at home, preparing for another amble, another useless amble. He had his peanut butter sandwich wrapped in cellophane with cucumber slices, and a bottle of Evian water. He was having early afternoon tea, a cup of strong Tetley's as usual, at the kitchen counter (still bright with natural pine, the glass cabinet on the end filled with local ceramics), which had become devoid of all sentiment by now. It used to be that John Henry had feelings that were sad and sweet, but now they were just simmering below everything, like a flame about to extinguish. The telephone rang then and he answered it without energy.

"Mr. J.H. Brackendale?" asked a man's husky voice. Funny how you try to determine everything about the call from the sound of the voice. As if you could read in the voiceprint itself what it is the person is going to say.

"Correct," he answered.

"Mr. Brackendale, this is Officer Nugent. I'm here with the file on Alberta Brackendale." John Henry straightened up; his back stiffened, his neck muscles tensed. He said nothing, just waited. "Your wife, Mr. Brackendale," Officer Nugent said then. "Your wife has been found."

"My wife has been found?" He wanted this repeated to him. That way you're sure you heard right. It's always possible you're starting to hear things.

"Yes, she's been found." Silence. "Mr. Brackendale, we'll need you to come down here to the station on Marine Drive. Can you come down here? Mr. Brackendale?"

That moment—that phone call in the middle of the day—was the part of the tape that repeated itself over and over in John Henry Brackendale's mind as he ran. He ran along the shoulder of the Sunshine Coast Highway along Wilson Creek up the hill and back again. He was jogging, but he knew he might as well call it fast walking because it wasn't much of a run. His white T-shirt was soaking from his profuse sweating, and his navy cotton shorts were flapping because they were so large and loose. On his head he had a sun hat, the type children wear when they're on the beach digging up wet sand with plastic shovels. It was in fact a child's hat belonging to Ruddy, his grandson. His daughter Stina gave it to him before he went out, saying that body temperature all went out through the head. That was after she decided she couldn't dissuade him from going for a run.

"Dad you run like spaghetti on somebody's fork," she complained to him. "You wiggle and jiggle your arms and head and legs like you've got no bones, just spaghetti arms, and you can't even run! Just stay home and stretch here, or maybe just walk. Don't even try to run. You can't. . . ." He was getting tired of her criticisms, really, although she meant well. Why shouldn't he go for a run like everyone else? And besides, the heart needed it.

Even more so because she was having one of her infernal garage sales. It was Saturday and she had them every Saturday all month long, from ten in the morning till three in the afternoon. God knows where she got all the stuff she sold; she said it was junk accumulated over the years. Well, if it was junk, why would anyone buy it? She took over the whole garage, and there was nowhere to park the car. John had to keep his car a block away, in front of somebody else's house because Stina had three whole tables rigged up in the middle of the garage with stuff on it and there was no getting into the place. She had an uncleaned Roman coin, a book called *Aunt Charlotte's Stories*, a St. Christopher Medal, a coffee mug with a ditty on it (*May God fill your life/ with sweet rewards/ as you have sacrificed* . . . and something more). Oh well, it was her house. He gave it to her, didn't he, and now he had to live with what he'd done. It was all right. She let him stay with her now. Her hubby Neil Parkington was gone, and her mother Alberta, John Henry's wife—she was gone too. That left

Ruddy, Stina and John, and they could work it out together. Help each other. It was a good arrangement—although not everyone's cup of tea. It wouldn't be everyone's cup of latté, no. They were three generations—three very different generations—and they each had a culture of their own. How they managed to fit three worlds under one small eight hundred square foot roof was a mystery worth probing. But they did, and good for them. Love can tie together the wildest differences, can't it? Love is the glue that binds—even if you're complaining all the time anyway! Let her complain about him. If she went on too long, well, he'd start complaining right back. But no, he probably wouldn't. Ruddy shouldn't be looking at his mom and grandpa quarreling. There were limits in all this—borders you didn't want to cross. Teach the kid family respect, that was more important. John Henry thought all these things as he jogged clumsily along where there was hardly any shoulder and where the cars just hurdled past him an inch away, heads of drivers turning to look at the weird jogger. Because he looked weird, all jiggly as he was, he knew that.

Ruddy was going on three now. Cute kid, but difficult as hell. His diet was the pits; even Stina admitted that. But she couldn't figure out how to change it. Ruddy refused to eat—basically refused. Whatever they put in front of him, he whined like a dog. Anything good, he simply threw it on the floor. Cooked eggs, oatmeal, sausages cut up into little bites, even pasta in whatever sauce. John Henry thought of various things: sticks of celery with peanut butter and raisins on top, which he called ants on a log; sour cream and cheese rolled up in tortillas with black beans and salsa, which he called bean pinwheels; but the kid stuck his fork into it and swept it to the floor, whining in his soprano voice. He sat in his highchair at the table, and the only thing he ate was dry Cheerios, spread out in front of him, and preferably not on a plate. He ate them with his dainty fingers one by one, and spread them out in different patterns. John Henry kept saying to Stina, "He can't grow up on Cheerios alone. It's no better than paper!" And she agreed but didn't have anything else, and meals always ended up with those Cheerios. Sometimes Ruddy took bread with peanut butter on it, but it had to be completely tasteless Wonderbread, and the peanut butter had to be Kraft, the kind they sweeten with sugar. John Henry had the secret thought that if Stina just left for a week, left the coast and went off on some vacation, and he was given complete charge of little Ruddy, the boy would be eating right by the time she got back. But while she was around, he couldn't presume on her mother-job. Even if it was a piss-poor job she was doing. Ruddy was always getting sick, colds and the flu nonstop, and John Henry was pretty sure it was because Ruddy had no antibodies in his malnourished little body.

Every day, John Henry got up, had his morning Black Ceylon tea with Bee Maid honey and speculated once again how to improve the child's eating habits. It was like a problem in the budget, a set of columns that wouldn't balance, that had to be thought and rethought all the time. He looked up recipes and tried to make them, but of course the whole endeavor ended up on the floor. It was hard not to get mad at the boy. Hard not to lose one's temper. But he couldn't do that. The boy ruled. The boy would hate him if he got angry! It would be John Henry Brackendale's ticket out of there because Stina would show him the door. She had her priorities in spite of everything, and her father wasn't at the top of that list. No, Ruddy was. Little Rudolph N. Parkington was at the top of that list. And his father Neil Parkington was at the bottom. (Neil was an ordinary guy, not cut out for extraordinary things. He wore suits religiously, brown ones, and glasses with brown plastic rims, kept his hair short and parted on the left side; he had a pleasant, nonthreatening smile—not a match for Stina in the first place, he wasn't). At least there was somebody there lower than himself. Small consolation, that was.

John Henry could tell that he'd started out too fast, but he didn't want to slow down. His breathing was getting hard, and he could feel a stinging in his throat like heartburn that was spreading all over his upper chest. His legs felt like they were very heavy, and after a while he could hardly lift them, but he pushed himself to and lumbered on. He was forced to go slower and ended up in a walk rather than a run, but he was not going to stop. That would feel like a defeat—he didn't know why he was capable of such guilt feelings toward himself (it's only a jog! he tried to tell himself)—but he didn't care when it came down to it. As usual after pushing himself like this, he would wake up with stiff legs and a sore lower back, aching thighs and cramping calves, and he would feel even older than he did before he started this jogging. On the other hand, he was proud of his perseverance. Especially since he couldn't really keep up the run, not to mention the uphill part as you got closer to the billboards for McDonald's and Remax, always showing happy elderly couples having Chicken McNuggets or standing in front of a brand-new house on the Shores. They always made John Henry think like a broken record whenever he passed them: *Why couldn't Albie and I have that opportunity?* His answer to Stina over the jogging issue was just the cholesterol thing. His doctor told him his cholesterol was too high and running would help bring it down. So he jogged, and there wasn't much Stina could say to that. After all, they'd been through enough already when it came to health issues. Stina didn't need another parent with health problems.

Because Alberta—Albie—took a long time, she did. She was only in her mid-fifties when she found out she had Alzheimer's. It seemed so unbelievable at the time. There didn't seem to be a thing wrong with her except the occasional memory problem. She seemed a bit hazy about certain things: suddenly, she didn't know how to turn on the washing machine and other times she substituted a strange word for a word she forgot; and then she would stop and out of the blue have no idea where she was. She started to go out in winter without a coat or forgot to put her shoes on, and there she would be in her slippers in the supermarket. But these were little things. John Henry didn't have a moment of "alert" until he opened the cupboard once and found a pile of dirty dishes in there—very uncharacteristic. When she was diagnosed (so long ago now!) she was very brave and practical about it. She called in the lot of them— Stina, her then-boyfriend Neil and himself, John Henry, her husband, and had a little family conference. She just said, "There will come a day when I won't recognize you; I won't know who you are, and I won't know anything. Let's just accept that. Even though we're going to do all they say with cholinesterase inhibitors and vitamin E and vitamin C, when the time comes and I have to be helped with everything, I want you to place me in a nursing facility somewhere where you won't be burdened with all that care giving."

Not only did she make that declaration in final definitive no-nonsense terms, but she started scouting around with him for a good place to end her days. They decided on a nursing home in West Vancouver, near Lighthouse Park, a low-lying building with a garden terrace and surrounded with a small forest of cedar and pine trees, and paving stones on the terrace with potted geraniums and hydrangeas blooming, and wisteria overhead and ivy lacing everything. Outdoor tables with sun umbrellas and overhead lighting for evenings made it look more like a cottage resort than a nursing home. It was even called the Lighthouse Rest Home. There was a view of Point Atkinson Lighthouse and Burrard Inlet, where the freighters and cargo ships are stationed all the time, dotting the seascape, and the sun sets over the misty haze and the whole picture becomes strangely purple and rose. And sure enough, when the time came, she moved into the nursing home, and John Henry spent four hours every day with her there. It was like he lived there himself. He walked over around noon, after her bath and breakfast were done and stayed with her until four. Sometimes they went outside on the terrace, and it soothed her, he thought, to know there was a park around where she could have a sense of real nature. Even when she no longer recognized him, when her eyes had become glazed over and her facial muscles had relaxed so she looked empty and tired, he stayed the full four hours. Besides, he thought she did know exactly who he was and what was happening on some level. He believed that—had to believe that.

When he thought about all that—let his mind sweep over the last decade fast like this—he ran faster. He picked up the pace, as if the energy of thinking about it could drive him on forever. It was just a shame—that's what it amounted to. A real shame, Albie's wasted life. She had class, that woman. They had a beautiful home in West Vancouver overlooking the neighborhoods below with the variously angled roofs and the crowns of trees—a few spots of red, white houses, gray, shingled roofs, a few low brick-facades, and in the distance the towering skyscrapers of the West End, and in the far distance snow-capped peaks, and on a good day hazy-blue sky getting paler as you looked down to the horizon. From wicker chairs on the deck they could see it all. Albie had the deck covered in a chequered flooring he had never seen before. But that was Albie: inventive. The living room was not big, but she knew what to do with it. The view was good so she had no curtains, but she put two large sofas, one against each wall, and they were heavy on the yellow. One of the sofas was so plush you practically disappeared in it. The coffee table filled almost the whole room. He warned her when she showed him the plan.

"This furniture will take up the whole floor space. There won't be anywhere to walk," he complained. "Shouldn't we get smaller things for a smaller room?"

"You'll see," was all she said. He had to trust her. But he was never sure whether it was her innate good taste or whether she was acting as a sick person, a person with Alzheimer's. He started walking then—walked along the shoreline and decided: it doesn't matter which it is. This is her life and she's got to live it, no matter what it costs. So he let her decorate, spend all that money, and it turned out classy. She bought some art that he was not sure about at all: one painting was an abstract thing with gold, red, blue and something in the middle that looked like a lantern of some kind, a glass box with a candle in it. He thought it was ugly, tell the truth, but up it went with everything else. Later he found out the thing actually had value. Now it belonged to Stina, and he had to look at it on her wall out here on the coast.

Stina's house—or cottage, best to call it—was perched on an incline above the seashore. The slope was so steep that it felt like the house could tumble any moment. Most of it stood on stilts, including the garage. It took John Henry the longest time to get himself to drive the car into the garage; he thought for sure the weight of the car would make the whole structure collapse. But it didn't. He got used to living on stilts. It was a ramshackle place, though, compared to the West Vancouver house.

For some reason, Stina was fond of junk. Real junk. She collected it like it was something valuable. As you entered her beach house, the first thing you saw was an old table that looked like it ought to be in the town dump. Except it had rather ornate legs. There was paint on it in places, but most of it was worn off. She had some old books on it for decoration (not even in English!) that looked like an old schoolbook series about a war between frogs and mice, among them *Aesopi Phrygis Fabulae* with woodcut vignettes and schoolboy notations on the margins—stuff no one would read, not even Stina. But they looked nice to her so she had them there. And junky tin containers with plants and pencils and what not, and even a pisspot! An old, white porcelain pisspot. When he saw that, he said to her, "Stina! Collecting junk is fine, but you've got to draw the line somewhere!" She reprimanded him in her usual way; made it clear she didn't have to take his views into account. He could take it or leave it. And then he took it. Like everything else in life, he took it. Stina's pisspot and Ruddy's Cheerios and living in a house on stilts where nothing was his own—he took it. John Henry Brackendale could feel his head getting extremely hot, like a balloon, and the pressure in his head was mounting (perhaps it would explode?). Perhaps he should slow down before he got a stroke. . . . He slowed down, started fast-walking, his limbs jiggling like spaghetti, he could see that, just like Stina said. Her description was pretty apt, yes it was.

As he jogged clumsily along the roadside, he could feel the flab on his stomach and arms and even under his chin flapping up and down like a tent in the breeze. His stomach, especially what they called love handles, was just wobbling around like milk. It wasn't that John Henry was all that fat. Not really. He was a thin-fat man. He was tall and thin but had this flab anyway. No muscle tone at all. He thought if he just kept running or jogging or walking, whatever you called it, he could replace some of the flab with muscle. Recently, he had acquired a desire to do that. "Don't ask!" was his response to Stina when she wanted to know what got into him. (He would certainly not give her any idea what fantasy was in his head now because, truth be told, he was starting to get the idea he could move on. He wasn't sure how this could be done, but lately he'd been thinking of one of his clients back in West Vancouver, a professor who was retiring in White Rock and who came to him for her taxes.

Élise, that was her name. Handsome woman, like Albie: elegant, with class. She would never look at him the way Stina did. Élise was from Rouen in France, where women paid attention to their looks. He knew she wasn't married: you get to know things when you do people's taxes.) John's skin was pasty too, he was pale, and Stina had the audacity to call him "the doughman." When Ruddy asked in his two-year-old manner, "Whassat?" she said, "It's the doughboy when he's grown up." Fortunately, Ruddy was too young to understand— but he wouldn't be too young forever. He'd probably adopt the nickname for him too, imitating his mother. All kids imitate their mothers for a period. Not until Ruddy was grown up would he understand why his granddad was flabby and pale. All those years spent sitting on an orange vinyl chair in Albie's room at the nursing home, doing very little except maybe a puzzle or a card game or reading to her from a book or watching her sleep—increasingly toward the end, watching her sleep—had made him like this. Stina should know better and stop making fun of him. . . .

There was of course that other reason, he hastily thought, for his flab. The reason that started when he was alone in the West Vancouver house and began staying up at night. It began with simple insomnia. He got up two or three hours after going to bed and turned on the television. Then he found a channel that showed old reruns, movies from the forties and fifties in black and white with Cary Grant and Gregory Peck as a young man and Audrey Hepburn and Ginger Rogers. He watched those night after night (*The Third Man* with Joseph Cotton; *High Noon* with Gary Cooper; *Grand Hotel* with Greta Garbo; *My Favorite Brunette* with Bob Hope), and then he'd make himself a bowl of Harvest Crunch cereal. First it was just a bowl one night, but he enjoyed it and it gave him comfort (the cold milk with the oats and nuts swimming in it had something primeval and comforting about it), and it became a nightly ritual to have one, sometimes two, bowls of cereal. He started to look forward to the nighttime because it was an escape from an increasingly depressing reality. The haunted memory of *The Pawnbroker* and the sultry relationship-drama of *Long Day's Journey into Night*, with Katherine Hepburn at her energetic-languid best, made him think there was a life out there somewhere. On Sundays toward the end, Stina and Neil, who had married by then, came over and cooked him a regular meal, and they ate together in the old dining room Albie had fixed up. Increasingly, Stina was lecturing him about getting out and doing more stuff and spending less time at the nursing home and all sorts of things she had in mind for him to do.

"Dad, you can't destroy yourself just because Mom is sick! Don't spend your whole life over in that nursing home. She doesn't even know you're there half the time—all the time even. She doesn't even recognize us any more. You need to go out—go to the theater or to a movie or see some friends sometime!" She meant well, John Henry knew that, and he didn't mind her saying these things. But she didn't know about his secret life now, did she, and how contented he had become watching black and white *film noir* with his bowls of cereal and the black cat curling up on that plush sofa, the one with the electrifying flower pattern on it that he hated to death at first but had come to love because it was Albie's idea. Anything to do with Albie as she was before he kept strictly in place: the perpetual bouquet of dandelions, all yellow and green, he continually renewed; the white candles in their porcelain candleholders he lit every evening the way she did when she was there; the cobalt blue bowl full of Ukrainian Easter eggs and antique Christmas ornaments he kept— the one he couldn't figure out at first why she wanted. He maintained everything the way she made it. Her lacy dark-yellow Chenille throw too, the one she sometimes put over her shoulders when the evenings cooled down—now he too, John Henry Brackendale, head of

Brackendale Certified Accountants of West Vancouver, British Columbia—put it over his shoulders to shield against the draft of late evening as if he were a woman getting dotty. If she had been a smoker, he would have preserved the ashes of her cigarettes in the ashtray. Occasionally, he sat there after the end of a movie, after the lovers had got married or their misunderstanding had been resolved and the villain had died. John Henry sat there feeling lonely, and he felt the lump rise in his throat like a case of heartburn and he shed some tears of his own. . . .

He was coming down the hill now and the jogging was easier, so he picked up the pace again. The air was hot, but a breeze blew a bit into his face, which was nice. His T-shirt was all damp, and he had a blister, but he wasn't going to stop because of that. The return trip was more gratifying, and at the end of it he could take a welcoming cool shower and have a cozy cup of Tetley's tea. The girls would be sitting out there in the driveway manning the junk ("You man the junk, girls!" he called out to them when he left for his jog. Stina and her new friend Carla George, who just moved up here from North Vancouver and lived down the highway; they both liked old junk), and he could sit on the back deck with Ruddy for a while. Stina sat there in the old garden chair with plastic weave that was quite torn and in shreds at the back, looking like Joan of Arc with her short brown hair and her intense eyes. She had that combination of strength and fragility: girl-warrior. Although she too was getting older, and it was showing in her attitude. She was exhibiting an older woman's attitude to things and getting more staid in her ways. It would all have worked out fine, John Henry felt certain of that, if Albie's story hadn't ended so badly. If it all hadn't come to such a disastrous, tragic finale! Why, Stina and Neil would probably still be married. John Henry knew the stress of those last eight months came in and broke their marriage like a disintegrating film, the kind that crumbles before your very eyes as you watch it: distressed and decomposed nitrate film self-immolating before you, the corrosive center getting spotty and the stain spreading and spreading until the whole thing is just one static-black blob with white flecks in it, melting before your eyes. . . . Stina blamed Neil for not keeping watch and not fixing the situation and going back to work instead, screaming at him "Fat lot you care!" And John Henry would not have moved up here either. He would probably have stayed in the old house and started to do what Stina always told him to do: get out there and meet someone or do something. But after what happened, it was too much hassle to even think of doing anything. There wasn't any energy left. Thank God Stina had already bought this place, so all she had to do was move into it. She would have been too confused and upset to start looking for coastal real estate and all that. After that incomprehensible ending.

It was on one of those late-nights with movies (*North by Northwest*, it was) when John Henry got the visit. Ever since, anyone knocking on the door at night or telephoning after ten struck him with terror. Actual panic overcame him with late-night phone calls. He was in the middle of the movie, Cary Grant and lovely Eva Marie Saint (*"I want you to leave right now. Stay far away from me and don't come near me again. We're not going to get involved. Last night was last night and it's all there was and that's all there is. There isn't going to be anything more between us. So please, goodbye, good luck, no conversation, just leave."*), and there was a knock on the door and he went to open it. Two policemen in uniform, their cruiser outside still running, the lights on too, beaming up the street. One of the officers had a roaming eye, immediately noticeable.

"Mr. Brackendale?" that cross-eyed one asked by way of identifying him. You wouldn't want to talk to the wrong person, not in a case like this. John Henry nodded and realized at the same moment that he was wearing a robe and slippers while they had outdoor clothes on, and this made him feel a little uncomfortable. "May we come in?" He let them in. After all, they were officers of the law. They stood at the midpoint between the entryway and the living room, next to the braided Ficus tree in Albie's wicker basket container. "Mr. Brackendale, your wife is at the Lighthouse Rest Home, correct?" To which John Henry nodded again. "We're here because we were called up to the home earlier regarding Alberta Brackendale. It appears she has disappeared."

"Disappeared? What?"

"Yes, it's strange but she seems to have wandered off the premises. We've been looking for her. She has Alzheimer's disease, am I correct?" John Henry nodded, but a tightening of his chest was occurring, and with it came a feeling that they shouldn't be standing there at all but should all be out looking. "She went out undetected, maybe for a walk or something, and left the premises. We've been combing the immediate neighborhood for her, but so far no luck."

"Who's *we*? How many people are out looking exactly?" John Henry thought there might not be enough people; maybe they only had a cruiser driving up and down Marine Drive when they needed a regular search team on foot.

"Started out us two, but we've got a troop of officers now, two cars and about five men on foot. We may need your help."

"I'll get dressed. Hold on!" John Henry ordered them to stay where they were so he could go back there with them. He ran through a hasty to-do list in his mind as he rushed into the bedroom and clumsily put on his blue jeans and chequered linen shirt and yellow wind jacket in a panic. He had to phone Stina and Neil. She might wander to the old house, so someone had to be here too. Neil ought to be involved right away because he's a lawyer. John Henry grabbed his cell phone as he put on his shoes and he went out with the officers. As they drove to the nursing home, he called Stina and told her. Neil agreed to come down while Stina went to the house.

After this followed the worst eight months of John Henry Brackendale's life. It was all a tight blur now, as he ran along the highway, making his way downhill again with physical relief. A long period of angst. Not a day or night went by that wasn't an extended panic. John Henry didn't know before then that you could go into a panic and then stay there. He always thought panic was a momentary experience. You panic, then it passes into something else. Usually action. That's why we have panic in the first place. Ask any anthropologist. It's to warn the system of impending danger and make you act. And he did act. But the panic never vanished because the action brought no result. There was an organized search. He couldn't fault the police with that. They started with the immediate vicinity—the streets and yards around the home itself. Then they extended it, spreading their net, they said, wider and wider (Sundance Crescent, Raindance Crescent, Tyee Drive, Klahanie Park, Clyde Avenue, Esquimalt Avenue, Capilano Indian Reserve. . . .), as wide as seemed reasonable to find one woman walking. Then they added the theory that someone might have picked her up in a car and driven away with her. So they got hooked up with other police centers in Vancouver, in Richmond, in White Rock even, and over to Chilliwack and Abbotsford, and north to Kamloops. Wherever they thought someone might take her. But it always seemed incomprehensible to John Henry that someone would drive off with her. She must be around here somewhere. Stina happened to agree with him on this.

Throughout those months Stina showed a side he hadn't seen before. She had the ability to be completely hysterical. John Henry and Neil agreed to try to keep her as far away from the day-to-day search as possible because little Ruddy was just an infant and the last thing he needed was all that hysteria in the air. But whenever Stina talked to the police, she didn't *talk*. She yelled and scolded, she hammered them and swore at them. Yes, she *swore at them*, as if it was all their fault. She could swear like a sailor. But John Henry couldn't fault the police with not looking. What he did fault them for, what he didn't forgive them for, was that they stopped. *They stopped looking.* After six weeks they said they had to put this case on the backburner and wait for something to show up. They couldn't spend all their resources on one sick woman who would, they figured, turn up in the end, somehow, somewhere. Then it was only John Henry looking. Stina was busy with her baby. Neil went back to work at Cinnamon & Wang in Burnaby. It was John Henry who kept wandering the streets of West Vancouver, every day, for hours at a time, peering into yards and investigating parks. He had taken to bringing a bag with snacks (things like Chex-Mix and Cracker-Jacks and sweet trail mix) and bottled water. He would not give up. It was a pilgrimage, a daily pilgrimage to find Albie because people don't just evaporate like mist. No, they don't. People don't just evaporate!

"Thank God you're back," Stina called up to him as he came down into the driveway where she and her friend Carla sat on their garden chairs. There was no one in the garage just then looking, but the people came at the rate of a couple every fifteen minutes. "Ruddy's being a pest. He always wants to run up to the highway! Can you take him to the back deck or something, Dad?"

"Sure thing, sure thing," he assured her, his arms limp at his sides and his knees perfectly weak from the exertion. "Let me take a shower first, though. Can you hang on while I do that? Ten minutes."

"Ten minutes then."

"We'll go to the beach or something." Ruddy was headed for the display of encyclopedias perched on a stool by the garage door. Stina jumped up after him. Carla sat watching them with a smile. They had heart-to-heart talks, those girls, John Henry knew that. They sat there all day talking up a storm. How did they have so much to discuss? He had his shower in the perfectly inadequate shower compartment. It felt like plastic, all of it. These beach houses were constructed as if they were supposed to wither away with the storms. In the winter it's a wonder they survive the onslaught of those gales coming in. He wiped his face and hair, put on a pair of white cotton pants, nice and loose, his leather sandals, a pale cotton shirt that let in lots of air. He felt refreshed. He would like some tea right now, but obviously Stina needed to get rid of the kid. They could take some Coca-Cola to the beach with them. A bucket and a spade and their identical sun hats. They could sit on a log, and the kid could be a bit freer down there.

He found Ruddy sitting on the floor in the bedroom smearing lotion on his arms and hands. He had a thick layer of white perfumed face cream on both his arms up to the elbow and all over his hands. It was Stina's Elizabeth Arden face cream, he could see that, a twenty dollar jar that Ruddy had just used half of.

"What are you doing, Ruddy?"

"I have mommy's lotion."

"Shall we wipe it off now?"

"Yeah." John Henry wiped the cream off his grandson's arms. Ruddy was fascinated by the procedure and stared transfixed at the way the lotion got off his arms and onto the towel.

"Shall we go to the beach now?" John Henry asked the kid.

"Yeah."

"Shall we take the bucket and put some stones into it?"

"Yeah."

"Would you like a glass of milk first?"

"Yeah."

"Are you going to not take that lotion again?"

"Pretty soon."

"Very good then." The two of them, one tall and dressed in clean white cotton, the other short, wearing knee pants that were so big they looked like a ballet skirt, and a yellow T-shirt and sneakers, took a cup of milk in a Donald Duck kiddie-glass and a Coke in a bottle, and maneuvered their way down the incline to the beach after calling goodbye to the women at the junk sale, where several people had suddenly swarmed in. He led Ruddy by the hand and took the very slow walk to the water surging onto the beach. They bent down and John Henry pointed out what looked like tiny minnows right in the water.

"Look at the little fish there," John Henry said, pointing at them. Ruddy put his face right down to the surface of the water so he could see better. "What are those, Ruddy? What are those? Are those little fish swimming?"

"Yeah." The boy pointed but then didn't have time to point; he had to investigate them up close. He sat on his haunches like an Indian sage and peered into the water, utterly transfixed. Whatever that boy looked at, he didn't just look at. He stared in a most fascinated manner, his mouth half open, his eyes rigid and intense. He pointed at everything that moved or glinted and said his favorite phrase: "Whassat?"

John Henry sat down on a driftwood log behind the boy and watched him crouching there. He thought again how sad it was that Albie didn't get to see her grandson. He was born well after Albie lost touch with things. She never really knew about him. But she would have enjoyed the child, and she would have had a successful way of dealing with the eating problem, he felt sure of that. Albie would have known what to do. But right now, it was just the two of them, and neither had any real experience of children and their nutrition. Stina wasn't made for this mother thing. That was clear as day. Stina should have been in the military or something. She should have been a mountaineer or an Arctic explorer or even a natural scientist. Her talents were being wasted. And John Henry himself had spent all his life with numbers and balance sheets in his accounting offices. They were unprepared for anything, really. Whatever went over the regular line they didn't seem to have the coping skill to deal with. And they had been tested! That was certain. Tested beyond comprehension, really.

Because when John Henry Brackendale got down to the station that strange day, he found out what had happened with Albie. She had gotten no further than the pine and cedar and scrub brush just outside the nursing home. She wandered into the woods and somehow, in all that ransacking, the six weeks of intense police search with dogs and the whole bit, and then the next six and a half months of relentless walking around in the neighborhoods with his pack on his shoulder, somehow, in spite of all that, they had missed her. There she lay. A man out walking his dog came upon her when the dog ran into the thicket. John Henry learned at the station that she had been dead a long time already. She had died in the first few days of being lost.

It was a chore to deal with Stina when she had to be told the news. John Henry telephoned Neil, who came down as well. They went to see Albie in the morgue—or what was left of her—and decided nothing good would come of letting Stina see this. John Henry remembered that whole time now with a numbness that comes of denial. Something in his mind went into a back chamber far removed from the rest of his senses, locked itself up there and threw away the key. He had feelings he knew he would never access—nor did he want to. The smell of those feelings leaked out, though, and he knew what they were about: anger. Not at the police, although he might have been angry at them for not being better at searching for missing persons. Not at the nursing home staff, although Stina was well rehearsed in blaming them for not looking after their patients. No, it was a bigger anger. At God, somehow. Even though he didn't believe in God, he had a right to be angry at God anyway. Why would a good woman like Albie, a *good woman* like Albie—she with the steel-colored shoulder-length hair, the high eyebrows and dark blue eyes, the well-molded neck, the finely chiseled nose and delicate, long fingers, with her soft smile (a serene smile that seemed to say, *Everything is the way it has to be.* No, that seemed to say, *Do not be afraid. God has come to test you so that. . . .*)—why would she be deprived of her senses and left to die alone and abandoned in the forest? Like that. With everyone looking in all the wrong places. Incomprehensible.

And as John Henry Brackendale thought about this once more, he found his throat tightening and the searing feeling inside his head, and the tears rising to the surface again. (Cruel irony it would be, he found himself thinking unexpectedly, but what if she had died in the woods by her own choice? What if she had picked the Lighthouse Rest Home specifically so she could do this at the end? What if she wanted it this way? *What if. . . .*) There is no God. That was the most obvious explanation. Fate is a cruel wheel that turns relentlessly, and whatever is on it drops off at random, into the churning sea of eternity. . . .

"Hi grampa," Ruddy's small voice was calling. The child had come up to where John Henry was sitting lost in thought.

"Hi, Ruddy."

"Hi, grampa."

"Shall we collect some stones, then?"

"Yeah."

"Let's take the colorful ones, shall we?"

"Yeah." They got the plastic bucket out and put it on the sand at John Henry's feet. Ruddy sat on the sandy ground. The forests of red cedar stretched behind them; eagles and ospreys sailed above; rainbow and Kokanee trout swam in the waters in front of them; the sunshine beamed down on them. John Henry Brackendale bent down and started picking up pebbles one by one. He took the ones that had the most promising color and shape and shine. One stone, two stones. Another stone. Soon Ruddy had figured out what to do as well and was putting stones one by one into the bucket, letting go a handful of sand each time. One stone, two stones. Three stones.

"We're doing well," he assured the boy. He was praising the kid for his work, moving stones like mountains, and just making sure he wouldn't pick up any of the bad feelings—wasn't he? And come to think of it, they were holding up. In their own way, like the house on those stilts. . . .

"Yeah," repeated Ruddy, moving pebbles clumsily from the warm, white sand into the bucket. "Doing well."

Under Other Skies

Tamara was coming home. She was a good-looking woman of fifty-five: tall, slender; with blue eyes and well-made features, though she had a fragile appearance too. People said she looked like she was just about to disintegrate, the way very dry paper crumbles at the touch. (Pasha said it made a man feel he had to be careful—and protective!) She used to keep her hair long and dyed pale blonde, but now it was cut boyishly short, and she no longer colored it. When she appeared suddenly with hair the color of ashes, people were surprised. But they got used to it.

Coming home was a strange way to put it now. She had been coming back and forth on this ferry for years. During term session she lived in an apartment in Calgary, where she worked as a professor of sociology. Other times she was on the coast, working at home and getting away from the academy. Now she was leaving the university for the last time and coming home for good. Her resignation had taken effect today; she had given notice last September. It was April now. She did not know what she would be feeling and thinking at this moment; she had no way of telling how she would be. Would her whole life flash before her the way they say it does when you die? Would she be standing on the deck of the ship, like she was doing now, right in the very front, leaning toward the coast across the murky water of the Sound, and all the moments of her working life would flare across the black heavens like shooting stars?

But there was more. There were things about her life only she knew. She was discrete, more circumspect than anyone she knew. No one anywhere knew the truth about Tamara's life. That was the plain fact of it: she had her life, with all its secrets, to herself. She savored it, like a pleasant taste or smell, or the feeling of soft Cashmere wool and mohair on her fingers. Her own life. No one knew, for example, that she had a secret lover. If they suspected, she would not say. But very few people asked, and for the most part, truth be told, Toma herself gave the matter little thought. She did not see him any more except *virtually*, when she opened the paper and he was in the news. She had not seen him for seven years now (except for an accidental meeting on an airplane; it was *awkward*).

They had first met at a symposium in Milan on "Society and the International Media," where he was giving a plenary address. So many years ago now. For him their relationship was a diversion, she suspected; but for her it was defining. In a way it was also very simple: he was a philanderer, but she was in love. She knew the truth, but *she didn't care.* Let me love whom I love and never you mind what his character is, she would like to say to her imagined finger-wagging friends and colleagues. . . . Frankly, she admitted finally that he might be a womanizer, but he made her happy. She was *happy* at the thought of him.

"I feel as if I've gone to heaven somehow," Toma was saying. She stretched under the white sheets. The walls of the room were cracked; she could see the paint chipped off in places and the raw stone showing through. She thought he was joking when he brought her here yesterday to an old, dilapidated farm on the plains of northern Italy, where the scorched earth was being plowed up, and to this cottage that was like a bombed-out ruin from the last war.

"Yes, my darling, we have come to heaven. Why not see it that way," he said with his broad smile. When he smiled his whole face lit up, like a room when the lights are switched on. He was holding a small tray with an espresso maker and a couple of tiny cups on it. A small, white plate with rock-hard Italian bread rolls on it, twisted into croissant-shape. He put the tray down on a wooden stool covered with splashes of different colored paint that had spilled and dried.

"Where did you get the coffee?" she breathed, surprised.

"From the concierge next door. She gave me the whole pot. For us." He poured the coffee and the tannin smell reached her. The orange morning light was seeping in. She really did feel this was a different universe. These were different skies. She was a different woman—not the humdrum Canadian academic any more, but a special being, an angel of the universe. He made the whole difference. Would she ever forget this moment? This night? Would she not exist in this moment forever?

The whistle blew and the boat began to skim away from the pier. Around on the far side of the steerage, Tamara noticed the outline of two thin, black figures kissing in the dark. They were holding each other against the crisp wind that was slowly starting. Another dusky figure, a woman with sweeping long hair and wearing a satin jacket, smoked a cigarette while she leaned against the railing. A middle-aged man in maritime clothing was peering into the sky over where the lifeboats where cached. *Nature's sweet ploy to reclaim you*—Toma remembered reading that somewhere about people in middle age and their relationship to nature. (That even applied to her now, hard though it was to believe.) The man stood by the small light at the solarium's outside wall. He had frizzy hair tied back with a scrunchie and wore glasses with oval frames. Toma could see his squarish face with its angular jaw. His hands were in the pockets of his coat, and he was looking out at the sky.

People did come out to watch the stars. Stars over the ocean are very different from stars over the land. Where no air pollution or city lights obstruct, you can see as far as two million light years away—all the way to the Andromeda Galaxy, she had heard. Someone told her that when you saw the red star Antares in the Scorpio constellation you were looking back five hundred years in time. On a night like this, she could see thousands of stars, not counting shooting stars, planets, meteorites. There was something about the Milky Way being less visible in the north than the south; something they called airglow, a luminosity of the atmosphere. The farther north and the higher the altitude, the more airglow illuminated the night sky. Down here at sea, it was dark as pitch. Toma looked up too: could one fathom the constellations: Perseus, Cassiopeia, Pleiades. . . . Pasha (her long-time companion and friend) once showed her the outline of stars she could learn to recognize. From the Big Dipper, she could go to Arcturus, then straight up to Polaris and the Little Dipper. Out right to Castor, Pollux below, farther down Regulus and then Spica. Spica was in Virgo, and on the Ecliptic—what he said was the path of the sun and the moon. When you are at sea, you enter the cosmos in a distinct way; there is no barrier between you and the stars except for the thin haze of what they call a *horizon*. The horizon of your imagination: the horizon of reality.

Tamara stood in the front of the boat because she wanted to reflect. This was a significant moment. She knew it was a special juncture. Intellectually, she grasped it, but she had not absorbed the palpability of that somehow. Whatever it meant to "absorb" something like this—when you change your life. When you come to yourself and realign your stars, put yourself in the right life for a change. She was perhaps waiting to feel it: that moment when it would come to her that she was in another life. Some sort of parallel life had started on another plane of existence, and she was now there. She was in it. On it. Journeying into the cosmos with God knew what awaiting her. She had taken this plunge and left everything behind. No one knew what her departure was really about. As usual, she told nothing to anyone. It was her own life, her own choice, and she wanted no one to know her private life. As they sailed farther out into the Sound, she could taste the tart salt in the cold wind. It was good. She felt like a thirsty desert dweller getting her first whiff of water. She told herself she had done well. She had put up with life. And she found a way to escape it without fuss, without rancor and without questions. She did not like making a commotion, a spectacle. She simply wanted to move quietly through the world and be able to go away if she discovered she was in the wrong realm. Now she had and here she was: in the right galaxy, the true solar system, with the stars at night.

It was more than simply quitting her job: what was happening to her was a metamorphosis in her whole being. She did not decide to change careers the way people decide to go on trips or buy a house. Instead it came to her the way a calling comes to someone who goes into the priesthood. As the ferry moved through the growing darkness, Tamara felt newly protected. In the distance the lights of Lions Bay down by the water's edge were visible, but getting smaller. She remembered how she herself had once been called to the priesthood. She answered; she wrote to the seminary and they wrote back, saying they would be "delighted" to have her there. What intervened? She did not remember what interfered with that plan, but something did. Another force interceded. She went on to teaching and wondered how the twists of fate can balance on a pinpoint. Instead of practicing at a church altar, she had her own personal altar in the office. On it she placed a piece of driftwood from the beach, a stone from the Rocky Mountains, a feather that fell from an eagle and dropped into the calm waters when she was canoeing with Pasha once. Toma did not question the changes of life. She never disputed these things. Her measure was the solidity of conviction, something she felt in the body rather than thought in the mind. She taught university until she knew it was time to go. So she went. She lived her life the way some people write novels: her life told her what to do, and life invented the plot, not the other way around.

"Looking for auroras?" a man's voice suddenly asked. Toma realized the frizzy-haired man in the nylon jacket had come over to the front railing.

"Are there any now?" she answered half-heartedly.

"Should be." He stood nearby, still looking out at the sky through his round glasses. He turned his face to her where she leaned against the wall. "There have been some great ones. Green amoebas wandering across the sky. Sometimes there's a bit of red on the outer edges—swirling, with spots and blobs and feathery rays going up. Quite something."

"I've seen some good ones in Alberta," Toma remembered. There was one night when she and Pasha were driving north of Calgary. There was such a rush of northern lights in the sky that people stopped their cars on the highway just to see the spectacle. "What are they anyway?" she wondered out loud.

"Auroras are protons and electrons in space that are raining onto the earth's surface," he answered.

"How do they come down like rain? Seems odd."

"Solar wind. Together with the earth's magnetic field. When the particles hit the atmosphere, they emanate atoms and molecules that make the air glow. The reds and the greens come from atomic oxygen. The blues from nitrogen."

Toma looked at the stranger more carefully. "Are you an astronomer or something?" she asked, realizing almost immediately she sounded rude.

"As a matter of fact," he laughed. They returned to being quiet; the silence of the sea was alluring. The man moved over to the other side to take a different view and stood there with hands in his pockets. Toma thought of the strange divergence of people she met on the ferry. So many different types live up here, she thought to herself, their numerous backgrounds converging. And her mind was flooding with memories at this hour as she stood looking at the stars over the Sound.

In the musky night in northern Italy, they walked together through the tall, dry grass. She was in sandals, and the straws and weeds on the roadside running beside the dry creek pricked her feet until they hurt. But she was oblivious— oblivious to pain! Her hand was inside his, that was all that mattered. He had thrown his jacket into the back of the Ferrari and rolled up his white shirtsleeves and loosened his collar. He pulled her toward an old ruin in the middle of the field. (Why were there so many ruins here? Buildings left to the weather and time and probably to the bombs of the Allied Forces, people scrambling in all directions to get away. . . .) The stone felt cold against her back, the uneven surface scratched her tender, sun-browned skin. But she wanted to lean against the cool stone and feel his full lips against hers and his hand tightly up her thigh, and she would allow her skimpy sundress to be removed; right there in the middle of the dry field she would allow him to make her completely naked and in love . . . the scent of rosemary in the night air, the sound of a palpable silence when the world stands still and only the rough bursts of his breathing on her neck, her hair, her shoulders and breasts. . . .

In the new morning, the one to come after this night under the stars on the ocean, she would have the dark coffee she put away at home. The beans glistened inside several old containers for nuts; Sumatran beans she kept on hand, tawny Mandhelings from the North Vancouver coffee shops. She had learned from the local coffee roaster that Sumatra coffees have their skins removed as soon as they are picked. The farmers ferment the slimy beans, then wash the fruit pulp next morning in the creek. But some of the ferment remains, and the beans have a fruity, chocolate taste. She would grind them and brew them. The house would be permeated with the sweet, malty, smoky infusion of morning coffee that reminded her of new leather and pipe tobacco. Her breakfast would be a *Fougasse* bread with savory and rosemary, warmed and dipped in Tuscan olive oil flavored with dried peppers. Bread and olive oil for breakfast. A Spanish breakfast. She would be in Spain, in Italy, soon enough herself. Toma had the strange feeling she was changing herself into herself. Paradoxically enough, the whole time she lived on the prairie, she had to be someone else (only with *him*, in *his* presence, had she been herself, the person she knew, Toma). In her working life, she found herself doing what others required her to do, not what she felt compelled to do herself. Dropping that persona now was like shedding a whole skin. Maybe she wore it all this time as a form of protection? She wanted no one to know her—to apprehend her as she really was. Perhaps she was shielding herself?

Strange things were happening in the last month before she left her position, her job, in the city. Everything was chaos. She took down her photographs of Linden trees and tough-skinned Coronation grapes on the vine and flogged off the Urban Barn frames. She sold her Sony stereo, and the absence of music made her dreary. She auctioned off the Panasonic VCR, and there was no entertainment. Everything went: her favorite cherry-red Ikea chair, where she spent most of her reading time. She moved about in her barren apartment feeling estranged from everything. Her office was being denuded as well: the books were in packing boxes, the files labeled "department memos" and "business correspondence" ready to be sent away. She lost track of mealtimes; it was Chinese food from the Ho Ho stand on campus—orange chicken and Chow Mein with celery and onions in Styrofoam containers. Then she lost control of her finances. She no longer knew what she had spent and when, after a lifetime of keeping track of every penny. At the university, she was writing off her associates one by one. As the days passed, their features became visible: where they had just been outlines in a hazy mindscape of many years of being in her life, now their faces became clear. They were not the faces of friends. People she had worked with for so long suddenly came into sharp focus and disappeared from view. It was uncomfortable, yet after a lifetime of false comforts, how easily they went!

Toma was noticing the frizzy-haired astronomer at the far railing. She decided to wander up to him and stand beside him for a moment. Present him with a question.

"As an astronomer, then," she said quietly, "what is the shape of the universe?" She often wondered about the possibility of parallel universes and other time zones. He looked at her not in the least surprised. Maybe it was the kind of problem that was on his mind all the time, Toma thought.

"Most astronomers would like an answer to that question too!" he laughed. Then he became more serious. "It's either spherical, a closed universe as they say, shaped something like a balloon, which means if you fly in a spaceship to the end of it, you're back where you started from. A spherical universe would expand and then contract again. Or else, it's flat. That means it expands in all directions forever, but all parallel lines are parallel and all triangles have a hundred and eighty degrees. Or, third possibility, it's open and has what's called a negative curvature."

"How can something be curved negatively?" Toma broke in.

"It would mean the universe is shaped like a saddle, where parallel lines end up diverging and triangles have less than a hundred and eighty degrees. An open universe would be expanding forever."

"Don't they know which shape?"

"Well, there are some good guesses. You can determine the shape of the universe by its density. Problem is, it's hard to figure out what the density actually is."

"What do you think it is?"

"I think the universe is probably flat." He was interested in this conversation, Toma could tell. It was such a curious thing to think of the universe as actually flat.

"That's so strange!" she muttered.

"In a way, yes," he mused. "What's your name?" he suddenly asked.

"Tamara. Yours?"

"Cameron. Dusty Cameron."

"Retired up here?" she asked him. It was a relatively popular place to retire in.

"Not yet. Soon, maybe."

"Where do you work?" She hoped she was not sounding too inquisitive.

"UBC. Professor, astronomy. And you?"

"Funny, I happen to be a professor too. Sociology. University of Calgary."

"Think of that! I just wrote a paper with a sociologist. On space. You're a long way from home."

"No actually, I *am* home," she laughed. "I've retired as of today."

"Congratulations!" he said loudly. They chuckled together, then stood in silence while the lights of Gambier faded to the right. Toma was captivated by the sense she had of being outside of time at this moment.

A young couple came to the front of the boat and plastered themselves against the balustrade. They were both lanky and thin; there was something brittle and featherweight about them. The boy was wearing dungarees and a leather jacket and had curly hair. The girl wore jeans, fringed cowhide half-boots, and she had a thin silk-knit sweater covering a short, midriff-revealing top. He was holding his arms around her to keep her warm. They were snuggling and laughing. Were they going home or going away? Toma was used to traveling home with strangers, visitors to the coast. People coming to see their parents or children, or just going on vacation. There was always anticipation and excitement in the air. Others were returning from vacations, like the man inside in the seating area with his snowboard and red face, contentedly exhausted from a ski trip to Grouse Mountain or somewhere like that. People were for the most part blithe and cheerful on this boat. Tamara had two known habitats for all those years, but only this one meant anything to her. The coast was where she had put down roots, and it was here she was vibrant and alert. In the other place, she was simply biding her time. She was almost inert there, if you could be such a thing. Not really in the moment. Dead. She was *dead* over there. The thought frightened her a little bit.

She had been noticing strange patterns—the pictures, motifs, templates—of fate itself. When you look back, you see them; she had done this before. It was like the strange formulations of chaos. Chaos theory and its odd determinisms. What you think is random turns out to be happening in nonrandom ways. Everything has a *shape*. For an instance: she joined the university faculty during the first Gulf

War, when the United States invaded Iraq. She left the faculty during the second Gulf War, when the United States invaded Iraq. The President of the U.S. was named Bush both times. Cycles like that were things you could never know until afterward. The stars too, which look so haphazard out there, have their patterns and cycles. They go around in their own paradigms. There is no knowing what any of it means, Toma reasoned. It just is. Another instance: when each of her parents reached the age of seventy-one, they died. And they both died of exactly the same thing at the age of seventy-one. She suddenly remembered her neighbor across the hall. On the first day of Ramadan, he brought a plate of food over when she came home from work. Warm bread with figs and dates and walnuts, under the cover of aluminum foil. She had the feeling he was waiting for her to come home, looking out the window to see her return, because she was no sooner home than he was knocking on her door. Something had to go out of the house, presumably: some gift, and this was his gift today.

Tamara was thinking these things because something had become obvious to her over the years: there was such violence enacted on the independent view, on independent inquiry, that the only way to respond was to stay focused. It was the individual's job to remain distinct. They had entered an era when *the personal really was the political.* That was her conviction. Keep your own voice; don't let anyone drown it out. Keep your own view, perspective, council. *Travel light,* she had started to tell her students. When you see something, say you see it, and don't let anyone allege you did not. She remembered reading a curious novel by Sally Vickers, *Miss Garnet's Angel.* Miss Garnet goes to Venice to retire after being a schoolteacher in England for decades. She has her first awakening in Venice: to art, to beauty, to people, to herself. But she functions at second and third hand to everything. She befriends a pair of young cousins who are metaphorically her angels because not only are they restoring a mural of angels, but they have the names of angels, and they cause a spiritual awakening within her. After hearing their story about the persecution of the girl's father and his resulting suicide, she has learned that *you didn't give in to a lie—you found resistance to it by establishing your own truth.* You have to counter with your own story. She also remembered the Hungarian poet George Faludi, when he came to Calgary to give a reading (in bare feet and with exploding white hair, like seraphim), saying the way to stay alive in a concentration camp is to keep intellectually active. Keep talking, keep memorizing poems, keep thinking, reading: keep your own world going. Those who did so, survived. Those who caved in mentally, died.

Leaning on the wheelhouse wall, her arms in the pockets of her Cashmere coat with a big, fur-lined collar, in her dark gray Russian-style winter hat, Tamara noticed a woman pacing past her at regular intervals. The woman was wearing a Drab jacket with several big pockets, what looked like Mudmaster boots, her head wrapped in a cloth turbanlike hat with beadwork on the side. She was "hiking" the ferry—something people did to get exercise, presumably after driving for too long. The woman was charging clear around the ferry deck, the whole length of the boat, at an accelerated pace. She looked determined, her face set in sharp concentration on something as she tramped on. Perhaps a problem she was trying to figure out? Maybe something serious had just happened? Or she could be walking off some sort of grief? Toma found herself thinking of the way Sally Vickers sneaked her wise remarks about life into the strange little novel about Tobias the angel. In retrospect, Toma remembered them as acutely wise somehow. The writer's comments on being lied about caught Toma's imagination: *one of those rational seeming lies which pose as morality because human beings like to think the worst of each other,* she wrote. Toma pondered now how that was not the case on a personal level only. It was true of everything. . . .

Somewhere in the back of her mind, Tamara had known she should clear out. Get off the carousel of "putting up with things" in the workplace and in private life. But when it came down to it, she was incapable. Could not move on. She tried to figure out why: she studied Foucault on imprisonment, on the military-prison complex that engulfs corporations. But it did not persuade. She studied Elaine Scarry on torture, on how abuse creates the sort of paralysis that disables and prevents people from doing the very thing that would help. But that did not quite satisfy either. Because the workplace was not, in fact, a prison, not a military, and she was actually not undergoing torture. It just *felt like it.* Was the fact that something felt like it enough to qualify? Then—again in an unassuming novel—she read what seemed like an answer. Ian McEwan's novel *Atonement,* which she was reading to relax in the evenings, had a girl-character who makes a big mistake in life. She goes off to learn to be a nurse during the war, and the nursing establishment is punishing. She explains to herself that *this enveloping regime paralyzed her— and she had no will, no freedom to leave. She was abandoning herself to a life of strictures, rules, obedience, housework, and a constant fear of disapproval.* That described something to Tamara. It also explained what was lurking in her working life—something she recognized.

Then what happened to break the spell? It was like divine interference. Pasha came from Moscow for a visit, went to Vancouver to get Tamara's SUV and drive it over the Rocky Mountains so they could use it on the prairies. It was in March. The weather was changeable: sometimes it was mild and the snow melted; occasionally, it was frosty and then suddenly extremely cold. A deep-freeze set in the day he flew west. He drove the car back, but crashed it when he got to Revelstoke. That day she was going about a regular round of teaching and meetings. She went to work, taught her class, met with her committee about curriculum reform and came home to cook a pasta pesto. She was looking forward to making pesto sauce with the fresh cilantro and parsley from the farmer's market and ground pine nuts and basil from the herb and vegetable stand at the organic market. She would watch the BBC news at six. There was no message on the answering machine, which made her wonder. Pasha usually left a message en route. When he did call, his voice was shaking.

"I've got bad news," he said in a voice that sounded like paper. Silence. Toma hated this kind of opening. In the seconds that followed, almost anything was possible.

"What happened, Pasha?" she said carefully.

"I've been in an accident," he said in the same tone of voice, "but I'm okay," he added hastily.

"You're okay!"

"I'm fine. But the car isn't."

"Never mind the car!" Everything is so clear at moments like this, she was thinking. That was the beginning of the end of this particular life. He'd hit an ice patch west of the Roger's Pass and lost control, he told her. The vehicle spun in circles, was rammed by another car hauling a trailer and both vehicles were smashed. The other driver was an art dealer, a Maurice Allard, driving his stuff from Vancouver to Montreal. Amazingly enough, the two drivers walked away without a single scratch. It was as if the plan (some divinely ordained plan or other) was to get rid of the car—only the car. The insurance agent later told her the stretch between the Skyline Bridge near Malakwa and the Roger's Pass summit was the most accident-prone section of highway in Canada. She started looking into it, and so far this year—halfway into the year—there had already been thirty victims. As she remembered this moment, she could tell the wind at sea was getting stronger. She let the cool breath of it stroke her cheeks. (*That which doesn't kill you will only make you wish it had. . . .*) Phrases from nowhere floated into her mind as the gale increased. She thought of that disaster and how catastrophes can hide blessings inside. And perhaps blessings hid catastrophes inside as well? It did occur to her that Pasha had an inkling of things she never told him—the way she lived in the memory of another man altogether and was acting out something that had been "emotionally transferred" without either of them knowing it. Those underground rivers of our psyches were there, though we would never see them. We would only see the evidence of them: a dry riverbed (like the dry riverbeds of northern Italy, the canals that ran under the road, the creek bed along the gravel road leading to the farm, dried out but expectant). When the car was wrecked in Revelstoke, she got money from the insurance company and she took it as an augury that said to her: *this is where the road ends. Get out while you can.* And she did. It was simple as that. That year, she later found out, on the Trans-Canada Highway at Revelstoke, there were seventy-two accident victims.

The loudspeaker on the ferry announced preparation for docking. The boat was taking a sharp left turn, as it always did when nearing the terminal in Langdale. *And now the day was over, and upon them fell the night. . . .* Tamara was remembering lines from *The Cid* for some reason. She stirred herself from her reverie and started down the steep outer stairs to the second level. She went inside. The ferry was full to capacity; fifteen hundred people, she heard once, could pack themselves onto this boat legally, and the crowd was jamming into the stairway to the car decks below, where the cars were lined up bumper to bumper. Toma joined them and went all the way to the bottom of the boat, where her bus was parked in the front. The driver was already at the entrance, examining people's tickets as they were reboarding, and the platform portals were opening as the ferry approached the dock. She got in the queue and onto the coach, where her attaché case lay safely on the seat. Some of the characters from the third deck got on the bus as well. The two ethereal lovers in their thin clothing came on and seated themselves in the front, where they continued to cuddle, holding hands under a camel-colored blanket. The woman who was smoking outside got into the back of the coach; her wavy, raven-colored hair reached down to her thighs, Toma noticed. The woman in the turban and army jacket who had been marching around the deck of the ferry now stood in the front in order to chat with the driver, ready to jump off shortly.

"Can I sit here?" a man's voice asked. Toma looked up and saw the pony-tailed professor-astronomer she had been talking with on the upstairs deck.

"Hi, sure." He sat down beside her and put a bag—a Ferrari Ruck Sack—at his feet. "How far are you going?" she asked him.

"Madeira Park. I have a cousin meeting me at the gas station on the corner, Frances Road or something."

"Vacation?"

"I'm going to be looking for a place," he explained. "I made some inquiries—need something with a big yard for a garden."

"You like gardens?"

"I've ordered three hundred and fifty tulip bulbs from Roozen Gaarde!" Dusty Cameron said laughing. "I have to get a place so I can plant them." He smiled broadly and looked at Toma.

"It's as good a reason as any I've heard for buying a place," she countered.

"I really love tulips—I've got orange Elites, yellow Yokohamas, coming in a month or so. Also bright red Apeldoorns and pink Ollioules—and Golden Apeldoorns. Let's see, then purple Caravelles and Pink Diamonds. Even white ones—Maureens, they're called. Some Negritas. . . ."

"This'll keep you busy for years!"

"That's my plan. The stars by night and the tulips by day."

Soon they were rolling off the ferry onto dry land again. The familiar bump as they drove onto the steel bridge, and again onto the concrete overpass, was a pleasant feeling. They motored up on the coastal marineway, which wound past the neighborhood cottages, with their lights on and smoke rising from chimneys. The turbaned woman standing by the driver was talking loudly so all could hear. She and the driver seemed to be old friends.

"Just a bit further," she was signaling by the front door. "You know they call it the red light district!" (Laughter.) "All the houses on this section of the One-O-One have red lanterns by the driveway, so we call it the red light district! Here!" The bus stopped and the woman cheerfully stomped out, yelling her thanks to the driver. Toma found herself tuning out momentarily, and through the dark glass of the bus window she imagined seeing the farmhouse between Parma and Ferrara somewhere.

She was lying half-raised under the white sheet in the heat of the morning, leaning on one elbow, looking out through the dim glass, yellowed with age and weather, at the verdant, opaque fields; half-rising from her bed like Lazarus, one knee raised, but not getting up and not lying down, in this expectant posture forever, leaning her head to the side, her hair falling down over her naked shoulder as he was positioning the small tray on the paint-spattered stool by the bedside.

"I want to stay here forever," she whispered, half to him, half to herself, and partly to the chipped and disintegrating walls.

"So do I, my darling," he said and leaned over her, put his sturdy arm around the back of her shoulders and pulled her up toward his lips. She had discovered during the night that his bones were heavy: his bones were heavy as rock. "So do I," he repeated. She thought in an instant of ways she could stay in this place, and her thoughts had no pattern and no logic. The evening before they had arrived in the middle of the night, but everyone at the farm was still up, some still outside in the rickety garden chairs, where they had been sitting drinking and smoking all evening long and waiting for the guests who would rent the run-down cottage next to the house,

where there was no electricity, and they arrived and lit an old candle that had been
dripping over a Chianti bottle, the way they used to in college in the sixties, and they
leaned and stretched and showered themselves on each other on the hard bed in the
dark, and there was a moon outside the window pale as a ghost, and she had begun
her departure from her dead life then and had continued rising toward the night sky
ever since. . . .

The bus moved on toward Gibsons. The village cafés on Marine Drive were open; people were sitting outside in the dark evening enjoying late tea and a smoke: "Howl at the Moon," washed pink with coyote silhouettes painted on the wall; "Leo's Tapas" with the tables outside (red and white checkered oilcloth covers and a sea-green canvas overhang above), the white wine sippers with sherry-soaked sausages on their plates; "Truffles Café" with its "WELCOME BOATERS!" sign in the window. Various objects decorated the front doors and front gates of the buildings they drove past. All small and simple. Little lanterns hung outside the cafés and open shops, fences and window frames painted in colorful folk art designs: pictures of yellow suns and blue moons and black-and-white cats in windows with wide whiskers. Chimes made of seashells, sculptures of drift-wood, steering wheels from sunken boats, painted masks. "Jack's Lane Bistro" on Gibson's Way, where the bus headed straight uphill, winding snakelike past narrow lanes going down into sleepy neighbor-hoods of old, wooden houses in the alder and fir trees. Tamara's mind was easing, and she felt a lot lighter already. She was being propelled into another life, another world: *The heavens are thine, the earth is also thine: as for the world and the fullness thereof, thou hast founded them.* As she looked out at the charcoal duskiness where the forest along the coastal high-way loomed, the Stygian twilight water of the Sound behind them, she thought that whatever was ahead was something entirely new.

"Perhaps you'd like to have coffee sometime?" The astronomer sitting beside her broke the silent thoughts flooding Toma's mind.

She looked at him. He was a pleasant man, also starting something new, she recognized.

"You mean during this visit of yours?"

"Yes. I'll be here for some time. Living up in Madeira Park at my cousin's. I'm on sabbatical this term." There was a brief silence while Toma thought this over. She didn't think very thoroughly or seriously. He was writing a phone number on a slip of paper. She took the number and put it in the pocket of her coat. "You can call me if you think you'd be all right with that?" he added.

"Sure," Toma said, smiling. "Sure. I think I'll do that. Give you a call." He smiled back and the coach wound its way north on the highway, bumping on potholes and screeching a bit on the hard turns along the dark sea and the even darker forests.

Every Shade of Meaning

Martha's brown hair ("goldenrod" Guy called it, trying to be poetic!) had grown long in recent months because she never had it cut any more. She had also hung up her racy jeans and her suggestive, mid-riff revealing, Lycra top (slinky and black with bronze metallic threads). Now she wore a big dress that was made for women who liked to hide inside frocks that looked like tents. (Hers was one of those Indian dresses that were popular in the sixties, she knew that; hippies liked to wear them, but now they were just fashionable ethno things people put on to make a statement and not for any real spiritual purpose like they used to.) Such dresses were usually made of cotton or rayon and had no waist, but spread out in a knee-length blouse (like a *kurta*) and sometimes loose pants under (what they called a *salwar*). Martha was only thirty-two, but the reason she resorted to this manner of dress (baby pink in color and decorated with hand-sewn bits of shiny metal) was obvious by now to anyone. She was five months pregnant. Soon it would be not only obvious, but downright cumbersome to get around, and the choice of dress would no longer be an actual option—it would be necessity. Martha wore no makeup—never did (even though she had been reading in a newspaper about spring fashion in Paris this year, and how there was a new line of makeup for men featuring lipstick men could wear with *insouciance*, it said). To each his own, she liked to say. It was a good say-ing, but hard to practice. Really hard—unless you were here on the coast where it was natural to practice your *owmess*. Your individual self was basically all you had out here. You were on your own. That was the reality of this place—and why she liked it here. She was here now, and she would never leave again!

Martha took the same bus every day from Davis Bay to West Sechelt because she went to work. It was in a new development up on Homestead Avenue, and she could get buses all the way up Northwest Bay Road to the corner, from where she only had to walk about four blocks. The house she worked in was the biggest one on the street—at least so far. They were always building up there. It was a Dodger-blue house with a small but busy garden filled with lots of plants and bushes (exotic plants, like *Spanish reed* and *cabbage palm*, trees Martha had never heard of before), a fish pond (with goldfish and minnows swimming), a fountain, three raised vegetable patches (for lettuce and tomatoes and radishes), some blackberry bushes and a shed covered in plastic. The inside of the house was painted in bril-liant violet red and turquoise, and the kitchen was bright magenta. Doreen, the woman Martha was taking care of there, had hired her brother as interior designer when she and her husband Bob built the place. This Don guy went wild and painted the whole house daz-zling fuchsia and screaming turquoise and orchid. How Doreen could live with that was a mystery. But it wasn't Martha's place to comment. She just went about the home doing stuff she was sup-posed to do. Doreen was dying of cancer and had Hospice coming in every afternoon. But Martha was there eight hours every day. She looked after Doreen, who was confined to her bed now, kept the place clean: she watered the plants, vacuumed rugs, ironed clothes, washed windows, cleaned the kitchen, changed the bed, fed the patient, answered phone calls, organized timetables for Hospice, called the doctor. . . .

Doreen slept most of the time, which was maybe her escape. She and Bob built the house for the "dream life." Both left their jobs in the city (Doreen was a cafeteria food service director at Golden Gate Hospital, and Bob was an account executive at Household International) and moved to their dream house. First thing you know, Bob got sick with lung cancer and died, and next thing you know, Doreen discovered she was sick with breast cancer, and now she was dying too. (One explanation Martha thought of often was that Bob and Doreen left their jobs—soul killing, mind-numbing jobs—*too late,* and that they already had the diseases they died of when they left). But the whole story just didn't make sense. It was like working every day in a weird senseless game somebody made up, where per-fectly good and innocent people went through such agony and heart-break and just plain *irony,* while other people—who were wild and wicked and manipulative—went through life like they had planned from start to finish for everything to work out smoothly. (And she had known some of those wicked people for whom things went so well. She had met them and rubbed shoulders, yes. But not any more. She was learning how to stay away!) Still, you had to wonder.

Martha thought of herself as an observer in all this. A life-observer. Not a real participant but *a being without substance,* as she said, like the woman she read about in the Robinson Crusoe novel, by that writer Coetzee, who was cast away with "Cruso" and Friday and then tried to find "Mr. Foe," who was really Daniel De Foe, so he could write the story of her adventure because she, Susan Barton, was *a being without substance* and such a being couldn't write a story. Even though she was pregnant, Martha could honestly say to anyone who asked that she didn't feel like she had a life, really. Obviously, something must have happened here, but it was nonetheless true: Martha had no life and she didn't want one. If it was this weird when you didn't have a life, look how much weirder it got when you actually had one. She didn't think she could deal with all those ironies. In a way she was perfectly happy with the worst-case scenario she was in. Because if you looked at it objectively, every woman's worst nightmare was to become pregnant and be alone. Women usually clung to the man no matter what (*no matter what*) just to avoid that scenario. But here she was, Martha Abernathy, pregnant and alone. And it wasn't so bad—after all that!

Martha's world came to a crossroads five months ago. That was how she thought of it: an intersection, where several lines from vastly different directions converge at a midpoint. Even though it took them months, even years or decades, to arrive, the different worlds collide in an instant; in the blink of an eye or a flash of a sunray, they meet, mesh and burst into a mushroom cloud of fate. The weird thing, Martha now thought when she considered it all, was that such a fateful moment is cataclysmic for only you. No one else experiences that same catastrophe. *It's yours alone.* Inside everyone's life is a network of roads and highways—some large and wide and some small and crooked, some just alleys winding along, some regular streets in straight blocks with corners—but these are the paths on which the various themes of your life are traveling. It's a web. A spider web, she was thinking, and you are at the center of it. (It was Guy who put this image into her mind: he was going on about Fritjof Capra and some sort of "web of life" idea, "synthesizing mind and matter." Guy was always finding something cultish to hang onto, but he never stuck. It would have been all right if he stayed with it, anything really, but he wafted about from one thing to another—*The Tao of Physics, The Science of Sustainable Living*—whatever answered his temporary spiritual wanderlust).

A mild breeze blew off the sea where Martha was standing at the bus stop. She could see the tiny waves bustling out on the Strait of Georgia between the coast and Vancouver Island on the other side. (She had heard that dogs happily swim in the ocean, but refuse to go in when it's overcast and they can't see the island on the other side. Do they really think they could swim across in an emergency? Whatever goes on in a dog's mind?)

Martha stood in front of the bus stop sign on Highway 1, directly below the Calvary Chapel. The chapel was located on a steep hill. A sign resembling a billboard announced the identity of the building; CALVARY CHAPEL, it said in big green letters. It was a new building, just barely finished. She could see how the blue-painted walls were literally gleaming from the newness. The parking lot was still gravel, and there were posts in for landscaping—railroad ties along the edge in zigzag patterns—but no flowers yet and no asphalt. Martha came to this bus stop every day, and she followed the progress of the building. She could read the "inspirational comment" posted out by the fence, overlooking the sea: *Look at your life, admit you are a sinner, genuinely desire to turn away from that sin, and ask Him to forgive you. . . .* What used to be up there instead of the sign for Calvary Chapel was a placard that said KINGDOM HALL, which was for the Jehovah's Witnesses. But they must have gone somewhere else.

Martha was not sure what the difference was between all these places of worship, as they were referred to. Or else they called them meeting places. Everyone knew about the Jehovah's people who come to your door (they probably had a hard time out here on the coast because people had decided they were in heaven already and it was hard to convince them there was anything better they needed to go to). And she knew that the Calvary group came from what others called Jesus people (and those who didn't like them called them Jesus freaks—but that was kind of intolerant. Martha couldn't help thinking: just because someone isn't like you doesn't mean he's a freak. . .). The only other thing she knew for sure was that they had ocean baptisms. They dunked each other in the Pacific Ocean down in California. Maybe it was at Costa Mesa. They had coffee houses where they sang and strummed guitars, and sometimes whole bands played. They were, she heard from Guy who knew them, real *street worshippers.* That wasn't bad, she thought to herself, was it now? Didn't Jesus himself practice squarely on the street? And his followers, weren't they also right on the street?

The spider web of life was something Martha was not aware of until the moment everything coalesced in the center. Only a few months ago she was living in St. Albert, just north of Edmonton, and things were normal. Nothing special distinguished the days for her. She went to work in her Toyota Corolla to the center of town, a long drive on Highway 2 she took every day. She was a loans officer at the Royal Bank in the Edmonton Center. She took her lunch in the Bistro on the main floor. Said hello every day to the shoemaker at the shoe repair kiosk by the pedway. She picked up deli food for her dinner on the way home (she liked the pita with roast turkey and honey mustard, or the turkey salad with peppers). She sometimes stopped to look at the jewelry displayed in the windows of Birks, especially the sapphire rings. She liked the names. Sapphire Solitaire;

Trillion & Princess; Three Stone Sapphire. Hers was a life led indoors. (Not as bad as Guy, though: he had no job and spent the day at the computer doing stuff like The Jesus Project, where he helped his church find encouraging messages for the inspiration board and collected testimonies from New Christians. He did that because he was nosy, Martha figured, not because his heart was in it). Her brother Steve was working a small farm north of Morinville; he was a specialist on annual ryegrass, the kind that was harvested as pastures in cool climates. It sounded pretty complicated, what he did: he knew all about levels of nitrogen and phosphorus and potassium, when the grass was cut, when the subsequent harvests were taken. . . . He also ran the Morinville Greenhouses off of Highway 2, north of the village.

Morinville was where their parents lived, just thirty clicks north of the city, a place a hundred years old (the St. Jean Baptiste Church with its murals of St. John the Baptist and the Casavant pipe organ from 1925—named after Father Jean Baptist. Morinvillians were proud of the history of their place, but it left Martha cold). Their sibling lives were the opposite of each other. Steve was married and had built himself a big house out on the barren plain. He was planting junipers and pines on the denuded lot, and it was all right in the summer. But in the winter it was cold and unfriendly to look at. The house was too big for him and Sandra. They had no money after the house was built, so they had very little furniture and no decorations at all. The walls were blank and chilly, painted white, as if it were a morgue. Then, instead of warming up the house with furniture and stuff, they had a baby.

When the baby was baptized, it was a big day for the whole Abernathy family. Everyone came down from the city of St. Albert, from the farms up toward Hinton, and from Lloydminster and Saskatoon. The extended family. All assembled to watch the first grandchild be turned into an anointed Christian: to go from Baby Abernathy to Jordan Abernathy, son of Steve Abernathy and Sandra Abernathy. Martha was there of course, helping out with the refreshments and getting the party ready because they were having everyone over to their house after the church ceremony, which was of course at the St. Jean Baptiste Church on 100 Avenue, where services were spoken in French. In any case it was a lovely church Martha always thought: the red-brick exterior with the white trim; a steeple that looked ornate and simple at the same time; the two mini-steeples on each side (gothic style, now a historic site, like so much else in Alberta). All the church events there were packed. Martha and Steve were not Catholic of course; they weren't anything. But Sandra was, and since Steve had married into a Catholic family, there was no help for it. Even so, Martha's family often went to the Catholic Mass at Christmas. It was part of Christmas Eve to go there first, then home for a big meal. So the Catholic Church was already familiar, and that made it easier for Steve to move into this way of life. Martha's first taste of a vague sense of discrimination was when she was not asked to stand as godmother to little Jordan. Because she wasn't Catholic—you had to be Catholic to stand godmother for a Catholic child. But Martha said nothing. What can you say, anyway?

The day of the baptism was confusing. They were leaving from two houses: from Steve's house north of town and their parents' house in the village, in two or three convoys of cars to the church. They had been running back and forth between the houses all morning, and little Jordan had been brought along some of the time and had stayed home some of the time, until Martha herself wasn't sure where exactly he was. But she knew Sandra was in charge. After putting out all the cups, some silver goblets for white wine, the white porcelain plates, the little forks and baby blue napkins, some roses on the table here and there, the name tags for place settings, getting coffee ready and glasses for pop and cranberry juice, Martha changed and joined the rest of them in the cars leaving from Steve's house. They were wearing white shirts and coral silk and satin tops with jackets over. Steve even wore a salmon-colored tie. (Guy's tie was the green of cheese mold, but he thought it was svelte. Guy had the idea he was always irresistible. A bit like his sister Sandra).

Sandra was over at her in-laws' house for a while as they were getting Jordan ready. He was going to be wearing a long white gown with a blue ribbon on it. Like a girl, Steve joked. But it was a formal baptismal ceremony, so no skimping. Martha was at Steve's house with Sandra, who came back from her in-laws'. Steve was at his parent's house with Jordan. Sandra didn't want Jordan to be in the middle of the reception preparations. She said there were too many cups and saucers, too much glass and porcelain, too many knives and forks and sharp things, and too much noise. So Jordan slept sweetly at their parent's house in his wicker bassinet with the frilly lace around it that Steve and Martha's mom had made. At two in the afternoon sharp, they loaded themselves in the family van at Sandra's house and headed for the church. Family members began arriving for the service at two-thirty. The van supposedly carrying the baby and the father arrived ten minutes later. They all went into the narthex of the church and made their preparations with the priest.

When Martha thought about it all now, it seemed like it could easily have happened. But at the time there was a real sense of incomprehension. Or simply that people act subconsciously. It had often occurred to Martha that accidents don't really happen at random: they are deliberate things set off at unspecified times. Interpreting chance events or desultory, haphazard occurrences was like trying to decipher a dream: there are clues and echoes and familiar patterns, but it all happens in an illogical sequence. Taken one at a time, though, each experience by itself may be quite ordinary.

As she stood on the highway, Martha saw the bus come up the hill toward her. It was a red, white and blue passenger bus, familiar by now as the handle on her own front door. The bus stopped and she got on. It was full as usual: a lot of pensioners (an elderly woman with gray hair in a bun and a huge birthmark over her left eye; a white-haired woman in a black T-shirt; a gentleman with black hair in a black suit and narrow tie), a lot of high school kids gossiping with one another (wearing T-shirts and making faces, girls in skimpy, tight dresses in bold colors), a lot of people like her transporting themselves to and from places of work (a couple in denim jackets; a fat woman with straight brown hair; two men in baggy khaki slacks and work shirts). Low paid working class, labor class. Martha had gone from white collar to blue collar in these five months, and she earned much less now. But she liked it anyway. How do you account for such things? She had no real friends here yet, although Doreen was very much a friend, if you looked at it right. Giving one person relief from pain was better than what she did at the bank. She never felt she was benefiting people there; she always sensed she was assisting the bank in taking advantage of its customers. That might not be true, but if she experienced it that way, it was true on that level, wasn't it?

Sandra, her sister-in-law, had several brothers, but one of them was more of Martha's friend than the others (until he stopped being her pal—relationships can end in an instant, they can). Besides, they all lived in places like Winnipeg and Los Angeles and Miami, and they all had big families. But Sandra's youngest brother Guy was still in St. Albert, and she had ended up in conversations with him many times, first at Steve and Sandra's wedding, then at the housewarming party in the new house outside of Morinville, then one Christmas they all spent together and finally at Jordan's baptism. Guy was an average young man, but he had a wild streak, he did. His brown hair was cut really short, and it stuck out of his skull like a porcupine. His nose was narrow and his eyes were too. His skin was pale and he was thin. Martha didn't like him. He was always trying to be clever. One time they ended up arguing about reincarnation. Guy was interested in Buddhism, but said he couldn't figure reincarnation. They were sitting in Guy's car because he had driven her home after the party and had parked on the street outside her house. (He knew she had stopped going out with Magne because Magne had already gone off to a university in Norway somewhere—but that didn't mean she had stopped thinking about him or anything. . . . But that was all over now, no going back.)

"Do you think Buddhists actually believe in reincarnation, or do they just pretend to?" Guy was saying rhetorically because he wasn't really expecting an answer from her.

"Yes, I'm sure they do."

"That can't be. How can you believe that stuff? Come on, tell me that! It's patently absurd."

"No, it's not absurd, Guy. You just aren't familiar with the concept, so it's only absurd to you. Think how absurd the whole idea of heaven and hell is for a regular Buddhist!"

"Heaven and hell are easier to comprehend," Guy insisted. He was intense, the muscles on his face were drawn and stiff, his lips clenched. That was when Martha started to wonder what was behind his interest in Buddhism. He wasn't just making idle chatter.

"Why are you so worried about this?" she asked him.

"I'm not worried about it!" Guy was laughing stiffly and looking at her as if she were hard of understanding. "I just don't get it—and I don't believe it's what anybody believes. In reality. It's just a thing they tell each other to make sense of nothing."

"*No*, it's not!" Martha was getting really upset at Guy. He was so stubborn, and he didn't care what she thought. He just wanted to pronounce his own views and force them on her. She knew that then, and she should have known to stay away from him later. At that moment in the car, all she wanted to do was get out of there. With Guy she had the sense that she was locked in a small room without windows and was breathing burning air.

Because Guy was the problem. Guy wouldn't let up on anything. Guy didn't take no for an answer. He was always propositioning her at those family gatherings. She always said no, but she said it too wimpishly. She would laugh when she refused or make some gesture to look like it wasn't a *serious* no, just a little no that couldn't be helped and wasn't her fault. . . . That was her first mistake, Martha was thinking. Why do girls and women feel guilty about saying no when they have to say no? Martha had not yet been able to say no properly. It was always said evasively, hoping the other person would understand. Hoping *he* would take the hint because the other person would usually be a man. But men didn't seem to take a hint. They were too dense, Sandra once said to her. Martha complained to Sandra about her brother Guy's coming onto her, as she put it then. How Guy wouldn't take a hint.

"He can't take a hint," Sandra said, "because he's a guy. He's a Guy guy!" Then she laughed her giggly girl-laugh. Sandra was quite a character in Martha's view: she had curly hair dyed white-blonde in Marilyn Monroe style, and it looked so wispy that it didn't even seem real. She had flighty and flirty mannerisms, always confused about where she put things or in what order things went. Martha couldn't figure out how Sandra kept a house going at all. She seemed so disorganized and distracted, and just plain *scatterbrained*. How did Steve put up with her? Martha wondered about that often. But you couldn't make your brother's decisions for him. He saw something in her, and it was true that she had good "family feeling," and that counted for something among her relatives.

But now Martha was living without any kin at all. They didn't know where she was, even. She didn't tell them. Just said goodbye all of a sudden—like she had been baptized anew and was following another song. She sent everyone a small letter on stationary she had bought in the shopping center downtown, with a picture of a basket of wildflowers. (She went so far as to put a passage from the scriptures, something from Peter, on the bottom of the note—just to confuse them and to catch Guy's attention: *To this you were called, because Christ suffered for you, leaving you an example, that you should follow in his steps. . .*). Her note said she was moving away to start a new life. That was all. She sent the same note to all her family, her friends and her employer.

The next day she got on the Greyhound bus. She didn't need to wait for results at the doctor's: she knew what had happened even before it actually happened. That's what they probably said "coming to Jesus" was like over in the Calvary Chapel. What else would it be? Those people who modeled themselves on the original Jesus story— where you had to leave everything behind and follow a new calling. It was not such a bad idea, Martha thought now. Not so bad.

She went over the day again. They got to the church and assembled around the priest in the vestibule. Sandra and Steve and the rest of them—but the baby wasn't there. They looked at each other in surprise.

"Didn't you bring Jordan?" Sandra said loudly. "Where's Jordan?"

"What do you mean?" Steve said loudly too. "Didn't you bring him with you?"

"No! Didn't you bring him? You had him!"

"No, you had him!"

"No, you did! Where is he?" Sandra was screaming by now. They quickly figured out that Jordan was still in the basement of Steve's parents' house, and Steve had simply forgotten in the rush and confusion. About five people scrambled into a car and raced back to the house. The rest waited at the church, anxiety rising. Martha was there waiting, and Guy started closing in on her then. He was shaking his head, muttering, "Man, Steve's in hot water now. He's in the dog house now, I can tell you that!" As if this were funny or something, because Guy was laughing in a way or at least smirking.

When they all came back, they had Jordan safe and sound, and he had just slept on down there, none the wiser. But whoever heard of forgetting to bring the baby to a baptism! Even Martha, flexible and amenable as she was (according to Guy!), found this development hard to swallow. Not that anyone was really in danger: it was mainly the symbolic value of the incident. It seemed to portend something, and she couldn't see what it was. She had a strong sense of anxiety, a sadness that was both sweet and frightening. It felt as though something was going to happen. Then, when nothing did happen, it was even worse. Waiting for a conflagration that doesn't come.

And when she thought about it, wasn't that what the Calvary Chapel people were all about? Didn't they go about warning everyone of the millennium when that happened? And nothing came of it. They went on about *Armageddon* and *the Last Days,* as if they could know (. . .*in the last days scoffers will come, scoffing and following their own evil desires.* . .). They couldn't know. People were not supposed to know these things. She had been to church often enough (read the Bible often enough, in fact) to know *it was not given to man to know* what only God could know. There was a plan, and it was supposed to be a surprise: the hour of your conception, your birth, your death, your funeral. Not for you to know. That's why some people didn't like abortion: too much control over something only God was supposed to control.

She, Martha Abernathy—formerly of St. Albert, Alberta, now of Davis Bay, British Columbia—had given abortion serious thought. She was not a church person, not a believer (a *believer*, whatever that was) in Jesus or in Mother Mary, as was Sandra and now even Steve. Though she kind of liked the idea of the Jesus freaks singing songs in coffee houses and worshipping on the street and saving the homeless and the destitute (soup kitchens, overnight hostels, drug rehab programs, needle exchanges, whatever was out there on the street). Even ocean baptisms appealed to her. Why should you let yourself be baptized when you're just an infant and have no clue what's happening? When you can never have a memory of your welcome into the fold? Why not wait till you're an adult and can do this in full consciousness? But she decided against abortion. Not so much from principle as from the realization that she liked what was happening to her. She liked the idea that she would be alone carrying a child without a husband, without a family—shunned, disrespected, shamed even. Making her living caring for a dying woman in her last days.

When Martha got to the West Sechelt stop, she stepped off the bus and walked up the road to Doreen's house on Homestead. It was uphill and more and more of a strain. But Martha was convinced this exercise did her good. The sun was out. Jaybirds were screeching. She would take some of the tomatoes off the plants today and make a tomato salad for Doreen even if Doreen couldn't eat much any more. She lay in her high bed mostly, staring at the purple ceiling, her lips grown puffy, her eyes glistening, her hair stringy, her thin body limp. But she had a peculiar smile. That was something Martha couldn't figure out. Why the smile? She lay there looking up as if she saw something no one else could see. Because there were always other people there: Betty from Hospice was there in the early morning (always dressed nice in cotton skirts with well-groomed white hair);

Andrew spent half the night there, also from Hospice (Andrew looked like he needed assistance himself, actually; he was thin and wan, his hair perpetually greasy, his beard straggly, his eyes bloodshot with shadows under them). Then Martha was there most of the day, with Betty coming back in the afternoons for three or four hours now. Later Andrew came in the evening again. Betty did lots of stuff in the kitchen, and also bathed Doreen and washed some of the laundry. Martha had to bathe Doreen in the middle of the day because she needed a bath every few hours. For that, she got Doreen to stand up. Then she dipped a cloth in lukewarm soapy water and wiped it across Doreen's sick body. Gentle strokes along the thin arms and the droopy diseased breasts and the wrinkly thighs. It was like washing the feet of visitors. Anointing them with perfume, like they did in ancient times. And Doreen stood there smiling a little bit, a slightly vacant stare into the distance in her pale eyes. Then Martha put a fresh shirt on her and helped her back into bed, with a bit of drink and a bite if she could take it.

When she got to Doreen's sky-blue house, there was a peculiar morning stillness. The lilies and roses were in white and yellow and pastel bloom out front. On the veranda all along the house, the nasturtiums and geraniums glistened in the morning dew. She let herself in and found Betty on the phone. Betty hung up and said to Martha right away, "She's a tad worse today. I'm calling Hospice. We may need a bit of help today." Martha understood. There was tension in the air all the time that this day would come, and then after that, more such days. Dying takes a long time. It can't be regulated. Women like Martha and Betty had been around since the beginning of days, Martha knew that. The women who wait. The women who serve and anoint and wait on . . . what? Death? God? Fate? The inevitable? Martha went upstairs to Doreen and saw what Betty meant. Doreen was very pale, breathing slowly. Some life had gone out of her face.

But when Martha stood there holding Doreen's darkly spotted hand, the sick woman suddenly turned and looked directly into her eyes. Doreen's eyes were almost sparkling; it was strange. Doreen smiled and squeezed Martha's hand and spoke with what sounded like happiness (or joy—perhaps it was joy) in her voice.

"I'll see you on the other side, Martha," Doreen said. So she knew her name after all. Martha had been sure the whole time she had been here that Doreen didn't register these things. Who knew what else Doreen had been taking in when they thought she was out of it or sleeping?

"Yes, we'll meet again over there," Martha said back, nodding as if she knew what she was talking about. They smiled at each other as if the deal were clinched. As if they had a date in the distance. When Doreen closed her eyes as if for sleep, Martha waited a bit. Doreen's breathing got irregular, and she took some gasps while her eyes remained closed. Then she just let go a big breath. All the while Martha held her hand. Doreen was lying eerily still. It took some moments for Martha to realize what had just happened. Doreen had died. Just like that: *She had died!* While Martha held her hand and participated in a big, bad joke about meeting on the other side—it was just something Martha said for fun or to make it easy on herself . . . not something she meant! She didn't mean it. She suddenly wished she could take it back and say something more honest . . . but then, she didn't know what that would be. Maybe this was good too? Maybe it didn't matter? Martha felt confused, and she discovered she was shaking, still holding Doreen's hand like this at her bedside.

After a while, Martha went back down to Betty, who was rinsing greens in the kitchen. She said nothing to Betty—didn't want to tell her. Not just now. They went about their business as usual: dusting, wiping, rinsing, laundering. As if nothing had changed. Yet there had been a change. From one minute to the next everything had changed. Martha stood at the front window looking out over the mountains of her new home, covered as they were with pine and cedar trees and dogwoods and hemlocks and snow-dusted on the peaks; she put her hand on her growing belly where that child whom she was going to acknowledge even though Guy wouldn't and couldn't because he was just a lost soul to Martha (lost to her, and she would never say the word for what he did on the night of Jordan's baptism when everything was in chaos and Steve was starting the long journey of punishing himself for being a *bad father* and the rift in their marriage started and Sandra had this edge on him he would never live down—how Guy came back to her house in St. Albert and knocked on the door in the middle of the night and she let him in stupidly, then couldn't get him out again; he forced her on the sofa in the living room, probably thinking she secretly wanted this. Isn't that what men like him really think? She was sure he thought *the girl wants it but can't say it because modesty prevents her from saying so?*) She was anxious about what was to come, about having the baby and raising it alone and not telling, never telling, a soul who the father of her child was. No one would never know. She was apprehensive about it and also looking forward to it. To be ruthlessly honest, she looked forward to it. As she looked at the snow-dusted mountains in the distance, she felt strangely alone and not alone at the same time. She wanted to own the moment. She would wait a little longer before telling Betty what happened upstairs—just so it could be hers alone a little longer.

The Road Between Wind and Water

"The thing is, Millie," Joanie was saying across the small cafeteria table in the back end of the ferry restaurant, *The Province* newspaper thrown onto the bench next to Millie (Joanie always read *The Province* because it had a more dramatic descriptions of the news), "the thing is, if a premier is acting like a hoodlum, he should be recalled! The man broke the law. Premiers shouldn't break the law."

"But didn't this happen in Hawaii? That's not Canada, so he didn't break the law here," Millie was saying. She was so *soft*, she was.

"Millie, you're a softie, sweetie. It doesn't matter if you break the law here or in the U.S., if you're a premier, you should be deposed. They can recall the governor of California, then they can recall the premier of B.C. Limits are limits, and people should have standards around here."

"Everybody makes mistakes, Mom," Millie was saying. She was full of excuses, the girl. Joanie always knew Millie was not good material for discipline.

"It's no good to be a bleeding heart liberal, is it now?" Joanie said admonishingly. She had put the breakfast plate aside and was on to her now cold coffee. If only one didn't have to go outside to smoke. Having a smoke here and now would have been just the thing. Millie was listening carefully to her mom, but she didn't seem to absorb it, really. Not in the right way. When Millie had a view, she kept it all her life. Once fashioned, it couldn't change. What made her that way? Joanie was wondering—not for the first time, either.

"Guppy says Jesus had a bleeding heart," Millie offered in a low voice.

"Oh, Guppy! Your grandma's just a crazy kook. She went to church when she was ten over there in Norway and never came out again. Somebody stewed her over with that gospel stuff!"

"You're too hard on Grandma, Mom. She can believe what she wants to, can't she?"

"Yea, sweetie, but it has to make sense, doesn't it?"

"Why?"

Joanie gave up for a moment. It was just like Millie to not even know why things should make sense. There should be logic to what you do and think. Things have to match up: the pieces have to fit. The knots have to get tied. Otherwise, where are you? But Millie didn't have any logic in her body, not an ounce of it. She went by her heart, as she said. Her *heart*.

"If you don't know that, this ferry ride isn't long enough for me to explain it, honey bun," Joanie finally answered. They smiled at each other. No one was ever going to say Millie wasn't the sweetest girl on Earth, in spite of everything. "But maybe I'll give it a try. You need to forget about emotions. You need to just look at the facts and realize sometimes your emotions are in the way. Your emotions aren't necessarily intelligent. They can lead you into difficulty, dearie."

"What about love? What about compassion? Aren't those emotions?"

Mother and daughter smiled at each other. This was not the first time they'd had this conversation, and Joanie knew why. They enjoyed talking. She enjoyed discussing with Millie, instructing her; it gave her a chance to be the teacher she never got to be. And Millie was always available for an educational conversation. She wasn't the busy type, like some of the other girls, running around between the shops and losing track of their money. No, Millie was modest about that sort of thing.

Joanie was trying to explain to her daughter what life was all about. She was always trying to explain things to her: how the plumbing in the house works, how babies get burped, how to prune a rosebush. Millie needed instruction in everything. Joanie had long ago accepted the fact that Millie was not going to shine in the intelligence department. Not in the looks section either because Millie was simply a little overweight—always had been and always would be. There was nothing Joanie or her father Artie could do about that, and they had long ago decided to let it go. Not that Millie needed to be a beauty queen or anything—she just would have benefited from losing a pound or two and getting some color. Because Millie was as pale as a sheet. She was born that way. Joanie's theory was that you worked at improving what you were given. But Millie was so placid. She just drifted along and made no effort at anything. In Millie's defense, she was a sweet girl. You had to love her anyway. The two of them were having traditional breakfast on the ferry (bacon and scrambled eggs and a stack of toast triangles too—a good deal on the ferry, only four bucks, and it kept you going till you came back on the three-thirty). They were going in on Friday as usual to visit Joanie's mom, who was in the palliative care unit of the Vancouver General. Poor Guppy! She had a former name, Grethe Haugen, but everyone just called her Guppy after she left that doctor husband of hers, who just happened to be Joanie's real father (but never mind!) and came to B.C., although heaven knows she could have used him and not the useless Nickie she did have (live and learn, she'd have to say). Guppy was never getting out of that hospital. Joanie went every Friday, and sometimes Millie came along, like this time. Sweet little Millie (not so little any more, but to a mom, no matter how big a child gets, she's always little).

Friday was the day the hospital set aside for all-day visits, so Friday it was. Joanie would have preferred the day to be a Thursday because it was always pretty congested coming back on Friday afternoon. But you did what you had to do when it came to your mom. Wouldn't Joanie like it if Millie did the same for her? That's what daughters do, and Joanie was making sure Millie learned that. It wasn't Millie's fate to do well in high school or to go on after that, but that didn't mean Millie couldn't learn. In fact, little Millie dropped out in her senior year—to have a baby, that's what. She had a baby with that pierced and tattooed Toronto guy they always called Hart, about whom no one knew a thing, and moved into one of the cheap apartments in Gibsons. Joanie and Artie thought that was the end, but sure enough, Millie just sailed along and later went back to night school and finished her diploma in another couple of years, going over to Chatelech high school on Wednesday nights, taking the courses one at a time. It's what Joanie's stepdad Nick used to say: what you don't have in brains, you can make up for with stubbornness. And Millie turned out to be real stubborn.

Joanie was talking to Millie about the politics of the day because Millie never read the paper either. Millie was wearing her loose blouse, as if she was pregnant, but she liked the soft cotton and the puffy sleeves. So let her wear it. After all, Millie was over twenty-one and you couldn't tell a grown daughter what to wear, could you? Millie's yellow hair hung down straight, the way they had their hair back in the sixties, and she had always kept it that way. Joanie herself was still more or less naturally blond, and she tied her hair up casually on top of her head, held up there with a wooden pin she once got at the ferry slip, one of those booths where they sell arts and crafts to people waiting. Joanie wore her usual gray sweatshirt top and jeans and sneakers. Why deviate from a good thing once you've found it?

Joanie sat back and let her mind wander a bit while Millie finished breakfast. The girl ate slowly too: everything she did was at a strangely decelerated pace, as if Millie's chemistry were different from others. She was inevitably late for things, never on time. She was at the table long after everyone else was finished and didn't seem to mind. When Joanie came to pick her up from school, back in the old days, she always had to wait till all the other kids were out. Finally, little Millie showed up, scraping her feet along the walkway from the school steps to the parked car. Being Millie's mom meant lots of waiting. Used to be she gave the girl heck for it, scolded her, raised her voice and all. But Millie didn't change because—guess what?—she couldn't. It just wasn't in her nature to be different, and finally everybody had to accept that. Now Joanie just turned the amps down, put herself in second gear instead of fourth and gave herself enough time around their visits to not be rushed. Millie just took her time—that's what Artie said. "The girl just takes her time with life, nothing to do about it."

Artie was spending all his time now helping out with that Visitor Center—doing something with curved rafters and tenon reduction and cutting red cedar. They built it right next to the library, a pretty building, all logs and shiny beams. But nobody got paid for a single nail or board or wire of it. They took a year to put it up: cement mixers mixing in the off hours; construction workers putting up the structure on weekends; people like Artie helping raise the bents (they even had a whetting bush on top of the last bent!), lifting and fitting logs week after week, putting shingles on, installing doors, putting on siding. Now it was all done, and they were *inaugurating* the place on Friday. They were having some sort of *gala dinner* with fancy clothes, and it was going to cost a hundred and seventy-five bucks per person. Per person, not per couple, this is. All the guys who helped build the thing had to pay for having dinner in it too. By all rights, Joanie figured they should at least be offered a free meal. But that's the way of volunteers. That's the meaning of the term: you do stuff for nothing. Volunteer. Artie said they should go because the money was going straight to the building costs, and they should contribute to it. He said they raised twenty-three thousand dollars at the dinner last year. They didn't ever get to go to anything fancy, and Artie said it was time they did. Whoever thought he'd think that way? Artie never spent a penny—didn't have any to spend. He lost his job four years ago at BC Hydro and never got other work. You couldn't get work if you were over fifty like Artie. What were they thinking, laying people off left and right? Now they lived on what Joanie was making at the Wheatberry Bakery and whatever they had saved. They had nothing when that was done—except Perseus of course. Perseus the Persian cat: a real, fluffy, flat-faced, ceramic-white, blue-eyed Rarity Tsesarevich Elisey.

They'd had Perseus for five years, and Artie sure took care of him! They first got him just for fun, but then folks from the Cat

Fanciers' Association started calling, wanting to breed Persian cats. Artie realized there was money in this, and he never looked back. The Association said they had fifteen thousand Persian kittens registered now. Problem is, Persians are groom-heavy and need shaving and combing and bathing. Then Joanie discovered Persians aren't the best at potty training either. Perseus got kidney trouble once too. It was more trouble than it was worth, Joanie thought: everything from fleas and earmites to ringworms. Artie was a fan, though. He knew everything now about ragdolls and Norwegian forest cats and Siberians and Selkirk rexes and British shorthairs and whatnot. He fed Perseus special cat food: Meow Chow you buy in a can. He combed the cat's fur every night and he made sure Perseus went for a walk every day. Usually, he didn't want to be the one holding the leash and had Joanie do it. She figured he was embarrassed about looking like a sissy with a cat on a leash. But Joanie held the leash all right, and the two of them walked the cat two or three blocks every day. The rest of the time the cat was indoors. It sat on the windowsill of the living room, sometimes draped on the back of the sofa with its paws and fluffy tail hanging down, looking out the window at the street life. Perseus never got tired of watching the cars and kids on the street outside.

Millie finally finished her eggs and bacon in her pensive way and pretty soon the voice at the loudspeaker was telling them to go to their cars. They weren't just going to visit Guppy this time. They were also going to stop at the Park Royal Mall to see if there wasn't something on sale for Joanie to wear at that *gala*—much as it wasn't her style to dress up. But Harvey and Carol and Stebbie were all going to be there, so who knew, it might be a good time. Joanie would rather just get together at the pub like they always did. At the Wakefield Inn, where they could sit around for a while at four in the afternoon and have a good time joking and laughing around one of those pinewood tables, or maybe outside when it wasn't too hot or too cold. They told a few stories, made a few jokes and went home at six for dinner. It was their Friday routine now—but this week it was going to be canceled for the dinner thing. Joanie doubted they would have more fun at that dinner than over a simple beer, but Artie said it wasn't the fun, it was the giving to the community that mattered. She wasn't sure where this community spirit of his came from now. He seemed immersed in it. But you didn't ask too many questions. Like the business of always wearing socks in his sandals. She got tired of telling him sandals were supposed to be for bare feet. But it never made him stop putting on heavy socks so she gave up trying. People just are what they are, that's the truth.

They went with the crowd down to the car deck, down the stairwell and out onto the main deck, where a cold sea wind blasted them as soon as they walked outside. The mountains of the mainland were looming overhead like giants in somebody's bad dream. As they wound their way to the Ford station wagon they had parked toward the front, Joanie saw someone she vaguely recognized going to another car on the bridge. It was *that woman*. Joanie had seen her a few times around the Visitor Center site. She was somehow involved with the Timber Framers Guild—maybe organizing their conferences and workshops about historic timber framing techniques. Maybe this new building was her special portfolio or something. Still, Joanie had a strong feeling of unease when she saw her. It wasn't that there was anything special. The woman (Joanie didn't even know her name) had never done anything strange or been anywhere noticeable that Joanie could remember. But she could tell her mind was puzzling all on its own, like a calculator gone insane. That woman seemed to emit signals Joanie didn't like. And as she and Millie got into the Ford, Joanie was realizing what was bothering her. What was upsetting her was, frankly, that this woman was—well, she looked like . . . what could she say? The woman looked like *a model*. She was like something cut out of *Vogue* magazine. She was tall and slim as a stick; she was tanned, and her skin was smooth as—well, as plastic or something. Her hair was long and dark and fell down her back, and was like what they say in the commercials: like *satin*. She was impeccably dressed in some blue summer dress that was short, above the knees, and only had straps to reveal her brown shoulders. Her lips were full, almost pouty, and her dark eyes were *big*.

Sitting behind the steering wheel with Millie beside her, Joanie suddenly felt really awful for no special reason she could figure out. She felt sick, frankly. Because it was dawning on her like a discovery when you wake up that there's a forest fire blazing right outside: it was flaring up before her as a real possibility that Artie was having a crush on that woman. That it was *she* who was really behind Artie's bout of good will toward the community. (Why else did he want to go to that conference at a place called Le Chateau Montebello?) He was there building away day after day because that woman, who looked like she ought to be in Paris or Milan and not here on the good old coast, came by all the time to see how the construction was going, talking to the guys, chatting and socializing and being nice. And it came as a cold sweat too that maybe this lady was what was behind Artie's desire to go to the *gala*. He wanted to dress in a suit and preen himself before this piece of female meat from elsewhere, who didn't even belong here. If Joanie was right, what really got to her was that Artie was willing to pay three hundred and fifty bucks just to get a chance to do that! Waiting for the cars to start driving off the ferry, Joanie decided to just talk. Say it, she told herself. The sooner this comes out in the open, the easier for everyone.

"Your dad has never been unfaithful to me, you know," she said to Millie, who was sitting silently in the passenger seat with her mind God knew where.

"Dad?" Millie repeated with some surprise. ""He wouldn't even know how."

"Listen to you talk, Millie!"

"It's true, he's too awkward."

"Awkward? What makes you say such a thing?"

"He's awkward—walking that cat for one thing. He walks like he's stiff as a board with his head in the clouds and his stomach sticking out."

"He doesn't have a stomach!"

"Yes, he does. Not so big, but he pumps it out when he walks that cat, like he's walking the Dauphin in the Versailles gardens."

"The what? You should stop reading children's books, Millie!" Millie didn't answer, and she was gazing out the window in a fog.

"Why are you thinking about Dad being unfaithful?" Millie said, turning her head slowly to her mom and looking straight at her. The line of cars started to move, but Joanie could easily converse because it was really slow getting onto the freeway with the new lights right as you headed up the ramp.

"Just that I saw that woman on the car deck and started putting one and two together. Just being practical, that's all. Better not to be naïve."

"You mean Caroline?"

"Is that her name? How do you know her name?"

"She's around. You think Dad has something for Caroline?" Now Joanie was more confused. How did Millie get to be so familiar with this stranger? Did she know something Joanie didn't?

"You didn't tell me how you know her so well," Joanie insisted.

"I don't."

"But you know her name."

"Yea. Well, she brought some stuff to the Salvation Army when I was working there, and I took her name down then. I just remembered it. Caroline Waits. Because she's kind of striking. And then I asked her when she came in again, she's actually half Greek and she's the illegitimate daughter of a poet from out east and he came to Vancouver to be closer 'cause he's really sick."

"You sure think you know a lot. Striking is it. That's the trouble."

"It's not trouble to be beautiful, Mom. It's good to be beautiful."

"Honey bun, get real. She's a looker and your dad is a male guy. Figure it out."

"Figure what out?"

"To tell you the truth, I think she's the reason he's always at the building site."

"So what if that's true?"

"So what?" Now they were well on their way down Highway 101, headed for the turnoff to West Vancouver and the Lion's Gate Bridge. They had lots of time because it was going to take them at least half an hour to get to the hospital. "I'll tell you what's *so* about it. It's not decent for a man who's been married twenty-six years to get interested in other women all of a sudden. It's not right and it causes trouble."

"Not necessarily," Millie was arguing. "When I was taking that literature class over at Chatelech High at nights, the teacher Mr. Rosen was telling us about this old Italian writer named Dante and how he said that beautiful things take you closer to God. I mean people who are beautiful can do that, just because they make you do better things."

"I never heard such nonsense!" Joanie was getting upset at her daughter all of a sudden. Could it be that in this kind of dispute, Millie would actually take her dad's side? Did the girl have no moral fiber at all? Was she a complete airhead about right and wrong?

"Sweetie, you have no idea what you're talking about. Whoever this Dante guy is, he doesn't know anything about real life. You should have been taking a course in practical thinking instead."

Millie was looking at her mom with a slightly unhappy expression, but it was only temporary. Mostly Millie just had a really calm face.

"I can think, Mom," she said softly. There was a longer silence between them as they drove down the highway. The car engine was humming, and the noise of the road surrounded them. The fancy houses on the hill above loomed into view. Millie continued in the same slow, careful voice: "I went to the North Vancouver Memorial Library and found this book called *The World as Will and Representation* or something, by a guy called Schopenhauer. He's a famous German philosopher from the eighteen hundreds. Mr. Rosen said he was really hard and all. So I borrowed the book and took it home and read it. I discovered that I understood it."

"You understood the book?" Joanie repeated in mock-surprise. "You actually understood some guy by the name of Schopenhauer. That's quite a feat."

"I understood him," Millie said again. She was half smiling to herself, as if she had some sort of secret that pleased her.

"Well, I don't like it if your dad has ulterior motives for doing good things, volunteering in building and then paying big bucks to have a fancy dinner, if it's really on account of some woman."

"It doesn't matter," Millie said again. "Whatever makes you do good things is good in itself."

"You've been talking to your grandma too much already," Joanie half-joked. "I got half a mind to leave you outside while I'm visiting Guppy, what with all her talk about being close to God and charity work. I tell you, thinking that way can get you really naïve. And you know what I call that in plain language? I call it stupid. Just plain stupid."

"Sometimes wisdom seems really stupid," Millie was mumbling, as if almost to herself.

Where did that girl get such crazy ideas? Joanie hated to think it, but you had to be practical in this life or else people went around taking advantage of you, playing you for a dupe. And in all practicality, it had to be admitted that Millie was a bit of an airhead. She was a sweetie, but she was all confused.

Thinking about all this put Joanie in a bad mood. In her view, there was nothing redemptive about that Caroline. She suddenly resented having to go into Vancouver like this every Friday. Why couldn't her stepdad do this instead? Nick was always in Abbotsford—where Joanie herself grew up and where Guppy should be if they hadn't closed down all the care centers everywhere. Now you had to stay far away from home to get treatment. Used to be you could get your medical care at home and your family could visit you. Not any more. Nick was getting obsessed with his harmonica playing and his group (he had collected at least twenty-five harmonicas by now and kept them in a display case like a spice rack!). He and Frank and Tom had harmonica, bass and keyboard, and were playing in churches and rest homes out there. Actually, they were playing all over the Fraser Valley. Now they were even making CDs. Nick was pretty fanatical about morality after being married to some much younger woman who ran off like hell with all his money, and after that what could be more important than visiting Guppy? Joanie didn't know.

It was as if that bolt of lightning that struck made them both senseless, both Nick and Guppy. They just weren't the same afterward. It was a weird thing that happened, it's true, but you'd think after a while people would get back to being themselves. They'd think about it and realize it was just one of those freaks of nature. Nothing symbolic or significant after all. But what could you expect, really: a church full of half-believers listening to a sermon by an ineffective pastor, and then, boom! Down comes a bolt of lightning out of the blue and hits the pulpit—just when the pastor has said, "Speak to us, Lord, and show us the way," or something like that. It was the kind of incident to put fear in the hearts of the superstitious. After that, Guppy was sick with her brain tumor and Nick was making up songs with titles like "Jesus Breaks Every Fetter" and "Nearer My God to Thee." Not only did Guppy have a brain tumor, but she had become half-crazed with protestant superstition. Joanie had to listen to this babble every time she went to the hospital. Artie said to just take it on board like it was the illness at work. Nothing more than that. He was right, he was. The tumor in Guppy's head was pressing on her good sense.

They parked the car in the 13TH Avenue parkade at the hospital and walked up to the fourth floor where the Palliative Care Unit was. To get there they passed through a double door with glass. You could see down the hall to the various rooms and the people wandering in the halls. Although these people were sick and couldn't go home, they were not always bedridden. They meandered about the thin hallway and clustered sometimes in twos and threes by the window at the end. For the most part, they looked like the miserable dregs of society they probably imagined themselves to be. People who felt completely abandoned—not just by society, but by God, no doubt, Joanie thought. They looked so helpless, desperate and vacant. It was uncomfortable to come here. Joanie never could learn to not mind it. She wished her mother could be transferred to a smaller, local hospital. She'd gladly have gone to Abbotsford twice a month instead of here. If Guppy were there, Nick could visit her every day. But that was not to be. Voters in this province, like she never tired of telling Millie, got what they voted for: a cutback government that took no care of its elderly and disabled.

As they reached the end of the hall, a very thin woman in a loose cotton dress and fuzzy slippers, with white hair and skin the color of sour milk and with some device in her nose, suddenly latched onto Millie. The woman flung herself on the floor in front of Millie and grabbed her loose slacks. "Pray for me!" shouted the old woman, looking up at Millie as if the girl were the Madonna herself. "Pray for me!" Millie stood there looking at the woman at her feet. Then, the most extraordinary thing happened. Instead of shying away or moving away in disgust, Millie put her hand very nicely on the woman's head, on top of her hair that was like a spider web, so thin and fine, and said, "Yes, I will. I'll do that for you." The old woman let go and seemed satisfied; she stood up again, fussing with the business of getting up on her feet. Joanie and Millie continued on their way to Guppy's room. Joanie was going to comment on the scene, but somehow no words came. She looked at her awkward, slightly overweight, pale daughter with the expressionless, calm face. What was *that* about? Joanie had to wonder.

Guppy was up, sitting in a green chair beside the bed, when they walked into her room. She was wearing a dark blue robe with a flowery blouse under—clearly dressed up for the visit. Her bone-white hair was neatly combed, and she had her glasses on. She even had regular shoes on and white socks. She obviously just had her morning bath routine and was newly dressed. She looked none too sprightly, though. Guppy had become very pale living in this place, and dark gray patches were forming on her face and arms. Her eyes looked like pools of blue water in a place that's been too dry for too long. When they walked in, Guppy looked up and smiled. They pulled up two chairs and seated themselves around her. Guppy was smiling wordlessly, first at Joanie, then at Millie, where she kept her gaze. There was an awkward silence for a bit. Then Guppy took Millie's hands in her lap and kept them there, holding her own hands gently over the girl's.

"Little Millie, little Millie, have you come to see me today?" Guppy intoned in her fragile, papery voice as she shook the girl's hands a bit for emphasis.

"Yes, I've come to see you, Grandma," Millie said. "Are you feeling all right?"

"I'm feeling all right, dear, sure," Guppy said again. Then they just sat there, the two of them, while Joanie looked on. They actually sat there like lovers. Like *lovers*—staring into each other's eyes as if they hadn't seen each other for a long time. Joanie couldn't relate to this. She seated herself by the open window and felt the warm summer breeze float in. She could hear the sounds of the city out there, in among the leaves of maples and chestnuts below.

"Tell me that story again," Millie was saying to her grandma. "I want to hear that story of the lightning." Guppy smiled knowingly but also happily. Joanie was feeling a little exasperated. She knew why Millie was asking for *that* story again, the one Joanie had heard already a hundred times. It was because Guppy was happy when she told it, and Millie was just trying to make her happy. But it wasn't right. It couldn't be—making the old woman go over that again and again. But she couldn't stop Millie from having whatever conversation she wanted with her grandma. It's a free country—still. Thank God for that. Guppy was preening herself for the tale—getting into her storytelling trance or whatever it was that came over her. She was talking in a way that made it sound like it just took place yesterday when actually it was at least five years ago.

"We were in the Bethel Church, you know, up on Gladwin Road," Guppy was saying in a voice that was like dry onion skin peeling off. "Just sitting there. It wasn't a special day or anything. Nickie almost didn't go that morning. I kind of had to drag him out on Sundays, you know." At this, Guppy chuckled. She was fond of Nick, clearly. That was one thing to be thankful for, wasn't it? Joanie was thinking to herself. Guppy was going on. "It was a hot day in the fall, when thunderstorms sometimes come in from the mountains out east. We weren't unprepared for a thunderstorm. That wasn't it. Sometimes we get one in the valley, and it comes with a lot of rain afterward too. The air was kind of heavy—made you a little light-headed. There was an orange haze over everything too. But we were sitting there and the pastor—oh, he was new, Pastor Corrie was, so young and just from seminary in Saskatoon—was giving his sermon, he was saying about God, *Light of the World, You stepped down into darkness, opened my eyes and let me see. . . .* It was a quiet morning—nobody comes out that early in Abbotsford, not even on the freeway. He was talking about how we don't see it when God talks to us, so we think he isn't there. Even when we see Him we don't recognize Him, you see. You know in the proverbs, dear. Where it says—*Every word of God is pure: He is a shield unto them that put their trust in Him. . . .*" Joanie decided she had to interrupt the story before her mom got too carried away.

"Mom, did you get your medicines this morning—the steroids?" she broke into Guppy's monologue. Guppy stopped short and seemed quite confused, but only for a moment.

"Yes, dear, they always remember the medications. But I don't know what good they're doing. It just makes me puff up like a balloon." Then she looked at Millie with the same appreciative face. "But what can you do? It's what they think is best, and so you let them, don't you, dear?" Millie nodded. They were quiet for a moment, then Guppy went on with her story. "I know why he was saying that—they were afraid of a thinning of the congregation, you know, a real thinning out. The old folks would be the only ones left. The young ones wouldn't see any reason to be coming. So they had a real nice Valentine's dinner there at the church—a buffet in the social room, with a big hoola hoop hanging from the ceiling to symbolize a wedding ring, you know." She chuckled at this softly. Joanie knew her mom often volunteered in the kitchen at the church. Guppy was going on. "I don't know what the young people go to any more—do you?"

Millie laughed a little. "Maybe they just watch MuchMusic on television," she offered. Guppy sighed, but not in a sad way. She made a sound that seemed to say the young people could do what they wanted, it wouldn't hurt them.

"But Pastor Corrie, you see, he was in the middle of saying this, and the thunderstorm outside picked up—we could hear the rain on the roof. It's a wood-construction church, after all. Then a bolt of lightning just came through the ceiling. It happened before we knew what next. A searing flash broke the roof and crashed the pulpit. It only lasted a moment, but there was a hole in the roof and the speaker's podium was broken, and there was a smell of charred wood and something electric, like a kettle you haven't washed out for too long. A tinny smell. The pastor stopped talking of course and just stood there in amazement. Speechless, really, because he could have been hit. The folks in the church, well, they didn't say a thing either. Everybody simply sat there like something had just dropped right out of the sky—which it did, you know." Guppy nodded to herself, but laughed silently as well. The story amused her, even though it also awed her.

"Did they give you breakfast, Mom?" Joanie broke in again, determined not to let this conversation get emotional.

"Oh, yes, but I don't have an appetite. They tried to get me to have yogurt."

"You should eat, Mom. It's the only way to be healthy. It won't help you at all to stop eating your meals." Guppy looked at Joanie tiredly.

"Whether I eat or not, it doesn't seem to matter, dear. It just doesn't matter. Things run their course anyway." Then Guppy looked at Joanie as if she saw her for the first time. "You seem grumpy today, my dear. Is there something the matter?"

"Mom's in a bad mood because she thinks Dad has got interested in another woman all of a sudden," Millie blurted out. Joanie was surprised and shocked.

"Millie!" she scolded to imply she shouldn't be telling their secret.

"If that happens, Joanie dear, it won't have been you that's done it," Guppy said slowly. "You're still a good wife and . . ." Guppy's voice trailed off and she slipped into a paralysis of a kind. She sat in her chair leaning to the side a bit, looking down, her glasses slipping from her nose onto her cheek, her hands holding Millie's in her lap, and she didn't move. Millie began to shake her grandma and whisper, "Grandma, Grandma, did you fall asleep? Grandma?" But Joanie knew what was happening. She had seen it enough times before. She rushed out into the hall to find a nurse. After a few minutes she came back with one of the nurses—someone new they hadn't seen on the ward before.

"She's got one of her seizures again," Joanie explained loudly. Then to Millie: "Honey, don't worry about it. She gets these all the time." The nurse removed Millie's hands from her grandma's lap, and Millie had to step away while the two women fussed over Guppy, saying, "Can you hear me, Guppy? Can you hear me, Mrs. Hemshaw?" She could of course. Guppy could hear and see everything; she was fully conscious, Joanie knew that. She just couldn't move, that's all.

Two hours later, Joanie and Millie were headed back over the Lion's Gate Bridge. They had managed to get Guppy back into bed after she got over her seizure. They were lasting longer now, Joanie couldn't help noticing. It used to be that her seizures lasted maybe one or two minutes. Now they went on for at least ten. The doctor said it might happen that she'd go into one of these and just not get out of it again. The seizure would simply take over. Guppie was also having seizures more often. It was the kind of thing you couldn't sit and wait for. You had to go on with your life, and if something was going to happen suddenly over at the hospital, well then, nobody could prevent it. They couldn't give her any more steroids. If they did, Guppy would just burst! She was already getting maximum dose. But going on with her life didn't seem so appealing to Joanie right now. Why should it? If your husband was just going to start stalking some model? Because that Caroline was of a different class. She wouldn't pay any mind to a guy like Artie. But the thing about Artie—and Millie got it from him, no doubt—he didn't know that. He thought he was . . . well, what did he think? That he was cooler than he really is? Artie was awkward, but he had these *pretensions.* Not like Millie, though. Millie had no pretensions at all. She was different that way. When they got to the Park Royal Mall in West Vancouver, Joanie just drove on up Taylor Way and didn't stop.

"Mom?" Millie said softly. "I thought you were going to stop here and look for a dress or something?"

"I decided not to!" It was unequivocal, nonnegotiable now. Joanie was not going to go into competition with that kind of thing. That sort of *fighting to keep your man* was so clichéd. Joanie had decided she would let Artie figure things out. He had to take her for who she was! Millie didn't say anything more. She seemed to know why instinctively or, more likely, she didn't know anything and had just drifted off into her own dream world. They drove on up the highway toward Horseshoe Bay. As they rounded the bend somewhere above Westmount Road, the mountain rose more sharply on the right, and on the left the view over the water in Burrard Inlet presented itself far below. It was really beautiful, that had to be admitted. The sky was a bit hazy—a tinge of rose in it—and the tankers anchored in the strait were sitting there like toys. The skyline of downtown Vancouver hovered in the background, peacefully. Joanie suddenly drove onto the shoulder and stopped the car. She put the gear into park and pulled the hand brake. The motor hummed low. The two of them sat there for a while in silence.

"Mom?" Millie whispered. She used the same voice she had used with Guppy when Guppy went off the radar. "What's the matter, Mom?"

"I just wanted to look at the view," Joanie announced. Her voice was false, she could tell that herself. Why was she trying to keep up an appearance with Millie now? Maybe she was just convincing herself she was all right? "The clouds are gathering up ahead," she said.

"Yea. Maybe we'll have thunder," Millie speculated out loud. Joanie guffawed a little hoarsely at that.

"Maybe another thunderbolt will hit something," Joanie said distractedly. They sat in silence for a while.

"I was reading this book on Nordic mythology over at the library," Millie then said, quite out of the blue, "and it said our ancestors used to believe there was a god for thunder. Name of Thor."

"Thor." Joanie wasn't paying attention, really.

"Yea. When thunder struck in the old days, it was Thor striking his hammer, and the sparks went out in all directions." She looked at Joanie again. "His hammer was something called *Mjollnir*, and the gods were in a place called Asgard."

"Was this Thor building stuff?" Joanie was trying to joke but it didn't come off.

"Maybe. He was just a god for regular people. Sort of a god for right and wrong."

"Well maybe he was building a visitor center in this Asgard place!" The suppressed emotion was coming out in Joanie's voice. "Maybe he had a Siberian cat he walked on a leash too!" Millie was looking at her mom, furrowing her brow.

"I think there's a wolf there. Called *Fenrir* or something. I don't now if the gods walked the wolf on a leash, though." Millie paused a moment, then said, "Actually, I think the wolf was sort of like a demon. He was the son of *Loki*. The gods chained him to a rock inside the earth called *Gjoll,* with this magic ribbon they called *Gleipnir.* . . ."

"You're sure reading a lot these days, Millie." Joanie was trying to make idle conversation.

"Well, it's true, though. That's what our Norwegian ancestors believed. They were sure that Thor would protect them from harm. They had special ceremonies for that." Joanie was looking at Millie now. Suddenly, it seemed to her that Millie might not be such an airhead after all. Maybe she actually had been learning something. All by herself at home, while the baby slept, and this boy Hart was up in Powell River working in a mill. Maybe all those trips to the North Van library were even educating her?

"Is this true?" she asked her daughter. She was asking quite seriously. Millie nodded.

"Yea." They were sitting in the car quietly. The clouds were forming more rapidly over the mountains, coming from Squamish it seemed. A wind was picking up. Soon it would be pushing the treetops around. Below, in a sheer drop with the stark-looking granite, the water seemed bleak in the afternoon sun. The haze filtered everything as if through a colored lens. The road to the ferry looked like a pale strip between the two, a ribbon that wound its way along the mountainside. "Yea," Millie repeated, lost in thoughts of her own. "That's what our ancestors believed." Joanie found herself gripping the steering wheel so tightly that her knuckles were turning white. She was getting pretty tense—just couldn't relax her muscles. A cramp was building in her right calf, where she pushed her foot on the gas. The cramp was traveling down into her toes, and her toes were curling up in pain, gripped by involuntary muscular contractions. She felt the back of her neck getting stiff.

"I feel like I'm losing control," she said awkwardly to Millie, apropos of nothing. "I feel as if I'm losing control."

"Control of what, Mom?"

"Just . . . just everything. First your grandma—she's my mom, she's always been there—first she's dying. Then you . . . you seem, well, going in some different direction, like I'm losing you to something . . . to your books or . . . I don't know. Then Artie, your dad— I think I'm losing my hold there too. . . ." She took a deep breath and let what she just uttered sink in. She didn't know she was going to say such things, let alone talk like that to Millie. She never talked like that to her daughter. She was the one who was always giving her daughter instructions. The girl needed advice—this was a case in point. Proved her point. Several moments passed while her daughter was looking at her a bit clumsily, obviously puzzled.

"You can't control everything, Mom," Millie then said, softly, in her gentle Millie way.

"It's just my own life I wanted to manage." Joanie was defending herself.

"You can't even control that, Mom. You shouldn't even try." More silence passed as the clouds had grown quite steel-colored and the rain began to come down. A storm was coming, that was clear. The rain would pelt onto the velvety orange-colored water below the Trans-Canada Highway. Joanie sat uncomfortably, feeling the muscles on her neck stiffen and the back of her mouth turning into a sore throat. She was just going to sit here until this passed. It would pass. She knew it would pass in a moment. It had to pass.

Angels Hide Their Faces

Daniel tried to reason with Rose. He set aside one evening in the fall after she had been writing again for a while and taking the blows too hard. To him, as a bystander and observer, this writing thing was a tough business and more trouble than it was worth. He sat Rose down at the kitchen table (the sapwood and heartwood tabletop she took such care in choosing back when she could enjoy their lovely home) and told her with as much empathy as he could find: "Rose, we've got to talk." She knew all his thoughts already but agreed to talk anyway. He put a bottle of Merlot and two glasses on the table. Rose had her light brown hair tied back in a short ponytail, and loose strands were hanging down the side of her face. She sat there in her coconut-colored blouse and rested her cheek in her hand. She just looked at him with that sad face of hers as if she were thinking *you don't understand.* Daniel resented the implication. What's to understand? You see someone being destroyed in front of you, what's not to understand about it?

"Just tell me, Rose," he said, "why you feel you have to do this? What exactly are you getting back?"

"If you write you're not counting every little thing you may or may not be getting back from it," Rose said.

"How's that? What is it you're *not counting*?"

"Whatever it is you mean. Money, for one. Good reviews or whatever."

"You mean number of readers. You're not even counting number of readers."

"No."

"So tell me you don't count number of readers, you don't count money paid to you, you don't count good reviews. What *are* you counting as a return on this investment?"

"You talk about this as if it were a problem in accounting or something."

"Well, in a way it is."

"No, it's not." And then she started with the tears. He could never talk with her about her writing without her crying. He simply didn't get it. He had to try, though. He marshaled his arguments.

"Look, I'm just trying to make this seem reasonable to me. As far as I can see, this is how it looks: you suffer once in your life, you suffer again when you write about it in such detail and you suffer a third time when readers either don't appreciate or understand, or downright dislike it. You're beating yourself up! What could be worth that?"

"You forget something. You forget that it's healing for me to write. It's also healing for me to have others participate in it. By publishing it as a book. And lots of people appreciate it. It's just that I get obsessive about bad reviews. I can learn to stop that. There are good reviews too."

"I think you're just opening yourself up to abuse. Setting yourself up for more pain."

"I think I'm staking a claim in the atmosphere, somehow."

He looked at her severely. What on Earth did she mean by that? "What do you mean?"

"I mean making myself heard. Making myself real somehow."

"Don't you feel real? What's going on?"

She sighed as if to say she didn't think there was much point in the conversation. "No. As a matter of fact, I don't. It's more important to me than all the other things you mention—more important even than being happy to feel that I'm real and that I exist."

"Can't you do that without you going though all this pain?"

"Apparently not."

That was the conversation. Daniel had gone over it again and again. He tried to look at all the angles. As far as he could see, Rose simply needed to do this. Her attitude was that he could support her or not, but she was in it for life. He felt a familiar surge of resentment. He had to admit—although only to himself because saying this to Rose would be just suicide—it was almost as if she cared more about her writing thing than about him. Maybe she was hoping it would all come together for her someday, but meanwhile she was willing to sacrifice her family and everything else. How could he be expected to keep putting up with this much longer? This being put aside, being less important to her than her writing? This excessive emotional life about something that was neither here nor there? Most people got obsessive like that about love affairs or something.

Whoever heard of having such feelings of betrayal and attachment over what you *wrote*? And it seemed people out there—readers and reviewers and even publishers and bookstore owners—didn't know what they were dealing with. Just didn't have a clue they had life and death in their hands. Or, if they did realize it, they had decided they didn't care. If that was the case, writers should know what they're getting into and take the consequences.

Daniel Card took a moment to pause by the window of the corner office in the second tower at Burnaby's Metrotown, where he worked on the tenth floor as the manager of his law office, Currier, Wang & Donaldson. He could see the gray and charcoal rooftops of the buildings below, the streets cutting at chaotic angles, the skyscrapers jutting up from the landscape, the occasional grove of green, bushy trees and parkland, and patches of water. It was overcast today but warm. At least the sun wouldn't be beating into his glass office and making it uncomfortably hot. He had learned long ago to wear only a light shirt under his jacket, so when the heat rose he could take his jacket off. Today was his fortieth birthday. He didn't know what Rose had planned, if anything. They had talked briefly about going out for dinner, but he couldn't be sure what condition he would find Rose in: mildly depressed? Depressed? Severely depressed? He could never be quite sure.

At the firm of Currier, Wang & Donaldson, it was Daniel's job to look after the details; he was good at that, and he knew it was the details that got you. Daniel was no theorist. He liked the solid ground of facts—like his father, Timothy Card, noted biochemist, retired fifteen years ago, getting on but still working. His father had made the transition nicely, setting up his office at home and continuing to be adjunct professor at Simon Fraser. They were going to get together next weekend to celebrate his birthday—he and Rose, his dad and his mom Gail. But it was only Tuesday today. The weekend seemed a long way off. It always did. Every Monday started like an elephant lumbering out of a muddy lake, where it's been cooling itself in the water, spraying itself as the sun's glow settles on the stale surface of the lake. He had seen images like this on the nature programs he and his dad watched when he was a kid. He still liked those images: the sandy banks of the water, the dry scrub grass, the elephant's trunk circling in the air, sending a cascade of droplets over its head while the sunset turned its face and the edges of its ears pink. Whenever something didn't go smoothly or he and Rose had disagreements, Daniel watched the National Geographic channel. It was comforting. It reminded him of when he was a kid and his parents took care of everything.

Now he was the one who had to take care of things. He liked it that way, but he had to admit that, even at age forty, he still wasn't used to it. He managed the whole firm and had his own clients as well. People looked to him for everything from invoices to court proceedings. He was taking on more clients now, and his aim was to move out of the managerial and into the purely legal work. Eventually, maybe in fifteen years or so, he could become a partner himself. Who knew? It would be Currier, Card & Donaldson because Joe Wang was going to be the first to go. He was the oldest. But Daniel was daydreaming, he knew. It's just that your fortieth birthday didn't come every morning. It turned out to mean more to him than he had anticipated, this business of turning forty. He felt like he was becoming an adult all of a sudden. Not that he wasn't before, it's just that when you turn forty the realization hits you on the head that you're not a kid any more. You've joined the ranks. The fun is over. You've got responsibilities, and no one will look after you if you don't. From now on, life will be a matter of just getting older and older and older. He'd be in this tower—this glass emporium in Burnaby—forever, having his lunch every day in the food court of the Metrotown shopping mall, the yogurt curried vegetables and tandoori chicken at the Indian food stand. Always taking his coffee break in the square outside by the sky train station, his Starbucks latté or mocha, always sitting on the bench, always watching the people file by as they came out of the train, professionals in their suits and heels standing around with cigarettes hanging from their lips and fingers, talking as if what they had to say was important. It wasn't. What they said to each other was seldom important: just inflated shoptalk. Daniel was more and more impressed by the sense that they were all living in a bubble of detail that, like the dot-com bubble, would just burst one day. This whole tower would blow—from the inside.

Tonight, if Rose's mood was not too low, they would go to the Italian restaurant down on Hamilton for dinner, the Villa del Lupo. It was a place they reserved for special occasions. They had dined there when his dad Timothy turned sixty-five and when his mom turned sixty (he remembered they'd had some sort of terrine of roasted vegetables and bufala mozzarella and saffron olive oil. . . .) They went there when Rose turned thirty-five. Now they might go on his fortieth. The Villa del Lupo had accumulated a lot of memories for him; it was where he proposed to Rose in the first place. He brought the engagement ring and gave it to her right there, during dinner. They had one of the private rooms, the one with the fireplace and the cozy round table with high-backed chairs. She put the ring on then and there. She was happy. That was a good memory because, on the whole, Rose had become very unhappy. You could see it in her drawn face—tense much of the time. Her pallid blue eyes were like water, and they somehow sunk into themselves. Her thin lips were drawn on her face like stiff pencil lines. Her dull blonde hair was lifeless, almost colorless. Her skin was pale. She looked stressed, like she'd been drained of vitality just recently. That sense of her, that the drain on her energy had to be recent, was something that somehow attracted him. It made him want to try to help. Of course, he'd learned he never could. She was beyond normal help. Rose's depression was deep, in some dark chasm all her own. Otherwise, though, you couldn't tell. Outwardly, she functioned well, was good socially and was a good companion.

The reason for Rose's trauma was so clear they didn't have to talk about it and never had. Perhaps it would be better if it were more complicated? But this was so cruelly simple. Rose's sister Emma had been abducted six years ago, assaulted and left to die in the woods outside of Saskatoon. Daniel could still feel the surge of sheer terror that went through them when the police officer appeared at the door—Officer Ainsworth, he said he was—a nice looking middle-aged policeman doing one of his horrid duties. *Notifying the family.* News like that makes you speechless. There isn't anything to say. Now Daniel and Rose sometimes just spent their evenings in glum silence: no music, no television, the dusk settling over the chestnut leather sofas and ottoman, the dark oak floor, the mahogany roll-top desk, the steel floor lamp in the corner by the French doors. Rose wouldn't turn on the lights, and he didn't force the issue. Let her go through this, however long it takes, was his attitude. He figured she'd slowly come out of it—but it didn't seem to be happening. She went into that dark cavern in her mind and simply stayed there.

Rose was a writer, a journalist doing op-ed and a little reporting. She worked freelance. When Emma was murdered, Rose stopped working and started on her book: *The Length and Depth of Water.* She told the story of Emma and her, right up to Emma's tragic end—until the moment Officer Ainsworth came to tell them the news. But submerging herself in writing the story didn't help Rose. The opposite happened: it was only after her book was published that Rose started to have nightmares. She woke up in a sweat, her heart pounding, even palpitating. Her nerves were frazzled, and she couldn't handle the smallest thing going wrong. Living with her became more and more of a strain. He didn't tell her that. It would be cruel, on top of everything else, to say you're tired of your wife's grief. But after a while he was. Truth be told, he got very tired of it. Daniel Card wished his wife would snap out of it, like they said. Just *snap out of it.*

Daniel started to worry more seriously the morning of the first review. What was it about reviews and writers? Some mysterious connection only they know about. To listen to Rose, you would think writing a book would be its own reward, and it wouldn't matter what one scribbling reader says in a newspaper. Especially when the book was something as personal as Rose's. But her friend Sally (Rose's journalist connection who worked for the *Vancouver Sun*) telephoned one evening right after *Water* came out and told her there would be a review in next morning's paper. That night Rose couldn't sleep. She tossed and turned, got up, made tea, watched TV, wandered around the house. After a while Daniel got up too. How was he supposed to sleep when she was roaming about like that? By five in the morning she figured the paper would be out, and she threw her yellow, over-sized raincoat over her blue pajamas with clouds all over them and went out in the car in her pompom slippers. Hair uncombed. Face puffy from no sleep. She drove away like crazy in the black morning, rain pouring down, to find a paper. Eventually, she found one and brought it home. There was this frantic sense about her, like somebody too hungry to eat properly. Just frazzled nerves. The review was bad. Said she was self-indulgent or something. Some librarian at Vancouver General Library named Julie Barthe wrote that thing, probably trying to score some points for herself at Rose's expense. How Daniel wished that idiot hadn't written those words. Couldn't the reviewer just say something noncommittal? Or write about the good things and forget about the other stuff? But no. This scribbler had to dwell on everything she didn't like about the book. Rose was crushed, and that really was the beginning. She hadn't recovered. She couldn't. No matter what Daniel said or did, Rose couldn't get over this review. It made Daniel want to go over and knock that woman down. As he stood there by the window looking at the white sky, Daniel felt the old surge of anger that had beset him. Still, the whole thing—book and all—was getting tiresome.

"Thought you'd be hard at work, son!" a booming voice Daniel recognized sounded from the doorway of the office. He turned around.

"Hey, Dad!" His parents didn't often come to his workplace. "What brings you all the way out here?" They gave each other that handshake-hug they'd been using for all these years. His dad was looking in great shape: the white hair and sky-blue cardigan, the hush-puppy sneakers. He looked like a man of true leisure.

"It's your birthday, isn't it?" his dad explained, smiling.

Daniel laughed dismissively. "I guess." Daniel tried to look non-committal.

"Just thought I'd stop by for the occasion. Maybe you'd be free for lunch or something."

"I'll check. Can you hang on?" Daniel went to Suzette at the front desk to look at his schedule, shifted a couple of appointments and told her he'd be out with his dad for lunch. Timothy agreed to meet him at noon downstairs in the lobby of the building, where all the executives stood around smoking. It wasn't something Daniel had expected: his dad didn't usually come by like this. Was something up?

Daniel "loitered" a bit inside his private office next to the meeting room. He called it loitering when he stole a few moments from the back-to-back schedule of meetings his days were usually composed of. He was seeing a client in a quarter of an hour—a new client who wanted something but who wouldn't tell Suzette over the phone. Something to do with a will. But Daniel felt he had more pressing things to think about just now. He really had to resolve this issue with Rose. But Daniel had become increasingly certain that her depression and paranoia about writing either had to be treated like an illness, in which case she should get proper help, or she should stop doing it. Mostly, he thought she should just stop. Everything would come out right again if she stopped writing and went back to being the girl he met on Kitsilano Beach so many years ago when they were students at UBC. They were bathing on the sand, knocking a beach ball around, joking and laughing with their friends. Eating Mexican on 4th Avenue. Dancing on the lawn in the backyard with the barbecue going and dahlias growing everywhere. Never for a moment did he anticipate her sinking into a quagmire he didn't understand.

He struggled to keep those early memories in mind but the hard moments of the recent past involuntarily and persistently crowded into his mind. As if they were devils inside him that kept taunting him. The time Rose asked him to leave the house so she could get some time to herself—when he actually had to stay over at his parents' place. The time she fell into this bout of weeping that wouldn't stop, no matter what he suggested. She kept on crying. She even suggested a divorce once. He had to persuade her she was just a bit depressed and the feeling would go away. Which it seemed to. But only for a little while. How was he—Daniel Card, lawyer, turning forty, who actually wanted a family—how was he supposed to live with this day after day? Sometimes when the thoughts came this way, they seemed like an old mantra. As if he were remembering these things simply to persuade himself that he *should* divorce Rose. Like his office mate next door, Neil Parkington, who divorced his wife. Was he just looking for a rationale? Daniel was afraid it would come to that. Maybe that's what he would give himself for his birthday: a divorce from Rose. Let her live with her words and books and her despair. It's what she wanted!

At this, Daniel was feeling self-righteous and even a bit cruel. He had a life too, didn't he? He put his head in his hands on the big desk. The schedule book lay opened before him; the white desk computer; the olive green tea cup; the white office telephone and, yes, his picture of Rose, a black and white photo his mother Gail took when they were first engaged. In the picture Rose had her old winning smile, and her hair was shiny and fell in waves over her bare shoulders. It was all so contradictory and unnecessary. This was the real Rose before she had been snatched and her place taken by this other Rose, this writer. This writer of books whom he didn't even know anymore and certainly didn't understand, who asked him to participate in a life-project that was not his own and which he didn't want to be involved in. Perhaps at lunch he'd actually own up and talk to his dad about it. He'd go ahead and tell his dad they were having problems. Get the matter out in the open. Maybe even say he was thinking about divorce.

His eyes were drawn to those two ceramic sculptures Rose gave him a year ago. Rose said they were angels, and she bought them for him to put on his desk, though they were hardly distinguishable as angels, looking more like two fallen figures leaning against a couple of boulders. They were glazed white, and their pale yellow wings, if that's what was behind their backs, were broken. Daniel couldn't imagine why she wanted him to have them. Maybe because she liked them herself. She got them at an auction. Sometimes she went to auctions just to pass the time. She said it was interesting to her: the strange tension in the air, the deadlines coming down to seconds, the mad grab for final bids, the strange collection of people, all with different agendas. No doubt it was the writer in Rose that made her interested. She said you get a good look behind the scenes of people's lives at events like that. Maybe you do. These sculptures were not bad as art goes, but he disliked the motif. They were sad. Why all this unhappiness? Rose had become downright attracted to unhappy things. She was also making a point of it: she had lost all color, never wore makeup or put on any jewelry or colorful clothes. She wore white and beige cotton and hemp. That was her style now.

All of a sudden Daniel found himself thinking of the Indian woman at the New Delhi Indian Cuisine, where he went every day for lunch. She was working in one of these offices somewhere and also took her lunch at the New Delhi. He didn't know her name. Had never talked to her. But she was so incredibly pretty. She was actually beautiful: her sleek black hair, her long slender neck, her shiny painted lips and filigree silver earrings. She wore silk suits and always had a scarf on in some bright version of pecan or gold. One evening when he was late getting out of the office, he passed her in the square between the two towers. She was rushing off somewhere in the most amazing skirt. It was a patchwork of lavenders and lilacs and turquoise, and she had a bright cerise shawl over a small top. The way her dress flew in the air was memorable—it was like she just descended from sky or something. Maybe he would sit down at her table some day. Get to know her. He could just take his tray over and ask if he could sit down. She was always alone, reading something in a magazine. He could do that. . . .

"Your client has arrived," Suzette was saying in her perky, high-pitched voice. She had opened the door during his reverie and was standing in the doorway. Daniel lifted his head from his hands where he had been lost in thoughts of this unknown woman at an Indian food stand. He didn't feel the least bit guilty—but he felt interrupted. Suzette was a big smiler, her hair dyed red and her low-cut neckline revealing the huge pewter and onyx pendant she always wore.

"I didn't hear you come in."

"I knocked, but you didn't answer."

"All right. Thanks anyway. Who is this guy?" She walked over in her black and white dress suit with a sheet of paper and put it on his desk in front of him.

"Name is Sanderson Waits. He's actually in a wheelchair."

"Oh." Daniel got up and moved the green leather chairs so there would be room for a wheelchair. The sun outside was getting starker, so he slung his suit jacket over the back of his desk chair. The two ceramic angels were almost hidden in the pile of manila folders and papers he hadn't been through yet, the post-it notes and his overflowing in-box. Suzette went out to get the man. Daniel had to push himself to return his attention to work. His mind had been wandering all morning and he was finding it hard to concentrate. It wasn't turning out to be a good day, this fortieth birthday of his. As he stood there pushing papers on his desk to the side, the man wheeled into the office. Daniel looked at him and walked over to greet him.

Daniel was taken aback. He had never seen such an unusual figure before. He had a full, snow-white head of hair that fell like silk over his forehead and down behind his ears, and wire-rimmed glasses under bushy black eyebrows. He was wearing all black: a dark cape over a shiny, satin shirt black as night. His trousers were charcoal and his leather shoes had the sheen of coal. He had very pale skin, ashen-blue eyes and his full lips had the most pleasant smile Daniel had ever seen. His hands were rugged, gripping the wheel of the chair as he approached the cherry wood desk. There was something wise and serene about him.

They shook hands. "I'm Daniel Card," he said. "You're Mr. Waits?"

"Doctor Sanderson Waits, yes."

"Pardon me, Doctor Waits." Daniel sat down in his desk chair. "What brings you here?" He watched while his new client fetched something from a briefcase he had perched on the chair back. A vague memory was materializing. A book Rose had been reading with a name on it something like this man's name. He remembered it because the author also had two last names. Rose had tried to get him to read it, but he never did. She was quite taken with the book, Daniel remembered that well. It was during the summer when they were having their worst rows. She was reading this book of poems from Greece, and the author was Sanderson something. Rose had repeatedly recited a line from that book that now popped into Daniel's mind, something like *who can decide, if not our readers—all five or fifty or five hundred of them, if a poet really has more than five hundred true readers at any given time. . . .*

"Well, I have something I'd like you to take care of," Sanderson Waits was saying. "A kind of final request, if you like."

"Sure," Daniel said. As he waited for permission to see what was in the papers, he decided to venture a question. "You wouldn't be a writer of books of poems, would you? I remember a poet with a name like yours." The man looked up and started laughing lightly, pleasantly.

"Why, yes. That would be correct."

"My wife was reading a book of Greek poems. Would that fit?"

"Yes, I lived on Santorini for quite a while. Published more than one book from that place."

"That's right!" Daniel said, remembering now. "It *was* about Santorini." The mention triggered another memory, but not as pleasant. The book was about having cancer or something and being in Greece, which was why Daniel refused to read it, no matter how many times Rose asked him to. He told her then he was not going to spend time indulging misery. What he wanted was for her to stop showering herself with books by people with diseases like cancer and AIDS, and people who have been assaulted in childhood, or whatever it was she was reading all the time. He looked inquisitively at this man who was very sympathetic, somehow. Daniel liked him instinctively, in spite of a sense of premonition that was growing.

"Well, I'm an English professor at McGill University," the man said by way of explanation. "I got cancer of the spine several years ago and went on medical leave. I've been back since, but I've had several treatments, and every time I do, I go on leave for a while. I had a place on Santorini and that's where I lived when I was recovering. I also lived in northern Italy for a while."

"Sorry to hear all that," Daniel interjected.

"Well, I did a lot of walking on Santorini and in Rimini before I was confined to this wheelchair, you know," he added and laughed lightly. "I had an increasingly hard time walking around. Not just because I was getting worse, but because the island of Santorini was getting worse too." He was smiling gently.

"Oh?"

"Yes." Sanderson Waits was looking directly at Daniel. "It's the tourism. So much there has changed—and for the worse, I'd say. Even though the water is still the color of crystal and the houses are chalk white and the roofs are all rust-brown, and the crooked olive trees are still there with arthritic branches and roots showing like veins up and down the trunks, it's less and less Santorini and more and more a tourist trap. The same plastic bags there as everywhere else."

"I see."

"But it served its purpose up till the end."

"Yes."

"What I've come to see you about," Sanderson Waits went on, "is something I've wanted to get off my chest for a while now. And I'm afraid I better get it done."

"That's fine," Daniel said. He was quite stunned by his client. Something engrossing about him.

"It's not my will as such."

"Oh, I thought it might be that."

"No, that was done in Montréal long ago, when I learned I had cancer."

"All right."

"This is an extra thing. What I want is for you to send a letter to certain people—but only after I die. I have a provisional diagnosis from my doctors, which tells me I don't have many months left. Perhaps as few as three."

"I'm very sorry."

"I don't have the energy right now to deal with the responses I might get from these letters. I really just want these people of mine—because they all mean something special to me—to receive my words to them specially and not have to respond."

"All right. How many letters are we talking about?"

"I have one letter, but I want you to copy it to twelve people. When you hear of my death—and I have left instructions that you are to be informed right away—I simply want you to send the letters in the post."

"Fine." Daniel found himself clearing his throat unnecessarily. Sanderson Waits handed him an envelope and then a list of names and addresses.

"Here is the list of the people to whom copies of this letter are to go."

"And do you want me to read it first?"

"If you wish. You should know what you send, although it's quite personal in nature. Nothing of concern to you legally, really. Just my ruminations as I go, so to speak." Then he leaned back in his wheelchair and looked at Daniel directly. "I'll leave a cheque with your assistant for the service," he added.

"That's fine, Mr. Waits—Doctor Waits, I mean. It all sounds a bit sad, but if I can help in this way, then that's what I'm here for."

"Good." He began to wheel his way out of the office. Daniel held the door open for him. As Sanderson Waits turned into the corridor, he looked back at Daniel and said, "Your wife is interested in poetry?"

"Yes. As a matter of fact, she writes poems herself."

"What's her name?"

"You wouldn't know her. Rose Carreras. She writes under the name Rose Carreras."

"Yes, I think I do know her," Sanderson Waits said hesitantly. "She wrote a book called *The Length and Depth of Water*, didn't she?" Daniel was surprised. Here was a knockdown surprise he hadn't expected.

"Yes, she did." His voice sounded strangely small to him.

"I read it," Sanderson Waits said. "It's a very fine book."

Daniel was clearing his throat again. "I'll tell her you said that."

"Please do. In fact, there was a time last year when it helped me a lot."

"Oh?"

"Yes. I found myself in the interesting predicament of grieving my own death. So to speak, I mean. I suffered the loss of myself, if you like. This is coming from a philosopher you understand—we're interested in these ironic things."

"I understand."

"And Rose Carrera's book, well . . . somehow it helped me get over my grief. It's interesting how accepting your own death is just as important as accepting the demise of others."

"I'll tell her you said that," Daniel repeated. This time he meant it.

Sanderson Waits was looking at him curiously from his wheelchair. He said, "You'd rather she write something like popular fiction, would you?" Daniel was stunned. Sanderson Waits said, "You know, playing music is not about melody, painting is not about drawing pictures and writing is not about plot. Real art is about all

sorts of other things. It's not about popularity or even money at all."
With that he wheeled himself toward to the waiting area and
Suzette's desk.

Daniel stepped back into his office and closed the door. He sat
down at his desk. His mind was blank. Something had occurred
here, but he hadn't processed it yet. So he sat in silence for a while.

Daniel met his dad Timothy as planned in the lobby of the second tower. The stone slab with its glass-encased directory stood in
the middle of the huge hall like a tombstone. The glass walls shone
in their coldness. When it rained the glass had a remarkable translu-
cency as slow waterfalls ran down them. The climate here was per-
fect for this sort of architecture, Daniel thought. A few people stood
outside smoking. It was a good day. No rain, warm temperatures,
although overcast. There was that whiteness to the world that comes
over everything this time of day when the clouds are high and not
too thick.

"I thought we'd go to the Balcony Lounge," Timothy said. Daniel
nodded. He wasn't feeling much like talking. When they got there,
they sat down outside under the glass-and-steel canopy. The place was
almost empty. White plastic chairs were grouped here and there
around plastic tables in the shade. The view up there was of haze and
bright sun over the cityscape. They selected cold turkey sandwiches
from a buffet inside and sat down at a table. Their iced tea arrived.

"You seem preoccupied," Timothy said.

"Oh, maybe."

"I asked you to lunch not just because it's your birthday, even
though that would have been occasion enough," Timothy explained.
Daniel looked at his dad inquiringly. "I noticed lately you haven't
quite been yourself. I don't know if you want to talk about it. But I
thought I'd at least give you a chance to."

"Well, thanks. I don't know what I could say."

"That's okay, son. No need."

Daniel found he was appreciating the shade and the quiet. "Rose and I have been having kind of a rough time lately," Daniel began. "Just the same stuff."

"Same stuff?"

"Yea, you know. Rose gets depressed really easily and worked up about things. She can't seem to settle down. Takes her writing too seriously." Timothy nodded but didn't say anything. "Or maybe I've been giving her a hard time. I mean I'm getting impatient with all this. I want her to forget about writing books and start thinking about life. What she's doing to herself."

"Can't you give her a little more time?"

"I'm trying. But I've given her—what?—five years already!"

"These things can take longer."

"Yea, but her grief or whatever it is has morphed into a writing obsession." Again, silence between them. Daniel was thinking in two different directions. He looked at his dad who was patiently waiting for whatever he had to say. Not interfering, just being there. "You know what," he then said. "This guy came to see me. This morning, just a while ago. This man in a wheelchair who has cancer and who's going to die."

"What is it about him you're thinking of?"

"He said something."

"Yes?"

"He said he'd read Rose's book. And that it helped him. I was thinking about this disagreement we have about why she should write these things. I mean, things that don't sell well and cause her pain. But then this dying man in his wheelchair actually got a lot out of her book. So I was thinking, it's for him she wrote it. I mean, she writes for people like him."

"I'm not sure I follow."

"I mean how every now and then what you've done makes a big difference to someone. The rest doesn't matter. You know what I mean?" As he was talking, Daniel noticed a pair of seagulls had landed on the white railing and were staring at them intensely—eyeing their food. A pigeon had begun walking in among the table legs.

"Yes, I think I do."

"If you can help that one person—or no, if you're communicating to that one person—then the effort must have been worth it. Maybe like people sending these signals in writing and not everyone getting them. Like a whistle only certain ears can hear. Maybe that's what Rose has been thinking all along."

"Maybe. It's a way of understanding her. But I think it's more than that. I think people who write poetry and the kinds of lyrical things Rose is writing, I think they just have a writing condition, if you know what I mean. I don't think it's a matter of needing to communicate with someone or anything evangelistic like that."

"Like a disease you mean?" Daniel couldn't help smiling at the suggestion. "But I'm thinking a little differently this morning. About a way in which Rose's addiction to this business does make sense. I wouldn't have been thinking this if I hadn't met this guy, Sanderson Waits."

"Sanderson Waits?"

"Yes. A professor and a poet. Cancer of the spine. Wheelchair." Timothy leaned back in the plastic chair. They ate in silence. Daniel was thinking he would maybe give his life with Rose another chance. He'd tell her about the writer who came to see him. Then forget about being upset at her. Just go out and enjoy life if he could. Leave the rest alone. Who knows, it might all still fizzle away anyway. Things might turn out all right by themselves.

After their lunch together, Daniel returned to his office. He had no appointments for an hour and had time to deal with the pile of papers on his desk. The sky outside looked as if a great forest fire were burning in the distance. He went through the rest of the day feeling as though the haze outside was inside his head. He flipped through the papers on his desk without accomplishing much. At four, he headed home in his Mazda coupe. He pulled into the driveway of their white house on 19 Avenue. It was an old building but looked very fine with white stucco and a dark tile roof, and inside, dark hardwood floors and a brick fireplace with built-in oak shelves. He found Rose lying on the leather sofa. She was wearing her sweatshirt and jeans, and her big slippers with teddy bear pompoms on them. Her hair had not been combed, and her expression looked tired as always. She was listening to Renata Tebaldi, a recording they got called "The Great Renata Tebaldi," digitized from old records. The flutelike voice rang through the air miraculously.

"I didn't make dinner reservations," Rose said.

"You didn't?"

"No. I didn't think we should go out."

"What do you want to do?" There wasn't anything in the fridge either, he knew that. They didn't go shopping specifically because they thought they'd go out today.

"What do I want to do? Hmm." She lay her head on the white sofa pillow. Daniel started putting his briefcase away in the study and taking off his shoes in the hall. "I think we should order a pizza," she then said.

"Order a pizza? On my birthday?"

"Yes." He sat down on the edge of the sofa.

"Rose, what have you done today?"

"Let's see. I got up. I had breakfast. Said goodbye to you. Turned on my computer. Looked at the screen. Looked at the screen some more. Read the paper. Sat on the steps outside. Had an apple and cheddar cheese for lunch. Checked my email. Answered two of them. Went for a walk. Took a nap. Looked at the screen again. Lay down."

Daniel could see she was being ironic. She'd had another of her bad days.

"Do we have some beer?" he asked her. She nodded. "Okay, we'll order a pizza and have pizza and beer," he suggested.

"In the park?" she asked him.

"You want to take all that to the park?"

"It's a way of going out too."

"Okay." He knew she was watching him for a reaction. She was testing him just to see what he would do. He was not going to get upset at her. Why should he? It was her right to do whatever she wanted. "It's all right," he then said to her. "Everything is all right."

"What do you mean *all right*?"

"Just that I'm not having any expectations, if that's what you mean. And I already went out today. Had lunch with Dad."

"Good."

"Rose?"

"Yes?"

"I met this guy today. Sanderson Waits." She sat up on the sofa.

"The poet?" There was surprise in her voice. He found it gratifying that she could still be surprised.

"Yes. The poet you were reading." She was all attention. Daniel was suddenly delighted. He didn't know getting Rose's attention like that could still delight him so much.

"What? Where? Tell me everything!"

"He came to my office today. Wanted me to do a job for him. He's quite remarkable."

"In what way? Tell me more."

"He's incredibly . . . what can I say? . . . charismatic. That's it. He's charismatic. And very dramatic. He wears this black cape and rides in a wheelchair."

"A wheelchair?"

"Yes. He lost the use of his legs to cancer."

"Really? Poor him."

"Well, there's more." Rose was waiting in tense expectation. Daniel was savoring this for some reason, her hanging on his every word. "He said he only had a couple or three months to live. He wanted me to take care of some last-minute business."

"Personal stuff?"

"Yes, seems quite personal."

"Poor him. He's such a great poet. When he dies, I don't know— there won't be any great poets alive." Daniel looked at her. He wondered at that. He didn't know she thought that highly of him.

"Actually," he went on, "Sanderson Waits mentioned you." She looked taken aback—as though she'd seen a unicorn.

"Me?"

"Yes, I mentioned you'd been reading his poems." Silence. "He told me he read your book."

"He did?"

"He did. What's more, he said it had helped him a lot. The mourning and grief part. He said it made it easier to face his own death. Something like that. . . ." But he couldn't go on because Rose was starting to cry. It wasn't the usual crying, though. She was happy. She was smiling even though tears were coming down. He didn't have to say anything more. He knew what her tears meant. He reached over and hugged her. As he held her, he thought of the first time he encountered a blue heron. The memory was like a photograph that's been packed away in an old shoebox in an attic somewhere, yellowed with age. It was on a science and nature program. He was six or maybe seven. The heron had a long neck and a yellow beak and was wading in the water. He remembered the shadow of the bird reflected in the water. He had to ask his dad to take him to the park where he could see a real heron. They went to Stanley Park and sat down on the ramparts and waited and waited for a heron to appear. Finally, his dad said, "I don't think it'll come today. We may have to go farther out. To the marshes."

"Marshes? Do they go to the marshes?"

"Yes, Danny, they go where there is shallow water and look for little minnows swimming there."

"They live in the marshes?"

"Yes. We'll go there soon," his father assured him. That was all right. Daniel remembered that was something he looked forward to.

*Other books by Kristjana Gunnars
from Red Deer Press*

The Prowler
Zero Hour
The Substance of Forgetting
The Rose Garden: Reading Marcel Proust
Night Train to Nykøbing